About Nicola Marsh

Nicola Marsh has always had a passion for writing and reading. As a youngster she devoured books when she should have been sleeping, and later kept a diary whose contents could be an epic in itself!

These days, when she's not enjoying life with her husband and sons in her home city of Melbourne, she's at her computer, creating the romances she loves in her dream job.

Visit Nicola's website at **www.nicolamarsh.com** for the latest news of her books.

What the Paparazzi Didn't See

Nicola Marsh

MILLS BOON

First published in Great Britain 2013
by Mills & Boon, an imprint of Harlequin (UK) Limited.
Harlequin (UK) Limited, Eton House, 18-24 Paradise Road,
Richmond, Surrey TW9 1SR

© Nicola Marsh 2013

ISBN: 978 0 263 23513 5

wable
ainable
the

Also by Nicola Marsh

Her Deal with the Devil
Wedding Date with Mr Wrong
Marrying the Enemy
Who Wants To Marry a Millionaire?
Interview with the Daredevil
Girl in a Vintage Dress
Sex, Gossip and Rock & Roll
Deserted Island, Dreamy Ex!

Did you know these are also available as eBooks?
Visit www.millsandboon.co.uk

TM

For Ange, Shanika and Kylie.
Thanks for the laughs and for providing me
with plenty of interesting book fodder!
Looking forward to some interesting research trips!

CHAPTER ONE

LIZA LITHGOW'S STYLE TIPS
FOR MAXIMUM WAG WOW IMPACT

The Lashes

The eyes have it. Whether attending a grand final at a stadium packed with one hundred thousand people, a glamorous nightclub opening or a BBQ with the team and their partners, bold eyes make a statement.

1. Prep with a hydrating cream.
2. Apply foundation over your lids.
3. Draw the perfect line with pencil then trace with liquid eyeliner.
4. Apply shadow of choice. Go for sparkle at night.
5. Finish with lashings of mascara.

If you need a little help in the lash department, extensions are the way to go. Individual fake lashes are pasted to your own, giving you a lush look that turns heads.

A full set of extensions takes about an hour. They last

3-6 weeks and will require refills at this time. Refills take 30 minutes.

The great thing about lash extensions is you choose whether you want natural or glamour. Though be warned: the longer-length 'glamour' lashes may result in questions like, 'Have you been to a fancy dress party?' or, 'Is there a *Priscilla: Queen of the Desert* revival at the local theatre?'

If you prefer *au naturel*, the key to luscious lashes is prepping with a good serum. Many cosmetic companies have them.

To open up the eye in preparation for mascara, eyelash curlers are essential. Best to heat them up slightly before applying pressure to the lashes for thirty seconds.

For more dramatic impact with mascara, wiggle the wand from side to side as you apply, ensuring good coverage at the base of the lashes. It's the density and darkness of mascara at the roots that gives the illusion of length.

And always, always, opt for waterproof. (You never know when your sport star 'other half' may shoot the winning hoop to win the national championship or kick the goal to break a nil-all draw in the World Cup.)

For a real wow factor with mascara, the darker the better. Black is best unless you have a very fair complexion, in which case brown is better.

Similarly with eyeliner. Stick to black at night and softer, smudged brown during the day.

For eyeshadow shades, stick to neutrals or soft pinks.
Let your lashes do the talking!

IF LIZA LITHGOW had to attend one more freaking party,
she'd go insane.

Her curves resisted the control-top underwear constriction, her feet pinched from the requisite stilettos and her
face ached from the perpetual smile.

The *joys* of being a WAG.

Technically, an ex-WAG. And loving the *ex* bit.

The reportedly glamorous lives of sportsmen's Wives
And Girlfriends were grossly exaggerated. She should
know. She'd lived the lie for longer than she cared to admit.

'One more pic, Liza?'

Yeah, that was what they all said. Not that she had anything against the paparazzi per se, but their idea of one last
photo op usually conflicted with hers.

Assuming her game face, the one she'd used to great
effect over the years, she glanced over her shoulder and
smiled.

A plethora of flashes blinded her but her smile didn't
slip. She turned slowly, giving them time to snap her side
profile before she cocked a hip, placing a hand on it and
revealing an expanse of leg guaranteed to land her in the
gossip columns tomorrow.

Hopefully for the last time.

Being a WAG had suited her purposes but she was done.

Let some other poor sap take her place, primping for the
cameras, grinning inanely, starving herself so she wouldn't
be labelled pregnant by the media.

With a final wave at the photographers she strutted into
the function room, pausing to grab a champagne from a
passing waiter before heading to her usual spot at any function: front and centre.

If this was her last hurrah, she was determined to go out in style.

She waited for the party peeps and hangers-on to flock, steeled her nerve to face the inevitable inquisition: who was she dating, where was she holidaying, when would she grant the tell-all the publishers had been hounding her for?

Her answer to the last question hadn't changed in twelve months: 'When hell freezes over.'

It had been a year since international soccer sensation Henri Jaillet had dumped her in spectacular orchestrated fashion, three years since basketball superstar Jimmy Ro had broken her heart.

Reportedly.

The truth? She'd known Jimmy since high school and they were the quintessential golden couple: king and queen of the graduation dance who morphed into media darlings once he hit the big time.

He'd launched her as a WAG and she'd lapped it up, happy to accept endorsements of clothes, shoes and jewellery.

For Cindy. Always for Cindy.

Everything she did was for her baby sister, which was why a tell-all was not on the cards.

She'd grown apart from Jimmy and when reports of his philandering continued to dog her, she'd quit the relationship when he wanted out.

The media had a field day, making her out to be a saint, a very patient saint, and the jobs had flooded in. From modelling gigs to hosting charity events, she became Melbourne's latest 'it' girl.

And when her star had waned, she'd agreed to be Henri's date for a specified time in exchange for a cash sum that had paid Cindy's carer bills for a year.

Being tagged a *serial WAG* had stung, as people who

didn't know her labelled her money-hungry and a camera whore.

She tried not to care, though.

The only people that mattered—her and Cindy—knew the truth.

And it would stay that way, despite the ludicrous sums of money being dangled in front of her for a juicy tell-all.

Yeah, real juicy. Readers would be distinctly disappointed to learn of her penchant for flannel PJs, hot chocolate and a tatty patchwork quilt.

As opposed to the rumoured lack of sleepwear, martinis before bed and thousand-thread sheets she slept on.

She had no idea why the paparazzi made up stuff like that, but people lapped it up, and judged her because of it.

What would they think if they knew the truth?

That she loved spending a Saturday night curled up on the couch with Cindy under the old patchwork quilt their mum had made—and one of the few things Louisa had left behind when she'd abandoned them—watching the teen flicks her sister adored?

That she'd prefer to spend time with her disabled sister than any of the able-bodied men she'd dated?

That every word and every smile at events like this were part of a carefully constructed, elaborate mask to ensure her popularity and continued work that would set up Cindy's care for life?

Being a WAG meant she could spend most of her time caring for Cindy; a part-time gig as opposed to a full-time job that would've taken her away from her sister.

It had suited their lifestyle, putting in infrequent appearances at galas or launches or openings in exchange for days spent attending Cindy's physiotherapy and occupational therapy sessions, ensuring the spasticity in Cindy's contracted muscles didn't debilitate her limited mobility completely.

She'd sat through Cindy's Botox injections into specific muscles to ease the pain and stiffness and deformity around joints, followed by extensive splinting to maintain movement.

She'd supported Cindy through intrathecal baclofen therapy, where a pump had been inserted into her sister's abdomen to deliver doses of baclofen—a muscle relaxer—into her spinal fluid to ease the spasticity and relieve muscle spasms in her legs.

She'd been there for every session of speech therapy, muscle lengthening and strengthening, splinting, orthotics, mobility training and activities of daily living management.

Putting on a façade for the cameras might have been a pain in the butt but it had been a small price to pay for the time she'd been able to spend supporting Cindy every step of the way. The financial security? An added bonus.

Cindy's care hadn't come cheap and if a magazine wanted to pay her to put in an appearance at some B-list function, who was she to knock it back?

She almost had enough money saved... After tonight she could hang up her sparkly stilettos and leave her WAG reputation behind. Start working at something worthwhile. Something in promotions maybe? Put her marketing degree to use.

Cindy had progressed amazingly well over the years and Liza could now pursue full-time work in the knowledge she'd put in the hard yards with her sister's therapy when it counted.

Cerebral palsy might be an incurable lifelong condition but, with Cindy's determination, her amazing sis had reached a stage in her management plan where the spasticity affecting the left side of her body was under control and she maintained a certain amount of independence.

Liza couldn't be prouder and could now spend more hours away from Cindy pursuing some of her own goals.

Though she wondered how many interviews 'serial WAG' would garner from her sketchy CV.

A local TV host laid a hand on her arm and she faked a smile, gushing over his recent award win, inwardly counting down the minutes until she could escape.

Think of the appearance money, she mentally recited, while nodding and agreeing in all the right places.

Another thirty minutes and she could leave her old life behind.

She could hardly wait.

Wade Urquart couldn't take his eyes off the dazzling blonde.

She stood in the middle of the room, her shimmery bronze dress reflecting light onto the rapt faces of the guys crowding her.

With every fake smile she bestowed upon her subjects, he gritted his teeth.

She was exactly the type of woman he despised.

Too harsh? Try the type of woman he didn't trust.

The same type of woman as Babs, his stepmother. Who at this very minute was doing the rounds of the room, doing what she did best: schmoozing.

Quentin had been dead less than six months and Babs had ditched the black for dazzling emerald. Guess he should respect her for not pretending. As she had for every moment of her ten-year marriage to his father.

A marriage that had driven the family business into the ground. And an irreversible wedge between him and his dad. A wedge that had resulted in the truth being kept from him on all fronts, both personally and professionally.

He'd never forgive her for it.

Though deep down he knew who should shoulder the blame for the estrangement with his dad. And he looked at that guy every morning in the mirror.

He needed to make amends, needed to ease the guilt that wouldn't quit. Ensuring his dad's business didn't go bankrupt would be a step in the right direction.

Qu Publishing currently stood on the brink of disaster and it was up to him to save it. One book at a time.

If he could ever get a meeting with that WAG every publishing house in Melbourne was clamouring to sign up to a tell-all biography, he might have a chance. Her name escaped him and, having been overseas for the best part of a decade, he had no idea what this woman even looked like, but he could imagine that every one of her assets would be fake. However, it seemed Australia couldn't get enough of their home-grown darling. He'd been assured by his team that a book by this woman would be a guaranteed bestseller—just what the business needed.

But the woman wouldn't return his assistant's international calls and emails. Not that it mattered. He knew her type. Now he'd landed in Melbourne he'd take over the pursuit, demand a face-to-face meeting, up the ante and she'd be begging to sign on the dotted line.

At times like this he wished his father had moved with the times and published children's fiction. Would've made Wade's life a lot easier, signing the next J.K. Rowling.

But biographies were Qu Publishing's signature, a powerhouse in the industry.

Until Babs had entered the picture, when Quentin's business sense had fled alongside his common sense, and he had hidden the disastrous truth.

Wade hated that his dad hadn't trusted him.

He hated the knowledge that he'd caused the rift more.

It was why he was here, doing anything and everything to save his father's legacy.

He owed it to him.

Wade should've been there for his dad when he was alive. He hadn't been and it was time to make amends.

The bronzed blonde laughed, a surprisingly soft, happy sound at odds with the tension emanating from her like a warning beacon.

Even at this distance he could see her rigid back, the defensive way she half turned away from the guys vying for her attention.

Interesting. Maybe she was nothing like Babs after all. Babs, who was currently engaged in deep conversation with a seventy-year-old mining magnate who had as many billions as chins.

Yeah, some people never changed.

He needed a change. Needed to escape the expectations of a hundred workers who couldn't afford to lose their jobs. Needed to forget how his father had landed his business in this predicament and focus on the future. Needed to sign that WAG to solve his problems.

And there were many. So many problems that the more he thought about it, the more his head pounded.

What he needed right now? A bar, a bourbon and a blonde.

Startled by his latter wish, he gazed at her again and his groin tightened in appreciation.

She might not be his type but for a wild, wistful second he wished she could be.

Eight years of setting up his own publishing business in London had sapped him, sucking every last ounce of energy as he'd worked his butt off. When he'd initially started he'd wanted a company to rival his father's but had chosen to focus on the e-market rather than paper, trade and hardbacks. Considering how dire things were with Qu Publishing, his company now surpassed the one-time powerhouse of the book industry.

He rarely dated, socialised less. Building a booming digital publishing business had been his number-one priority. Ironic, he was now here to save the business he could've been in competition with if his dad had ever moved into the twenty-first century. And if he'd been entrusted with the truth.

Not that saving Qu mattered if Babs had her way.

The muscles in his neck spasmed with tension and he spun away, needing air before he did something he'd regret, like marching over to stepmommy dearest and strangling her.

He grabbed a whisky from a passing waiter and downed half of it, hoping to eradicate the bitterness clogging his throat. Needing a breather, he made his way to the terrace that wrapped across the front of the function room in wrought-iron splendour.

Melbourne might not have the historical architecture of London but the city's beautiful hotels, like the Westin, could hold their own around the world.

He paced the marble pavers in a vain attempt to quell the urge to march back into that packed function room and blast Babs in front of everyone, media be damned.

Wouldn't that go down a treat in tomorrow's papers? PUBLISHING CEO BAILS UP SOCIALITE STEPMOTHER, a real page-turner.

He wouldn't do it, of course. Commit corporate suicide. Qu Publishing meant too much to him. Correction, his dad had meant everything to him, and Wade would do whatever it took, including spending however long in Melbourne to stop Babs selling his legacy.

Qu Publishing needed a saviour. He intended to walk on water to do it.

He cursed and downed the rest of his whisky, knowing he should head back inside and make nice with the publishing crowd.

'Whatever's biting your butt, that won't help.'

Startled, he glanced to his right, where the bronze-clad blonde rested her forearms on the balcony, staring at him with amusement in her eyes.

Blue. With tiny flecks of green and gold highlighted by the shimmery dress. A slinky, provocative dress that accentuated her assets.

The whisky he'd sculled burned his gut. His excuse for the twisty tension tying it into knots.

Her voice surprised him as much as her guileless expression. Women who dressed like that usually wore calculating expressions to match their deliberately sexy garb and spoke with fake deference.

She sounded…amused. Concerned. *Normal*.

It threw him.

He prided himself on being a good judge of character. Hadn't he picked Babs for a gold-digging tart the moment his dad had introduced her ten years ago?

His people radar had served him well in business too, but something about this woman made him feel off-kilter. A feeling he wouldn't tolerate.

He needed to stay focused, remain in charge, to ensure he didn't lose the one thing that meant anything to him these days.

And as long as she was staring at him with that beguiling mix of fascination and curiosity, he couldn't concentrate on anything.

'Can't a guy have a drink in peace without being accused of drowning his sorrows?'

He sounded abrupt and uptight and rude. Good. She would raise her perfect pert nose in the air and stride inside on those impossibly high heels that glittered with enough sparkle to match her dress.

To his surprise she laughed; a soft, sexy sound that made his fingers curl around the glass as she held up her hands in a back-off gesture.

'Hey, no accusations here. Merely an observation.'

A host of smartass retorts sprang to his lips and he planned on using them too. Until he glimpsed something that made him pause.

She was nervous.

He saw it in the way her fingertips drummed delicately on the stem of the champagne flute she clutched. Saw it in her quick look-away when he held her gaze a fraction too long.

And that contradiction—her siren vamp appearance contrasting with her uncertainty—was incredibly fascinating and he found himself nodding instead.

'You're right. I was trying to take my mind off stuff.'

The corners of her mouth curved upward, the groove in her right cheek hinting at an adorable dimple. 'Stuff?'

'Trust me, you don't want to know.'

'I used to worry about stuff once.'

Intrigued by the weariness in her voice, he said, 'Not anymore?'

'Not after today,' she said, hiding the rest of what she was about to say behind her raised glass as she took a sip.

'What happened today?'

Her wistful sigh hit him where he least expected it. Somewhere in the vicinity of his heart.

'Today I secured a future for someone very important to me.'

He didn't understand her grimness or defensive posture, but he could relate to her relief. When he secured the future of Qu Publishing in memory of all his dad's hard work, he'd be pretty damn relieved too.

'Good for you.'

'Thanks.' She smiled again, sweet and genuine, and he couldn't fathom the bizarre urge to linger, chat and get to know her.

She wasn't in his plans for this evening. Then again, what did he have to look forward to? Putting on a front for a bunch of back-slapping phoneys and gritting his teeth to stop from calling his stepmother a few unsavoury names?

He knew what he'd rather be doing.

And he was looking straight at her.

'Do you want to get out of here?'

Her eyes widened in surprise before a disapproving frown slashed between them. 'You've got to be kidding me? I make polite small talk for two seconds and you're propositioning me?'

She shook her head, her disgust palpable.

'Let me rephrase that.' He tried his best smile, the one he used to win friends and influence colleagues. Her frown deepened. 'What I meant was that I've had a long day. Landed in Melbourne this morning, had to attend this shin-dig for work tonight and I'm tired of the schmoozing.'

He waved towards the balcony. 'Considering you're out here to get away from the crowd, I assume you've prob-ably had a gutful too?'

Her wary nod encouraged him to continue when he should cut his losses and run.

'The way I see it, we have two choices. Head back in there and bore ourselves silly for the next hour or we can head down to The Martini Bar in the lobby and unwind before we head home—I mean, before we go our sepa-rate ways.'

The corners of her mouth twitched at his correction.

'What do you say? Take pity on a guy and put him out of his misery by saving him from another interminable stint in there?'

Damn, he'd made a fool of himself, blathering like an idiot. What was it about this cool, classy blonde that had him rattled?

He'd had her pegged wrong and he, better than anyone, should know never to judge the proverbial book by its cover.

'So you weren't propositioning me?'

Was that a hint of disappointment? Mentally chastising himself for wishful thinking, he mimicked her frown. 'Sadly, no. I'm too jet-lagged to—'

He bit off the rest of what he was about to say when her eyebrow arched.

Yep, he was stuffing this up royally.

'To what?'

At last, she smiled and it made him feel oddly excited, as if he wanted to see her do it again.

'To muster up enough charm to ensure you couldn't say no.'

She chuckled and he joined in.

'I like a guy with confidence.' She laid her champagne glass on the ledge. 'Let's go get that martini.'

He didn't have to be asked twice. 'You really made me work for that acceptance.'

As he gestured for her to take the stairs ahead of him she cast him a coy glance from beneath her lashes. 'Didn't you know? You need to work your butt off for anything worth having.'

'Is that right?'

'Absolutely.' She nodded, strands of artfully curled golden silk falling around her face in gorgeous disarray. 'Nothing better than nailing a challenge.'

He bit the inside of his cheek to prevent laughing out loud, finding her utterly beguiling. In contrast to her sex-kitten persona, she was forthright and rather innocent if she hadn't picked up on that nailing remark.

Then he made the mistake of glancing at her and saw the moment her faux pas registered.

She winced and a faint pink stained her cheeks, making him want to ravish her on the spot.

'That didn't sound too good,' she said, wrinkling her nose.

'Now we're even,' he said, wondering what they'd come out with after a few drinks under their belts. 'My mistaken proposition, your nailing suggestion.'

'Guess we are.' She eyed him speculatively, as if not sure what he'd say next.

That made two of them.

'Maybe we should stick to coffee tonight?'

'Why's that?'

That dimple flashed adoringly again. 'Because with our strike rate, who knows what'll happen if we have a martini or two?'

He laughed. 'I was thinking the same thing.'

'Coffees it is.' She nodded, expecting him to agree.

But there was a part of him that delighted in flustering this woman and he couldn't help but wonder how she'd loosen up with a few drinks inside her.

He leaned in close, expecting her to retreat a little, his admiration increasing, along with his libido, when she didn't.

'Actually, I prefer to live on the edge tonight. Why don't we have a martini or two and see what other verbal gaffes we can make?'

'As long as we stop at the verbal stuff,' she said so softly he barely heard her.

'Any other mistakes we make? Not our fault.'

'Oh?' He loved how she did the imperious eyebrow quirk.

'Haven't you heard?' He lowered his voice. 'What happens in The Martini Bar stays in The Martini Bar?'

With a surprisingly wicked twinkle in her eye, she nodded. 'That's if we stay in the bar.'

With that, she took to the steps, leaving him trailing after her, more than a little captivated by this woman of contrasts.

A woman whose name he didn't know.

Ah well, he'd have all night to discover it if he was lucky.

CHAPTER TWO

LIZA LITHGOW'S STYLE TIPS FOR MAXIMUM WAG WOW IMPACT

The Lips

For the height of sophistication and glam wow, the perfect pout is where it's at.

Having a palette of colours for various looks is essential.

Co-ordinate colour with outfits.

Go bold with fire engine red for an awards ceremony or pastel pink for the season opener.

Keep lips soft; that means no lip liner!

For a fabulous femme fatale pout, preparation is key.

1. Gently exfoliate lips with a soft-bristled toothbrush.
2. Moisturize with a specialized lip balm.
3. Use a lip-fix cream which prevents colour bleeding.
4. Apply lipstick once. Blot with tissue. Re-apply.

For a subtle look, pat lipstick on with a fingertip.

For bold lips, apply with a lip brush.

Blot.

Reapply.

If you want a plump pout without the injections, try lipsticks with inbuilt 'plumpers'. These innovative ingredients are proven to increase lip volume by forty percent. Amazing! They also hydrate and restore collagen over time.

A dab of gloss in the middle of the lower lip is a subtle touch that adds real wow!

LIZA COULDN'T REMEMBER the last time she'd been out on a date.

One that hadn't been orchestrated as some huge PR stunt, that was. She'd attended the Logies, Arias and Brownlow Medal galas on the arms of a TV personality, a rock star and an up-and-coming footballer respectively. And on each occasion had been bored witless within the first ten minutes.

So what was it about this guy that had her laughing and fluffing her words and interested in spending some one-on-one time with him?

She'd made her required appearance at the book launch; she should head home, get out of this designer dress she'd been begged to wear and curl up with her e-reader and the latest juicy romance.

Instead, she watched *him* place their martini orders, shocked she didn't know his name, thrilled she didn't particularly care.

She never had fun or did anything on a whim. Ever.

Her life for the last ten years since her mum had absconded when she was eighteen and left Cindy in her care had been about weighing decisions carefully to see how they would affect her younger sister.

Everything revolved around Cindy and while Liza never begrudged her sis anything, knowing tonight would be the last time she'd have to put on her *fake face* had lifted a weight from her shoulders.

She could be herself from now on and Mr Martini had been in the right place at the right time. More than that, he'd intrigued her, and she couldn't say that about many men.

She'd watched him morph from uptight and judgemental to cool and a little goofy, with a hint of underlying sexiness that made her long-neglected hormones sit up and howl.

When was the last time she'd had sex? Probably not since she was with Jimmy, because while Henri had paid for her arm-candy status for a year, she wouldn't go *that* far as part of their deal.

And if she couldn't remember exactly, it meant it had probably been during the good period with Jimmy, which hadn't been the last year of their relationship. The year he'd progressively withdrawn, establishing emotional distance before the final break.

Her mum had done the same over the years. In both cases, their abandonment hadn't come as any great surprise but had hurt all the same. Hurt deeply.

But tonight wasn't the time to dwell on her issues. Tonight was perfect for something else entirely.

She did a quick mental calculation…. Could it really have been four years since she'd been with a guy?

Maybe that explained her irrational urge to push the limits with Mr Martini. He'd be ideal for a celebratory fling, a little fun on a night where she felt like dancing down Swanston Street with her arms in the air.

Not that she'd had a one-night stand before but the way

she was feeling right now? Edgy. Dangerous. A little out-rageous. It could very well be a first tonight.

He stalked towards her, his ebony suit highlighting lean legs, broad shoulders, impressive chest, and she squirmed a little.

What would it be like to explore beneath that suit? To feel the warmth of a man's skin next to hers? The heat of passion? The yearning to lose herself in pleasure?

Cindy was her world and Liza never regretted assuming responsibility for full-time care, but it was at times like this she wished deep down for something she'd never have: a guy to come home to, a guy to warm her bed, a guy who wouldn't abandon her when the going got tough.

'You must really have a hankering for a martini,' he said, taking a seat next to her, far too close as a few synapses zinged with the need to touch him.

'Why?'

'Because you have an odd look on your face, like you want it real bad.'

Uh-oh. He could see her desperation? Not good.

'I'm thirsty,' she blurted, wishing the waitress would hurry up and deliver their damn drinks so she wouldn't have to stare into his knowing dark eyes.

'And I'm curious.'

That made two of them. She was curious as to why she'd agreed to this and why the hell she wanted him to be part of her freedom celebration tonight.

'How could two intelligent people like us, about to hav-ing a scintillating conversation, still be strangers?'

'Not anymore.' She stuck out her hand. 'Liza Lithgow.'

'Wade Urquart. Pleased to meet you.'

As his palm touched hers and his fingers curled around her hand, Liza could've sworn every sane reason why she shouldn't indulge in a night of incredible sex with this guy melted clean away.

'Your name sounds familiar.' He frowned, releasing her hand after lingering too long. She wasn't complaining.

'I'm hoping the next words out of your mouth aren't, "Haven't we met some place before?"'

He laughed. 'No need for glib lines. You're here, aren't you?'

'True.'

And with the dim lighting, the smooth jazz spilling softly from discreet speakers behind them and a gorgeous guy eyeing her speculatively, she was right where she wanted to be.

For tonight. Tonight, she was in the mood for celebrating. Shedding her old life felt amazing.

'Why did you agree to have a drink with me?' The waitress deposited their drinks and he raised a martini glass in her direction. 'You seemed to be in your element at that party.'

'Haven't you ever faked it?' She clinked her glass to his. 'What you see isn't always what you get.'

He stared at her over the rim of his glass, a slight groove between his brows. 'Have to say, you're an intriguing woman, and I can't figure you out.'

She shrugged. 'What's to figure out? We're two people who wanted to escape that party; we're having a drink, end of story.'

'Is it?'

His gaze locked on hers, potent and smouldering, and her breath hitched.

She took a sip of her martini, needing the alcohol to loosen her tightened vocal cords. 'You're expecting an epilogue?'

'A guy can always live in hope,' he said, downing his

martini and placing the glass on the table in front of them. 'Honestly? I've had a crappy six months, my dad's business is under threat and I haven't met anyone as captivating as you in a long time. So excuse me if I don't BS you.'

Liza valued honesty. Most people didn't know the meaning of the word. How many times had friends, who'd hung around under the misguidance she'd take them places because of her lifestyle, vanished when they'd learned she had a disabled sister?

Stupid morons acted as if cerebral palsy were catchy. And they didn't stay to be educated either.

Even Jimmy had been awkward and stilted around Cindy, despite Liza explaining cerebral palsy was a physical disability caused by injury to the brain before birth.

Cindy had a milder form, with only the left side of her body affected by the debilitating spasticity that left her hand, elbow, hip and knee clawed, and some speech problems. She had been lucky in escaping ataxic—uncontrolled—movements and athetosis, the writhing movements.

Sure, the spasticity in Cindy's elbow, wrist and fingers made daily tasks like eating, dressing, writing and manipulating objects difficult, but they'd learned to cope best they could. Countless occupational therapy sessions had seen to that. And the ongoing physiotherapy to prevent deforming contractures made Liza eternally grateful for the job she'd had for the last few years.

After tonight, not anymore.

Having Wade clearly articulate what he wanted impressed her. Scared the bejeebies out of her, but definitely impressed her.

'Want to talk about the crappy six months or the business?'

'Hell no,' he said, loosening the knot on his tie and unbuttoning the top button of his shirt to reveal a hint of deliciously tempting tanned skin. 'The only reason I'm in Melbourne is to sort all that stuff out, but considering I arrived this morning it can wait 'til tomorrow.'

'Then why show up at the party at all?'

'Because sometimes we have to do things we don't want to.'

His frown reappeared and she had a feeling he did a lot of that. He'd been frowning when she'd first seen him on the balcony, deep in thought, incredibly serious. It was what had made her approach him. Because she used to look like that all the time when she didn't have her game face on, the one she donned along with her make-up before a public appearance.

She'd frowned a lot over the years, worrying about Cindy. About her care long term should anything happen to her, about her sister's health, about her financial security.

The latter had driven her to go to great lengths. Heck, she'd tolerated posing as Henri Jaillet's girlfriend for twelve months when most people couldn't stand longer than a few minutes in the egotistical soccer star's presence.

But those days were over. She'd invested wisely over the years and tomorrow, when her investment matured, financial security would give her the peace of mind she needed to get more carer help, leaving her more time to sort out her own future.

Why wait until tomorrow?

The thought wasn't exactly out of left field. She wouldn't be sitting here if she hadn't already contemplated celebrating her newfound freedom tonight.

But how did this work? She couldn't take Wade home; she'd never expose Cindy to that unless the guy meant something to her. Even Jimmy had hardly visited and she'd known him since high school.

Though that had been more due to Jimmy's unease around Cindy than not wanting to see her. She hadn't pushed the issue with him, content to protect Cindy from any vibes she might pick up from Jimmy. But it had hurt, deep down, that her boyfriend wasn't more open-minded and didn't care enough about her to accept Cindy as part of the package while they dated.

'Another drink?'

She shook her head. 'No thanks. After the champers I had upstairs, any more of this and who knows what I'll do?'

'In that case, maybe I should insist you try every martini mixer on the menu?'

She smiled, glad his frown had disappeared, but a little intimidated by his stare, the probing stare that insisted there was intention behind his teasing quips.

'You could try, but you'd have to carry me out of here.'

'Not a problem. I have a suite upstairs.' He winked. 'You could recover up there.'

Guess that answered Liza's question about how she'd go about *celebrating* with Wade.

The old Liza would've laughed off his flirtation and changed the subject.

The new Liza who wanted to kick up her heels for the first time in for ever? Surely she couldn't pass up an opportunity like this?

'Is that an invitation or a proposition?'

'Both,' he said, capturing her hand between his, the unexpected contact sending a buzz shooting up her arm. 'Am I in the habit of picking up women I barely know at parties? No. Do I invite them back to my place? Rarely.'

He raised her hand to his lips and brushed a soft kiss across her knuckles, making her yearn for more. 'Am I hoping you'll say yes to spending the night with me? Absolutely.'

Liza had a decision to make.

Do the sensible thing, the responsible thing, as she'd done her whole life.

Or celebrate her new life, starting now.

'Do I accept offers to spend the night from guys? No.' She squeezed his hand. 'Have I had a one-night stand before? Never.' She slid her hand out of his. 'Do I want to spend tonight with you?'

She took a steadying breath and laid her hand on his thigh. 'Absolutely.'

CHAPTER THREE

LIZA LITHGOW'S STYLE TIPS
FOR MAXIMUM WAG WOW IMPACT

The Shape

The key to WAG wow is making the most of what you have.

Learn how to show off your best assets and how to visually change the body parts you'd rather hide.

Always, always, dress to suit your shape.

PEAR

a) Wear dark colours on the lower half of your body.

b) A-line skirts that skim the hips and bottom are flattering.

c) Accessorise with scarves, necklaces and earrings to draw attention to the upper half of your body.

d) Avoid light coloured trousers or anything too tight on your bottom half.

BUSTY

a) Go for flattering necklines with tops and dresses: turtlenecks, shirt collars, boat necks, V necks.

b) Go for high-sitting necklaces as they draw the gaze up.

c) Avoid baggy tops with no shape as they can make you look heavier and avoid anything too tight across the chest.

SHORT

a) Dresses ending above the knee are best.

b) Wear fitted tops and trousers (straight or bootleg).

c) Avoid cropped length pants as they make legs look shorter.

TALL

a) Wear different colours top and bottom to break up the illusion of length.

b) Wear horizontal stripes.

c) Wear well-fitted layers that skim the body.

d) Adding a wide belt can help create a nice shape.

e) Avoid wearing pants that are the incorrect length.

Remember, the key to appearing confident in the clothes you wear is to be comfortable.

How many times have we seen women tugging up their strapless bodices or tugging down their micro-minis? It's not a good look.

When you strut into a room, being confident in your body and the look you've created is half the battle!

As LIZA STARED out over the lights of Melbourne glittering below, she had second thoughts about her decision.

Was she really in Wade's suite, about to indulge in her first one-night stand at the ripe old age of twenty-eight?

She still had time to bolt. She'd thought it rather cute when he'd mentioned making a quick trip to the convenience store across the road, and it reinforced his assertion that he wasn't in the habit of picking up women or expecting to have sex his first night in Melbourne.

But while he was buying condoms, she was mulling over reasons why this might not be such a good idea after all.

She maintained strict independence for a reason. Depending on anyone for anything inevitably led to heartache.

Not that she'd be depending on Wade for anything, but letting her guard down came with a price. It left her vulnerable to *feeling*, and having her defences weakened, even for a short time, made her skittish.

She'd loved her dad. He'd abandoned her without a backward glance.

She'd depended on her mum. She'd eventually left too.

She'd thought sweet, easygoing Jimmy would always be there for her. He'd done a runner too.

No, it was easier maintaining aloofness, not letting anyone get too close. And that was exactly what Wade would be doing shortly…getting exceptionally close.

Ironic, it wasn't the prospect of some stranger seeing her naked that had her half as anxious as the thought of being intimate with him and enjoying it too much.

She'd never been a needy female and had tried to instil the same independence into Cindy despite her physical limitations, yet there was something about how much she wanted to be close to Wade tonight that terrified her.

She could blame it on her impulsive need to celebrate and do something completely out of character.

Or she could admit the truth, albeit to herself. That she

craved a connection, even if only physical, for just one night.

The soft swoosh of the key card in the lock had her fingers clenching on the windowsill.

So much for escaping.

He entered and her tummy fell away in that uncharacteristic swoop that signalled she really wanted this guy.

She tingled all over from it, her nerve endings prickling and putting her body on notice, a heightened awareness that made her want to rub against him, skin to skin.

Then it hit her.

She'd never been so attracted to any guy before. Not even Jimmy, whose body she'd known in intimate detail from the time they'd lost their virginity together in the back seat of his car at seventeen.

Because of the clothes she wore and the persona she presented to the world, guys assumed she was an easy mark. Even while she'd been dating Jimmy and Henri—albeit platonically in his case—guys had hit on her.

Fellow soccer and basketball stars who assumed WAGs were up for anything. Commentators and managers and agents who thought WAGs would do anything for stardom and recognition, including accept outlandish proposals.

The whole scene had sickened her and, while she'd seen enough hook-ups at parties in her time, she'd never been remotely interested.

What made Wade Urquart so special that she wanted to rip her clothes off the moment his sizzling-hot gaze connected with hers?

'Glad you're still here.'

He closed the door and slid off his jacket, where she caught sight of a tell-tale box bulging from the inside pocket. What looked like a surprisingly large box for what she'd envisioned as a brief interlude.

Her skin tingled again.

'I contemplated making a run for it.'

'What stopped you?'

He stalked towards her, stopped less than two feet away. 'This.'

She laid a hand on his chest, felt the heat from his skin brand her through the expensive cotton of his shirt.

He didn't move as her palm slid upward. Slowly. Leisurely, as she savoured the contours of hard muscle, desperate to feel his skin.

He watched her, his gaze smouldering as her fingertips traced around his nipples, his breathing quickening as her fingers skated across his pecs, along his collarbone and higher.

When her hand reached his neck, she stepped closer, bringing their bodies less than an inch apart.

She could feel his heat. She could smell his expensive citrus aftershave. She could hear his ragged breathing.

She'd never wanted anything as badly as she wanted Wade at that moment.

With a boldness she'd had no idea she possessed, she tugged his head down towards her and kissed him.

The moment their lips touched Liza forgot her doubts, forgot her past, forgot her own damn name.

She couldn't think beyond their frantic hands and loud moans. Couldn't get enough of his long, deep, skilled kisses.

Her body ignited in a fireball of passion and she clung to him, eagerly taking the initiative, pushing him down on the bed so he lay sprawled beneath her like a fallen angel.

His lips curved into a wicked grin as she shimmied out of her dress.

Another first. Letting a guy see her naked with the lights on.

She didn't like being seen during intimate moments.

She spent enough of her life in the spotlight, being scrutinised and evaluated, she didn't need it in the bedroom too.

But this was a new Liza, a new life.

Time to shed her old habits and take what she wanted.

Starting with the sexy guy beckoning her with a crook of his finger.

'Bronze is your colour,' he said, propping on his elbows when she straddled him.

'I like to colour coordinate my outfit and underwear.'

'While I appreciate the effort—' he snagged a bra strap and tugged it down, trailing a fingertip across her collarbones and doing the same on the other side '—I'd prefer to see you naked.'

He surged upward so fast she almost toppled off, but he wrapped his strong arms around her waist, anchoring her, holding her deliciously close. 'Now.'

She cupped his face between her hands and stared into his beautiful brown eyes. Eyes that held shadows lurking behind desire. Eyes that intrigued.

She briefly wondered if they were doing the right thing. Before ignoring that thought.

She wanted to celebrate her new life tonight. Having an exciting, impulsive fling with a hot guy who made her pulse race with the barest touch?

What a way to do it.

She inched towards him and murmured against his mouth, 'What are you waiting for?'

Wade knew Liza had vanished when he woke.

It didn't surprise him. He'd half expected her to disappear when he'd gone condom shopping.

Even now, after six hours of sensational sex and a much-needed two hours' sleep, he couldn't quite believe she'd stayed.

He'd known the moment they'd started flirting she wasn't the type to deliberately reel a guy in with the intention of a one-night stand.

She hadn't toyed with her hair or used fake coy smiles or accidentally on purpose touched him as so many women who came on to him did.

She hadn't pumped up his ego or been impressed by his trappings. How many times had women made a comment on his expensive watch, thinking he'd be flattered? Hell, even Babs couldn't go past a thirty-thousand-dollar watch without making some remark.

How wrong he'd been about Liza.

He'd likened her to his stepmother when he'd first seen her surrounded by lackeys at that party. The two women couldn't be more different.

Thoughts of Babs had him glancing at his watch and leaping out of bed.

He had a board meeting scheduled for ten this morning. A meeting he couldn't miss. The future of Qu Publishing depended on it.

While one-night stands weren't his usual style, Wade knew better than to search for a note or a business card or a scrawled phone number on the hotel notepad.

But that was exactly what he found himself doing as he glanced around the room, hoping for some snippet that indicated Liza wouldn't mind seeing him again.

He might not be in the market for a relationship but his time in Melbourne would be tension-filled enough without adding frustration to his woes.

He'd been lucky enough to meet an intriguing woman who made his body harden despite the marathon session they'd had. Why not stay in touch, date, whatever, while he was in town?

He might not know how long that would be, or how

long it would take to ensure the publishing business that had been in his family for centuries was saved, but having someone like Liza to distract him from the corporate stress would be a bonus.

A quick reconnaissance yielded nothing. No contact details.

Disappointment pierced his hope. By her eagerness and wanton responses he'd assumed she'd had a good time too. And if she wasn't the one-night-stand type, why didn't she leave *something*? A note? A number?

Ironic, for a guy who didn't trust easily, he'd pinned his hopes on a virtual stranger trusting him enough to leave her contact details?

Then again, she'd trusted him with her body. A stupid thought, considering he wasn't naïve enough to assume sensational sex equated with anything beyond the heat of the moment.

A glance at the alarm clock beside the bed had him frowning and making a beeline for the bathroom.

He had a boardroom to convince.

Time enough later to use his considerable resources to discover the luscious Liza's contact details.

In all the years Shar, Cindy's caregiver, had stayed over, Liza had never needed to sneak past her 'the morning after'.

By Shar's raised eyebrows and smug smile as Liza eased off her sandals and tiptoed across the kitchen, only to be caught out when Shar stepped out of the pantry, the time for sneaking was long past.

Liza had been sprung.

'Good morning.' Shar held up a coffee plunger in one hand, a tin of Earl Grey in the other. 'Which would you prefer?'

'Actually, I think I'll hit the shower—'

'Your usual, then.' Shar grabbed Liza's favourite mug and measured leaves into a teapot. 'Nothing like a cuppa to lubricate the vocal cords first thing in the morning.'

'My vocal cords are fine.'

Liza cleared her throat anyway, knowing the huskiness came from too much moaning over the hours that Wade had pleasured her. Repeatedly.

Shar grinned. 'Good. Then you can tell me who put that blush in your cheeks.'

Liza darted a quick glance at Cindy's door.

'She's fine. Still asleep.'

One of the many things Liza loved about Shar was Cindy was the carer's priority. Liza had seen it instantly when she'd interviewed Shar for the job after her mum had left.

Liza had been a hapless eighteen-year-old, used to looking out for her younger sister but shocked to find herself a full-time carer overnight.

She'd needed help and the cerebral palsy association had come through for her in a big way. Organised respite care, assisted with ongoing physio and occupational therapy and sent part-time carers to help.

Liza had known Shar was the best when Cindy took an instant liking to her and the older woman didn't patronise either of them.

At that time Liza hadn't needed a mother—she'd had one and look how that had turned out—she'd needed a friend, and Shar had been all that and more over the years.

Liza couldn't have attended functions and cultivated her WAG image without Shar's help and they'd eased into a workable schedule over the years. Liza spent all day with Cindy and Shar came in several evenings a week, more if Liza's WAG duties had demanded it.

Liza had been lucky, being able to devote so much time to Cindy and support them financially. And when her investment matured today she'd be sure to give Shar a massive wage increase for her dedication, loyalty and friendship. And increase her hours to include days so Liza could find a job in marketing. One that didn't involve marketing herself in front of the cameras.

'Sit.' Shar pointed at the kitchen table, covered in Cindy's scrapbooking. 'Start talking.'

'Damn, you're bossy,' Liza said, not surprised to find a few muscles twanging as she slid onto the wooden chair.

She hadn't had a workout like that in...for ever.

Though labelling what she'd done with Wade a workout seemed rather crass and casual.

The passion they'd shared—the caresses, the strokes, the exploration of each other's bodies. She'd never been so uninhibited, so curious.

She knew the transient nature of their encounter had a lot to do with her wanton playfulness—easy to be bold with a guy she'd never see again.

So why did that thought leave her cold?

On waking, she'd spent an inordinate amount of time studying his features. The proud, straight nose with a tiny bump near the bridge, the dark stubble peppering his cheeks, the tiny scar near his right temple, the sensuous lips.

Those lips and what they'd done to her...oh boy.

'On second thought, I need more than a caffeine shot to hear this story.' Shar stood on tiptoe and grabbed the tin box storing their emergency brownie stash.

While Shar prepared the tea and chocolate fix, Liza wondered if she'd done the right thing in bolting. She had no clue about morning-after etiquette. Should she have left a thank-you note?

When she'd slid out of bed and done her best not to wake him, she'd dressed in record time yet spent another ten minutes dithering over a note. She'd even picked up a pen, only to let it fall from her fingers when she'd stared at the blank hotel paper with fear gripping her heart.

As she'd looked at that paper, she'd been tempted to leave her number. Before reality had set in. Wade hadn't questioned her or made polite small talk. He hadn't been interested in anything beyond the obvious. And that was enough of a wake-up call for her to grab her bag and get the hell out of that hotel room.

One-night stands were called that for a reason. That was all they were. One night.

The uncharacteristic yearning to see him again? To have a repeat performance of how incredible he made her feel? Not. Happening.

'Right, here we go.' Shar placed a steaming cup of Earl Grey in front of her along with two double-choc-fudge brownies on a side plate. 'Get that into you, then start talking.'

Liza cupped her hands around the hot cup and lifted it to her lips, inhaling the fragrant bergamot steam. Earl Grey was her comfort drink, guaranteed to make her relax.

She'd drunk two pots of the stuff the morning she'd woken to find her mum gone.

It hadn't been a shock. Louisa had been an emotionally absent mother for years before she'd left. Guess Liza should be grateful her mum had waited until Liza had turned eighteen before she'd done a runner, leaving her the legal guardian of Cindy.

Crazy thing was Liza had long forgiven her father for running out on them after Cindy's birth. Men were fickle and couldn't stand a little hardship. She'd come home from her first day of school to find her dad shoving belongings into his car in front of a stoic mum.

Louisa had cried silent tears, holding a twelve-month-old Cindy in her arms, while her dad had picked Liza up, hugged her tight, and told her to take good care of her sister.

And she'd been doing it ever since.

While Liza might have forgiven—and forgotten—her dad, she couldn't forgive her mum as easily. Louisa had watched Cindy grow. Had been a good mum in her own way. But Liza had seen the signs. The subtle withdrawing of affection, longer respite visits away from the girls, the scrimping and saving of every cent.

Her mum hadn't left a note either. She'd just walked out of the door one morning with her suitcases and never looked back.

If Louisa expected Liza to be grateful for the birthday cards stacked with hundred-dollar bills that arrived every year on Cindy's birthday, she could think again.

Cindy needed love and caring, not guilt money.

Thankfully, with what Liza had done over the last decade, Cindy's financial future was secure and they no longer needed her mum's money.

Now she needed to start doing stuff for *her* and first item on the agenda involved finding her dream job. One that didn't involve schmoozing or showing her best angle to the cameras.

She sipped at the tea, savouring the warmth.

'Could you drink that any slower?' Shar wiped brownie crumbs off her fingers and mimicked talking with her hand.

Liza placed a cup on the saucer and reached for a brownie, when Shar slapped her wrist. 'You can eat later. I want details, girlie.'

Liza chuckled. 'Better tell you something before you break a bone.'

Shar's hand continued to open and shut, miming chatter. 'Still not enough of this.'

'Okay, okay.' Liza leaned back and sighed. 'Henri's book

launch was every bit as boring and pompous as him. I was
doing the rounds, talking to the regular people. I got bored
as usual.'

Then she'd stepped out onto that balcony and her life
had changed in an instant.

Melodramatic? Hell yeah, but no matter where her future led she'd never forget that one incredible night with
Wade at the Westin.

'And?' Shar leaned forward and rubbed her hands together.

'I needed some fresh air, headed outside, met someone.'

'Now you're talking.'

Liza sighed. How to articulate the rest without sound-
ing like a floozy?

'Shar, you know Cindy is my world, right?'

Shar's eyes lost their playful sparkle and she nodded,
sombre. 'Never seen anyone as dedicated as you.'

'Everything I've done is for my little sis and I'd do it
again in a heartbeat, but last night signalled a new beginning for me and when the opportunity to celebrate presented itself? Well, let's just say I grabbed it with both
hands.'

Shar let out a soft whoop and glanced at Cindy's door.
'Good for you.' She leaned forward and wiggled her eyebrows. 'So how was he?'

Liza made a zipping motion across her lips. 'No kiss-
ing and telling here.'

Shar reached across and patted her forearm. 'All I can
say is about time, love. You're a good girl, dating those
dweebs to secure your financial future, making the most
of your assets. About time you had a little fun.'

'There was nothing little about it,' Liza deadpanned,
joining in Shar's laughter a second later.

'Hey, Liza, is it Coco Pops time?'

Liza's heart squished as it always did at the sound of Cindy's voice from behind her bedroom door. There was nothing she wouldn't do for her baby sister.

'You know the drill. Weet-Bix as usual,' Liza called out, draining the rest of her tea before heading to the bedroom to help Cindy dress.

'Are you going to see him again?' Shar asked as Liza paused with her hand on the doorknob.

Liza shook her head, the disappointment in Shar's expression matching hers.

Silly, as Liza didn't have time for disappointments. She had a secure investment about to mature, a new career in marketing to embark on and an easier life ahead.

No time at all to reminisce about the hottest night of her life and what might have been if she'd had the courage to leave her details.

'Trade you a pancake stack for the Weet-Bix,' Cindy said as Liza eased open the bedroom door.

The moment she saw Cindy's beaming, lopsided smile, Liza wiped memories of Wade and focused on the number-one person in her life and her sole motivation.

Life was good.

She didn't have room in it for commanding, sexy guys, no matter how unforgettable.

CHAPTER FOUR

LIZA LITHGOW'S STYLE TIPS
FOR MAXIMUM WAG WOW IMPACT

The Classics

You don't need money to create a WAG wow look. Designer bargains, vintage chic and good accessories can create an outfit that will have the paparazzi snap-happy.

To create a timeless, elegant look consistently, it's worthwhile investing in a few classic pieces, the items in any WAG's wardrobe that will always be in style.

- Little black dress. (A staple. Buy several: different lengths, necklines, fitting. The classic LBD is a lifesaver and can be combined with various jacket/shoe combinations to give the illusion of many different looks.)

- Jacket. (Make sure it's expensive and tailored. It will last for ever.)

- Heels. (Black patent leather stilettos will never go out of style.)

- Sunglasses. (Brand names are classy. Enlist

the help of an honest shop assistant to ensure the shape/size suits your face.)

- Boots. (Black and brown leather boots can be worn with anything and everything. High heels and flats in both recommended.)
- Striped top. (Black and white stripes are a staple. Dress up or down.)
- Ballet flats. (Perfect to pop into your bag to use at the end of a long day at the Spring Racing Carnival or a long night of dancing.)
- Trousers. (Tailored black and beige will go with almost anything. Wide leg is elegant. Bootleg flattering.)
- Belt. (Thin, black leather. Classic.)
- Cardigan. (Cream cashmere, can't go wrong.)
- Clutch. (Smaller than a handbag yet makes a bigger statement.)
- Handbag. (Must carry everything including the kitchen sink but bigger isn't always better. Co-ordinate handbag to your outfit and shoes. Choose neutral colours: black, tan, brown. Mid-size with handles and shoulder strap best.)
- Jeans. (Discover which style suits you best and stick with it. But for maximum WAG wow, have denim in various cuts: skinny, bootleg, boyfriend, etc.)
- Trenchcoat. (Double-breasted, belted, beige. Classic.)
- Watch. (For timeless elegance, invest in an expensive watch. People notice.)
- Bling. (Take the 'less is best' approach. Dia-

mond stud earrings. Thin white gold necklace.
Unless your sports star partner wins the World
Cup or Olympics for his team, then get him to
buy you a diamond mine and then some.)

WITH CINDY ENGROSSED in her electronic tablet, Liza ducked
into the shower, something she should've done the moment she'd arrived home to scrub off the lingering smell
of Wade's aftershave.

Maybe that was why she hadn't? For the moment she
towelled off, slipped on her skinny jeans and a turquoise
long-sleeved T-shirt, and padded into the kitchen to say
bye to Shar, she missed it—his evocative crisp citrus scent.

Irrational? Absolutely, but it wasn't every day an amazingly hot guy left his designer aftershave imprinted on her
skin.

The perky hum died in her throat as she caught sight of
Shar waving a stack of messages at her.

'These are for you.'

Liza raised an eyebrow. 'All of them?'

Shar nodded. 'I didn't want to bombard you when you
first came in.'

'More like you wanted the goss and knew those would
distract me.'

'That too.' Shar grinned and handed them over. 'Looks
like some editor from Qu Publishing is mighty persistent.'

Liza groaned. 'Can't those morons get a clue and stop
badgering me?'

'Doesn't look like it.' Shar pointed to the message slips
in her hand. 'All those are from her.'

'No way.'

Liza flicked through the lot, twelve in all. Nine yesterday when she'd been out in the afternoon and later at the
party, three while she'd been in the shower this morning.

'She said she'd call back in ten minutes.'

'Like hell.' Liza stomped over to the bin and dumped the lot. 'I'm sick to death of being pestered by this mob and I'm going to put a stop to it.'

Shar punched the air. 'You go, girl.'

Liza grinned. 'While I'm kicking some publisher butt, maybe you should stop watching daytime TV?'

'Careful, cheeky.' Shar shooed her away. 'You've got an hour before I need to leave, so hop to it.'

Liza didn't need to be told twice.

No way, no how, would she ever sell her story. Cindy needed to be protected at all costs and the last thing she wanted was a bunch of strangers reading about their lives and intruding.

For they would, she had no doubt. There'd be book tours and blog tours and a social media explosion if she told all. It was why these Qu Publishing vultures were hounding her. They knew a best-seller when they saw it.

Laughable, really. What would they say if they knew the truth? That she'd invented a fake life to protect her real one?

That every event, every lash extension, every designer gown, had fitted a deliberate persona she'd cultivated to get what she wanted.

Lifelong security for her little sis.

And when her financial adviser rang today and gave her the good news about her investments maturing, she could put away her lash curler and hair straightener for ever.

Yeah, the sooner she set this publisher straight, the better.

She yanked on black knee-high boots and shrugged into a sable leather vest with fake fur collar. While being a WAG had been a pain, some of the perks, like the gorgeous designer clothes she'd got to keep on occasion, had been great.

She'd miss the clothes. She wouldn't miss the rest.

Time to hang up her stilettos and set the record straight.

Wade strode into the boardroom with five minutes to spare then spent the next thirty listening to a bunch of boring agenda items that could've been wrapped up in half that time.

He wished they'd cut to the chase.

The future of Qu Publishing depended on a bunch of old fuddy-duds that wouldn't know a profit margin if it jumped up and bit them on the ass.

The members of the board were old school, had been best buddies with his dad and, in turn, were *rather fond of his delightful wife Babs.*

When the chairman had articulated that little gem at the party last night, he'd wanted to hurl.

Was Wade the only guy who could see through her fake wiles?

By the board's decision to back Babs in her quest to sell Qu Publishing? Hell yeah.

He knew it would take a monumental effort to save this company. From the accounts down to the staff, Qu needed a major overhaul. And to do that they needed a cash injection, in the form of a mega best-seller.

Which reminded him. He needed to sign that WAG to a contract today. He'd up the ante with a massive cash injection from his own pocket, a hefty six-figure sum she couldn't refuse. From what he'd heard in snippets from memos, her sordid tale would be a blockbuster. Serial WAG, dated an international soccer star and a basketball player, a media darling from magazines to TV, a practised socialite who'd appeared everywhere in Australia from all reports.

He couldn't care less if she'd dated the entire Socceroos

team and what she'd worn to do it but that kind of gossip drivel made the average reader drool. And sold books.

Thankfully his company had branched out into the lucrative young adult market and were making a killing but Qu readers expected factual biographies, so no use getting too radical when he'd probably only have a few months tops to save the joint.

Yeah, he needed to get that WAG to sign ASAP. He'd get straight onto it, once this meeting wound up.

'And now, gentlemen, we come to the last item on the agenda.' The chairman cleared his throat and glared at Wade as if he'd proposed they collectively run down Bourke Street naked. 'As you've seen from the proposal Mr Urquart *Junior* emailed us yesterday, he wants to give the company three months to see if it can turn a healthy profit.'

Wade bristled at the emphasis on junior. He'd paid his dues in this company in his younger days, had done a hell of a lot more in London where his business was booming compared to this languishing one.

Thoughts of the disparity saddened him and pricked his guilt as nothing else could. If he hadn't been so pig-headed, so stubborn, so distrustful, he could've helped his dad while he had the chance. Could've done a lot more, such as mend the gap between them *he'd* created. A regret he'd have to live with for the rest of his life. A regret that would be eased once he saved Qu.

'To do this, he proposes Qu Publishing will have a *New York Times* best-seller on its hands within the year, along with accompanying publicity blitz in the form of social media, television and print ads.'

A titter of unease echoed around the conference table and Wade squared his shoulders, ready for the battle of his life.

No way would he let Babs win. She'd made a laughing

stock out of his dad; damned if he sat back and let her do the same to his dad's legacy.

'We usually put agenda items like this to a vote.' The chairman steepled his fingers and rested his elbows on the table like a presiding judge. 'But I don't think it's necessary in this case.'

Wade clenched his hands under the table. Pompous old fools. 'Gentlemen, if you'd let me reiterate my proposal—'

'That won't be necessary, Wade.'

The chairman's use of his first name surprised him, but not as much as his dour expression easing into a smile. 'Every member here knew your father and respected what he achieved with this company. But times are tough in the publishing industry. The digital boom has hit our print runs hard and readers aren't buying paperbacks or hardbacks like they used to. Economically, it makes sense to sell.'

Wade opened his mouth to respond and the chairman held up his hand. 'But we admire what you've achieved with your company in London. And we like your ambition. Reminds us of your father. So we're willing to give you three months to turn this company around.'

Jubilant and relieved, Wade nodded. 'Thanks for the opportunity.'

'We understand the profits won't soar until we have that promised best-seller on our hands, but if you can prove to us we'll have that guaranteed hit with buyers' pre-orders in three months, we won't vote with Babs to sell Qu. Got it?'

'Loud and clear.' Wade stood, ready to hit the ground running. His first task? Get that WAG to sign on the dotted line. 'Thanks, gentlemen, you won't be sorry.'

He'd make sure of it.

The idiots were stonewalling her and Liza wasn't happy.

'You won't take no for an answer. Your editors won't

take no for an answer so I'm taking this to the top.' She leaned over the receptionist, who, to her credit, didn't flinch. 'Who's your boss?'

The receptionist darted a frantic glance to her right. 'He can't see you now.'

'Like hell.' Liza strode towards the sole double doors where the receptionist had looked.

'You can't do that,' the perky blonde yelled and Liza held up her hand.

'Watch me.'

Liza didn't stop to knock, twisting the doorknob and flinging open the door before she could second-guess the wisdom of barging into a CEO's inner sanctum unannounced.

They were relentlessly harassing her; let them see how they liked getting a taste of their own medicine.

The editors wouldn't listen so the only way she'd get this mob to leave her alone was to have the order given from the top.

However, as she strode into the office her plan to clear up this mess hit a major snag.

For the guy sitting behind a huge glass-topped desk, the guy barking orders into a phone, the guy clearly in charge of Qu Publishing, was the guy who'd set her body alight last night.

Wade stopped mid-sentence as Liza barged into his office like a glamazon bikie chick.

She wore tight denim, a clingy long-sleeved T-shirt, a black leather vest and the sexiest knee-high boots he'd ever seen.

By her grim expression and wild hair, make that an avenging bikie chick.

He'd expected to never see her again. Had secretly hoped he would.

After the crappy year he'd endured—learning his dad hadn't trusted him with the truth about his heart condition, accepting how far their relationship had deteriorated, his dad's death, Babs's sell-out plans—maybe the big guy upstairs had finally granted him a break.

'Set up a meeting with the buyers and we'll discuss covers and digital launch later,' he said, hanging up on his deputy without waiting for an answer.

He stood, surprised by Liza's stunned expression. Wasn't as if they were strangers. She'd obviously sought him out, though the dramatic entrance was a surprise.

Most people couldn't get past Jodi, the receptionist, he'd been told. His dad had raved about her and from what he'd seen of her work ethic in half a day, the woman was a dynamo.

Maybe Liza had been so desperate to see him she couldn't wait?

Yeah, and maybe that WAG would saunter into his office any second and give him her completed biography bound in hardcover.

'Hey, Liza, good to see you again—'

'*You're* the CEO of Qu Publishing?'

She made it sound as if he ran an illegal gambling den, her eyes narrowing as she crossed his office to stand on the opposite side of his desk. 'Oh, it all makes sense now. That's why you slept with me.'

She muttered an expletive and shook her head, leaving him increasingly clueless as he waved away Jodi, who'd stuck her head around the door, and motioned for her to close it. Jodi mouthed an apology before doing as he said, leaving him alone with an irate, irrational woman who stared at him as if she wanted to drive a letter opener through his heart.

He wished he'd stashed it in his top drawer once he'd done the mail.

'Time out.' He made a T sign with his hands and gestured towards the grey leather sofas. 'Why don't we sit and discuss this?'

Whatever *this* was, because he had no idea why she'd gone crazy on him for being CEO of Qu and what that had to do with having great sex.

Her lips compressed in a mutinous line as she marched towards the sofas and slumped into one, ensuring she sprawled across it so he had no chance of sitting nearby.

Ironic, when last night she couldn't get close enough. And the feeling had been entirely mutual.

Even now, with confusion clogging his head, he couldn't switch off the erotic images.

Liza straddling him. Underneath him. On her hands and knees in front of him.

The sweet taste of her. The sexy sounds she made. The softness of her skin. The intoxicating rose and vanilla scent that had lingered on his sheets.

Their night together had been sensational, the most memorable sex he'd had in a long time.

Hell, he was hard just thinking about it.

Then he looked into her dark blue eyes and saw something that shocked him.

Betrayal.

What had he done to make her look at him as if he'd ripped her world apart?

'You used me,' she said, jabbing a finger in his direction before curling it into a fist as if she wanted to slug him. 'Proud of yourself?'

'I don't know what you're talking about.' He poured a

glass of water and edged it across the table. 'Can we back-track a little so I have a hope in Hades of following this bizarre conversation?'

'Drop the innocent act. The moment I walked in here and saw you, everything made sense.'

Her fingers dug into the leather, as if she needed an anchor. 'Why you asked me to have a drink with you last night, inviting me back to your suite, the sex...' She trailed off and glanced away, her blush rather cute. 'Totally freak-ing low.'

She thought he'd used her. Why? None of this made sense.

'From what I remember, you approached me on that bal-cony. And from your participation in the phenomenal sex, you were just as into it as me.'

Her blush deepened as she dragged her defiant gaze to meet his. 'What I don't get is why you'd think I'd sell my story after I discovered your identity?'

She shook her head. 'Or are you so full of yourself you thought I'd remember the sex and sign on the dotted line?'

Pieces of the puzzle shifted, jiggled and finally aligned in a picture that blew his mind.

'*You're* the WAG we're trying to sign?'

'Like you didn't know.' She snorted in disgust. 'Nice touch last night, by the way. "Your name sounds famil-iar"? Sheesh.'

Hot damn.

Liza Lithgow was the WAG he needed to save Qu Pub-lishing.

And he'd slept with her.

Way to go with messing up big time.

'Liza, listen to me—'

'Why the hell should I?' Her chest heaved with indignation and he struggled to avert his eyes. No use fuelling her anger. 'You *lied* to me. You *used* me—'

'Stop right there.' He held up his hand and, amazingly, her tirade ceased. 'Yeah, I knew Qu Publishing was pursuing a WAG for a biography but I had no idea that was you.'

'But I told you my name—'

'Which I had vaguely heard but, come on, I'd only landed in Melbourne for the first time in six months a few hours earlier. I'd come into the office briefly before heading to that party. So yeah, I'd probably seen your name on a document or memo or something, that's how it registered.'

He leaned closer, hating how she leaned back. 'But everything that happened between us last night? Nothing to do with us publishing your biography and everything to do with...'

Damn, wouldn't do any good blurting out what last night had been about. He didn't need her feeling sorry for him. He needed her onside, ready to tell her story so the board gave Qu more than a temporary reprieve.

'With what?'

At least her tone had lost some of its vitriol.

'With you and me and the connection we shared.'

'Connections can be manufactured,' she said, her steely stare speaking volumes.

She didn't believe him.

When he'd first glimpsed her last night he'd associated feminine and bimbo in the same sentence. Then when she'd spoken to him, he'd re-evaluated the bimbo part pretty damn quick. He never would've thought her attractive outer shell hid balls of steel.

'Maybe, but the way we burned up the sheets last night?' He winked, trying to charm his way out of this godforsaken mess. 'I wasn't faking it. Were you?'

At last, a glimmer of softening as her shoulders relaxed

and her glare lost some of its warrior fierceness. 'Forget last night—'

'Big ask,' he said, continuing with his plan to use a little honey rather than vinegar to coerce her into giving him a fair hearing. 'Don't know about you, but the way we were together last night? Pretty damn rare.'

She glanced away, but not before he glimpsed a spark of heat in those expressive blue eyes.

'And have to say, I was pretty disappointed this morning to find you gone, because I would've really liked to...'

What? See her again? Pick up where they'd left off? Prove their attraction extended beyond a first-time fluke?

Best he stop there.

He needed this woman onside to save his father's business. A business he should've seen was floundering before it was too late. Before his prejudices had irrevocably damaged his relationship with his dad and ended up with him not knowing his dad was dying before he could make amends.

Saving Qu, saving his dad's legacy, was the one thing he could do to make this semi-right. He could live with the guilt. He couldn't live with knowing he hadn't given this mission his best shot.

Her gaze swung back, locking on his with unerring precision. 'Look, I'll admit we shared something special last night. But I don't have room in my life for complications.'

He should drop this topic and move on to more important stuff, like getting her to sign. But he couldn't help teasing her a little. Maybe if she loosened up he'd have more chance of convincing her Qu Publishing were the only mob in town worth considering for her tell-all tale?

'And that's what I'd be if I called you for a date? Dinner? A movie?'

She nodded. 'You're a nice guy but—'

'Nice?' He winced. 'Ouch.'

She rolled her eyes. 'Your ego's not that fragile, considering you picked me up at a party after knowing me less than ten minutes.'

'And you're not as immune to me as you're pretending considering you agreed to a drink after knowing me less than ten minutes.'

'Touché.' The corners of her mouth curved upward. 'Let's forget last night and move on to more important matters, like why your office is bugging me constantly and won't take no for an answer.'

'Glad to hear the editors are doing their jobs.'

Her mouth hardened. Maybe he'd taken the levity a tad far?

'You think this is a joke?' She shook her head, her ponytail swishing temptingly over one shoulder, reminding him of how her blonde hair had looked spread out on the pillows and draped across his chest. And lower. 'I can't count the number of phone calls to my mobile. And now someone in your office has used underhanded tactics to discover my *unlisted* number and I'm being pestered at home? Poor form.'

She sighed and a sliver of remorse pierced his resolve to get this deal done today.

'I hate having my private life invaded and it's time you and your cohorts backed off.'

He should feel guilty but he didn't. While Liza didn't fit the typical WAG profile, she couldn't live the life of a famous sportsman's girlfriend without loving some of the attention. And having her private life open to scrutiny came with the territory.

All he wanted was to delve a little deeper, give his readers something more and they in turn would give him what he needed most: money to save Qu.

'What if we don't back off?'

He threw it out there, expecting her to curse and threaten.

He wasn't prepared for the shimmer of tears that disappeared so fast after a few blinks he wondered if he'd imagined them.

'Two words for you.' She held up two fingers. 'Harassment charges.'

Idle threats didn't scare him.

But the guilty twist his heart gave at the sight of those tears? Absolutely terrified.

He didn't handle waterworks well. Even Babs's crocodile tears at his dad's funeral had made him supremely uncomfortable.

That had to be the reason he'd gone soft for a moment and actually considered backing down after seeing Liza's tears.

'Maybe if you gave us a chance to explain our offer, you may feel differently?'

Her expression turned mutinous. 'There's nothing you can say or do that will convince me to sell my story.'

Okay, he was done being cool. He'd tried the truth; she hadn't believed him. He'd tried charming her; she'd lightened up for a scant minute. Time to go for the jugular. And do his damnedest to forget that his lips had coaxed and nipped her in that very vicinity last night.

'A ghost writer, a mid-six-figure advance, a more than generous royalty percentage, all for a story that most people have probably heard before?'

Her glacial glare dropped the temperature in the room by five degrees. 'It's called *private* life for a reason. I don't give a flying Frisbee what people surmise or print or think about me. As of last night I'm done with all the hoopla so you and your cronies can invent a fictional story for all I care.'

The first flicker of unease soon gave way to fear. Wade

never took no for an answer, not in the business world. But Liza's adamant stance put a serious dent in his confidence he could woo her to Qu.

He needed her biography.

Failure wasn't an option.

'Look, Liza, I'm sure we can come to some type of mutually beneficial agreement—'

'What part of *you can take your offer and stick it* don't you understand?'

With that, he watched his final chance at saving his father's legacy stride out of the door.

CHAPTER FIVE

LIZA LITHGOW'S STYLE TIPS
FOR MAXIMUM WAG WOW IMPACT

The City

Depending how famous the sportsman, WAGs get to travel, but home is where the heart is. Here are my tips for getting to know beautiful Melbourne.

1. Acland Street, St. Kilda. (An iconic street lined with cake and pastry shops. Dare you to stop at trying one! And on Sundays, check out the market on the nearby Esplanade.)

2. Lygon Street, Carlton. (The Little Italy of Melbourne, a street lined with fabulous restaurants and cafés. Try the thin-crusted pizzas and the espressos. You won't be able to walk past the gelato outlets without succumbing!)

3. Victoria Street, Richmond. (If you love Vietnamese food this street is for you. Choose from the many restaurants filled with fragrant steam from soups and sizzling dishes. And if you love to shop, check out nearby Bridge Road with its many brand outlets. Bargains galore!)

4. Southbank. (Stroll along the Yarra River and try to decide which fabulous café you'll dine in. Or check out the funky shops.)

5. Docklands. (If you like to eat by the water's edge, this area is for you. Many restaurants, many nationalities.)

6. Dandenongs. (The mountain range just over an hour from the city, where you'll find many quaint B&Bs, craft shops and cafés to explore. Also home to the iconic Puffing Billy steam train, which takes you on a leisurely ride through the lush forest.)

7. Phillip Island. (If you like cute animals and the beach, you'll love this place. Stroll the surf beach and, at night, check out the fairy penguins.)

8. Federation Square. (In the heart of the city, Fed Square is home to restaurants, cafés and cultural displays.)

9. MCG. (WAGs in all sports codes have usually visited the Melbourne Cricket Ground at some stage. Home of the AFL Grand Final, watched by millions around the world. A visit to the sports museum here is worth it.)

10. Little Bourke Street. (In the heart of the city, Chinatown in Melbourne, lined with fabulous Chinese restaurants. Hard to choose!)

11. Chapel Street, South Yarra. (About ten minutes from the city, you'll find an eclectic mix of boutiques, restaurants and cafés here. Worth strolling to people-watch alone.)

12. Queen Victoria Market. (Food and fashion bargains, with everything in between. A fun way to pass a few hours.)

13. Daylesford. (This quaint town is in the heart of 'Spa Country'. The amazing baths at neighbouring town Hepburn Springs are a must visit. The area is home to gourmet food and artists. Visit the Convent Gallery for a combination of both.)

14. Brunswick Street, Fitzroy. (An eclectic mix of cafés, boutiques and clubs.)

LIZA HAD MADE it to the elevator when her mobile rang. Considering her hands shook with fury, she wouldn't have answered it if she hadn't been expecting her financial adviser's call imparting good news.

Her investments had matured and Cindy was set for life. The figures she'd crunched for long-term ongoing medical and allied health care had terrified her but now, after years of careful saving and investing, she could rest easy in the knowledge that should anything happen to her, Cindy would be financially secure.

It made every blister from impossibly high stilettos, every sacrificed chocolate mousse so not to gain weight, every artful fend-off from a groping sleaze worth it.

Ignoring the death glare from the receptionist, she fished out her phone, checked the number on display and hit the answer button.

'Hey, Walden, good to hear from you. I've been expecting your call.'

A long silence greeted her.

'Walden?'

A throat cleared. 'Uh, sorry, Miss Lithgow, this is Ullric.'

Okay, so Walden's assistant had called instead. A first,

but not surprising considering Walden had a full schedule whenever she'd tried to slot in a meeting lately.

'Hey, Ullric. I'm assuming you have good news for me about my investments?'

Again, a long pause and this time a finger of foreboding strummed Liza's spine.

'About that…' His hesitancy made her clench the phone. 'Afraid I have some bad news.'

Liza's heart stalled before kick starting with a painful wallop. 'I don't like the sound of that. What's happened?'

Ullric blew out a long breath that transferred into annoying static. 'Mr Wren has disappeared and his clients' funds are gone.'

Liza's legs collapsed and she sagged against the nearest wall.

This couldn't be happening.

A delusion, brought on by the shock of discovering Wade had potentially used her.

Though she wasn't prone to delusions and Ullric's pronouncement underlined with regret seemed all too real.

'What—how—?'

'The fraud squad are investigating. His assets have been seized, but from what I've been told the client funds have been siphoned into offshore accounts.'

Liza swore. Several times. The only words she could form, let alone articulate.

'I'm sorry, Miss Lithgow. The police will be in touch and I'll let you know if I hear anything—'

Liza disconnected, the mobile falling from her fingers and hitting the carpet with a muted thud.

Her life savings.

Gone.

In that moment every stupid awards ceremony and dress

fitting and magazine article she'd endured flashed before her eyes in a teasing kaleidoscope of humiliation.

Everything she'd worn, everything she'd said, for the last umpteen years had been to build a sizable nest egg for Cindy in case something happened to her.

And now she had nothing.

Tears burned the backs of her eyes and a lump welled in her throat.

What the hell was she going to do?

A pair of expensive loafers came into view and her head fell forward until her chin almost touched her chest. Great, that was all she needed to make her failure complete. Wade Urquart to witness it.

'I think this belongs to you.'

He picked up her mobile phone and held it out.

Liza was bone-deep tired. Exhausted to the core, where she'd regularly drawn on a well of courage to face the media, the crowds, the critics.

But she had to leave here with some snippet of dignity intact and right now, sitting in a crumpled heap on Wade's expensive carpet, she'd lost most of it.

'Here.' He dropped the mobile into her open bag and held out his hand. 'Let me help you up.'

'I think you've helped enough,' she muttered, but accepted his hand all the same, grateful for the hoist up, for her legs still wobbled embarrassingly.

'Are you okay?'

She couldn't look at his face, didn't want to see the pity there, so she focused on the second button of his crisp pale blue business shirt.

He'd lost the tie, a snazzy navy striped one that had set off his suit earlier. The fact she'd noticed? A residual tell from her WAG days when it paid to be observant about the latest fashion. And nothing at all to do with the fact she could recite every item of clothing he'd worn last night and what he'd looked like without it.

When she didn't answer, he placed his hand under her elbow and guided her towards his office. 'Come with me.'

Liza wanted to protest. She wanted to yell at the injustice of busting her butt all these years, and for what?

But all the fight had drained out of her when she'd hung up and it wouldn't hurt to have a glass of water, muster the last of her meagre reserves of courage and face the trip home.

Home. Where Cindy was.

Damn.

She'd had their future all figured out.

Now she had nothing. She now needed to find a job, and pronto. The idea of trying to juggle a new job and how it would affect Cindy's care, without the security of money... Pain gripped her chest and squeezed, hard.

The tears she'd been battling welled again and this time spilled over and trickled down her cheeks.

Wade darted a glance her way but she resolutely stared ahead and dashed away the tears with her other hand.

Thankfully, he didn't question her further until he'd led her to the sofa she'd so haughtily vacated five minutes earlier and closed the door.

He didn't speak, setting a glass of water in front of her and taking a seat opposite, giving her time to compose herself.

His thoughtfulness made her like him. And she didn't want to like him, not after what she'd discovered today.

In fact, when she'd huffed out of here she'd assumed she'd never see him again—and had steadfastly ignored that small part of her that had been disappointed at the thought.

She gulped the water, hoping it would dislodge the giant

lump of sadness in her throat. It did little as she battled the hopelessness of her situation.

Her new life? In ruins.

Cindy's safety net? Gone.

She'd been screwed over by some smarmy financial adviser whose balls she'd crush in a vice if she ever laid eyes on him again. Yeah, as if that were likely.

Her financial ruin meant she was back to square one, but no way could she don designer outfits and start prancing around on some egotistical sportsman's arm again.

Mentally, she couldn't take it any more. Physically, late twenties was getting old for a WAG and she was done with the paparazzi scrutiny.

Which left her plum out of options.

'Want to tell me what happened out there?'

'Not really.' She topped up the glass from a water pitcher, grateful her hand didn't shake.

'I don't think my offer was that repugnant so it had to be something else.'

'It was your offer.'

The lie tripped off her tongue. Better for him to think that than know the truth.

That she'd lost her life savings and had no way out of this disastrous situation.

'You're not a very good liar.'

'How would you know?'

He raised an eyebrow at her acerbic tone. 'Because contrary to what you believe, I actually spent time paying attention to you last night and I reckon you've got one of the most guileless faces I've seen when you let your guard down.'

Damn, how did he do that? Undermine her with insight when he shouldn't know her at all?

'I can't talk about it.' She shook her head, tugging on the

end of her ponytail and twisting it around her finger. 'Besides, it's my problem. There's nothing you can do about it.'

'Sure?' He braced his elbows on his knees. 'Don't forget, if you're ever in a bind all you have to do is accept my offer and you'd be set for life.'

As his words sank in, Liza's hand stilled and she flicked her ponytail back over her shoulder.

No. She couldn't.

But what other option did she have?

Agreeing to a tell-all biography would replenish her lost savings and ensure Cindy's security.

Relating a few stories to a ghost writer had to be less painful than going down the fake tan/lash extensions/hair foils route again.

She wanted to pursue a career in marketing and accepting this book deal would allow that.

The only catch was Cindy.

Liza didn't want the world knowing her private business and she wanted to protect Cindy at all costs. She'd done a good job of it so far, keeping her public persona completely separate from the reality of her home life.

Any publicity shots and interviews with Jimmy had been done at his palatial apartment, same with Henri. It had been important to her, deliberately misleading the press to think she lived with the sports stars so they wouldn't hound her or, worse, follow her.

Not that she was ashamed of the modest Californian bungalow she shared with Cindy, but her goal to ultimately protect Cindy at all costs meant she wanted their real home and the life they shared to be off-limits to the public.

The guys had never mentioned Cindy in interviews either, though she knew that had more to do with them not wanting to be tainted—even by association—with a disability they couldn't handle or had no knowledge of rather than her request.

Jimmy and Henri were too egotistical to want to field questions about their girlfriend's disabled sister so they'd pretended Cindy hadn't existed. While their apparent disregard had hurt, it had been exactly as she wanted it.

Her protecting Cindy over the years had worked, but how could she sustain that in a biography?

She had physically invented a façade all these years, playing up to the image of the perfect WAG.

What if she invented a story to go with it?

It wasn't as if she hadn't done it before when she'd been interviewed. She'd give a few scant details, an embellishment here, a truth stretched there. No one would be wiser if she did the same in her biography.

She could lay out the basics of her upbringing and focus on the interesting stuff, like her relationships with Jimmy and Henri. That was what people were really interested in anyway, the whole 'what's it like dating a famous sports star?' angle.

Yeah, she could do this.

Continue her WAG role a little longer, but behind the scenes this time. Had to be easier than strutting in front of A-listers and faking it.

But she'd told Wade to shove his offer so appearing too eager would be a dead giveaway something was wrong, and she didn't want him prying.

If she had to do this, it had to be a strictly business deal. From now on, her personal life was off-limits. Unless it involved inventing a little drama for the ghost writer.

'What if I was crazy enough to reconsider your offer? What would it entail?'

He masked his surprise quickly. 'We'd have a contract to you by this afternoon. Standard publishing contract with clearly stated royalty rates, world rights, advance, no option to your next book.'

Next book? Heck, she could barely scrimmage enough suitably juicy info for this one. Though she'd love to publish a book raising the awareness of cerebral palsy and give an insight for carers. It was something she'd considered over the years: using her high profile to educate people regarding the lifelong condition.

But then she imagined the intrusiveness on Cindy's life—the interview requests, the demands, the interference on her schedule and the potentially damaging physical effects linked to emotional fragility in CP sufferers—and Liza balked.

Cindy thrived on routine and the last thing Liza wanted for her sister was a potential setback. Or, worse, increased spasticity in her muscles because she got too excited or too stressed. Most days were hard enough to get through without added complications and that was what spotlighting her sister's cerebral palsy could do.

Embellishing her so-called glamorous life and leaving Cindy out of it would be a lot easier.

'How much is the advance?'

He named a six-figure sum that made her head spin.

Were people that desperate to read a bunch of stuff about her life?

Considering how she'd been occasionally stalked by paparazzi eager for a scoop while dating Jimmy and Henri, she had her answer.

'The advance is released in increments. A third on signing, a third on acceptance of the manuscript and a third on publishing.'

'And when would that be?'

'Six months.'

She laughed. 'You're kidding? How can you publish a book in six months?'

'Buyers are lined up. Ghost writer ready to start tomorrow if you can. Week-long interview process, two weeks writing the book, straight to copy and line editors, then printers.'

Liza knew little about publishing but marketing was her game and she'd interned at a small publishing house while at uni. No way could a book get turned around in six months.

'Do you have a marketing plan?'

A slight frown creased his brow. 'Have to admit, Qu is lagging in that department at the moment. I want to bring the company into the twenty-first century with online digital instalments of books, massive social media campaigns, exclusive digital releases on our website.'

'So what's the problem? Hire someone.'

He tugged at his cuffs, the first sign she'd seen him anything but confident since she'd arrived. 'Turnaround time on this book is tight.'

'I'll say.' She shook her head. 'Six-month release date? Impossible.'

'And you can say that with your extensive publishing experience?'

She didn't like his sarcasm, didn't like the fact it hurt more.

'Matter of fact, I interned for a publisher during my marketing degree.'

'Next you'll be telling me you're applying for the job.'

And just like that, Liza had a bamboozling idea. For the first time since that soul-destroying phone call earlier, hope shimmered to life and gave her the confidence to make her idea happen.

'That's a great idea. Why don't you give me the marketing job on this book and I'll make sure it's the best damn book this company has ever published?'

He fixed her with an incredulous stare. 'Let me get this straight. You want a publishing contract *and* a marketing job here? After basically telling me to stick my offer—'

'Call it a WAG's prerogative to change her mind.' She smiled, hoping it would soften him up. 'What do you say? Do we have a deal?'

'What we have here is you not telling me everything and then having the cheek to try and coerce me into giving you a job too.'

'Take it or leave it.'

Yeah, as if she could afford to call his bluff.

If he left it, she'd be back to strapping on her stilettos and smiling for the cameras again. She shuddered.

Those sensual lips that had explored every part of her body eased into a smile.

'You drive a hard bargain, Liza, but you've got yourself a deal.'

Liza could've hugged him.

She settled for a sedate shake of hands, though there was nothing remotely sedate about the way her body buzzed as his fingers curled around hers.

That part of her plan where she kept dealings with Wade strictly business?

Would be sorely tested.

CHAPTER SIX

LIZA LITHGOW'S STYLE TIPS
FOR MAXIMUM WAG WOW IMPACT

The Big Chill

Melbourne is renowned for its chilly winters but that doesn't mean WAGs need to lose their wow. Here's how to beat the big chill:

1. Even though your body isn't on show as much, maintain moisturised, smooth skin. Indulge in home-made natural masks made from egg whites, avocado and honey. Exfoliate dry heels, lavish with moisturiser and wear warm socks to bed. Continue to drink two litres of water a day. Evening events will continue throughout winter and you need to be at your glamorous best.

2. Surround yourself with warm textiles at home. Fluffy throws and cuddly cushions, perfect for snuggling inside.

3. Choose to stay home occasionally rather than doing the constant social whirl of nightclub openings, theatre and movie premieres. Curl up with a hot chocolate and watch DVDs.

4. Stay warm. Invest in a pair of snug Uggs and a cosy blanket to cover yourself with while curled on the couch.

5. Scented candles are perfect for creating a winter ambiance. From vanilla to cinnamon, infuse your room with warmth.

6. Whip up a feast. Check out new cookbooks. Invest in a slow cooker. Surround yourself with fresh ingredients and herbs. And enjoy the results of your labour while whizzing around a warm kitchen.

7. Relax. Take a long, hot bath, slip into comfy clothes, pour a glass of red and curl up on the couch with the latest best-seller.

8. Warm up. On rainy days, get active. Whether yoga at home or a local Zumba class, having a workout is good for the mind, body and soul.

9. Rug up and take a walk. Head to a local park or the beautiful Botanical Gardens near the city.

10. A rainy day is perfect for all those little jobs you've put off: sort through your old photos, spring clean your closet, organise your filing cabinet. You'll feel satisfied and warm by the end of it.

11. Pep up your wardrobe. Investing in a few key pieces will glam up your look. A good quality woollen coat and black high-heeled and flat-heeled knee-high boots can be used for many seasons.

12. Check out other sports. While WAGs get to attend all her partner's games, why not learn

about a new sport? Melbourne is the home
of Australian Rules Football in winter. Pick
a team. Don the colours and show your pa-
triotism.

13. If all else fails and the cold is getting you
down, book a weekend away to escape and
make sure it's somewhere tropical. Winters
in Queensland are notoriously mild and after
a two-hour plane trip you could be soaking
up the sun.

WADE HAD GIVEN up figuring women out a long time ago.

He dated them, he wooed them, he liked them, but that
was where it ended. Any guy who lost his head over a
woman was asking for trouble.

He'd seen it firsthand with his dad.

Not that he'd begrudged the old man happiness. Far from
it. Quentin had raised him alone after his mum died when
he was a toddler, devoting his time to his business and
Wade with little room for anything else.

Then when Wade had started uni Babs had come along
and his dad had been smitten. Wade had been appalled.

He'd seen right through the gold-digging younger
woman; probably why Babs had hated him on sight. The
feeling had been entirely mutual.

But Wade had seen the way his dad lit up around Babs
and while he'd tried to broach the delicate subject of age
differences and financial situations, one ferocious glare
from his dad had seen him backing down.

They'd been married within a year and, as much as Wade
hated to admit it, Babs had been good for Quentin. They'd
had a good ten years together but Wade had left for London after two.

He couldn't pretend to like Babs and he saw what the barely hidden animosity did to his dad. It caused an irrevocable tension between them and while neither of them mentioned it, it was there all the same.

Wade had stayed away deliberately, only catching up with Quentin on his infrequent trips to London, invariably alone. They talked publishing and the digital revolution and cricket but Wade never asked how Babs was and his dad never volunteered the information.

The fact he hadn't seen his dad in the fifteen months before his death? And that Quentin hadn't trusted him enough to tell him the truth about the heart condition that had ultimately killed him? The biggest regret of Wade's life and the sole reason he was here, trying to save the company that had meant the world to his dad.

He should've known about his dad's dodgy heart. He should've had the opportunity to make amends for deliberately fostering emotional distance between them.

Instead, guilt had mingled with his sorrow, solidifying into an uncomfortable mass of self-recrimination and disgust.

He didn't trust easily and his scepticism of Babs had ultimately driven his dad away.

He'd regretted it every day since his dad's funeral.

Hopefully, saving Qu would help ease the relentless remorse that he'd stuffed up royally when it came to Quentin.

While Wade had left Qu a long time ago, he kept abreast of developments and when rumours of employee dissatisfaction, low sales and financial strife reached him in London following Quentin's death, he knew what he had to do.

Throw in the fact his dad had barely been buried before Babs had started flinging around terms like 'white elephant' and 'financial drain' in relation to Qu, and Wade had had no choice.

He'd appointed his deputy as acting CEO in London and hightailed it back to Melbourne as fast as he could.

Just in time too, judging by the board's lukewarm response to his plans to save the business.

As for his confrontation with Babs before the party yesterday...he'd been right about her all along.

Thank goodness his dad had been smart enough to leave a very precise will. Babs got the multimillion-dollar Toorak mansion and a stack of cash. He got the business.

But sadly, the bulk of his dad's shares had passed on to Babs too and that meant they now had equal voting rights with the board.

If she whispered in the right ears—and she had from all accounts—if it came to a vote they'd sell Qu Publishing out from under him.

He couldn't let that happen. He wouldn't, now he had Liza on board.

Thinking of Liza brought him full circle back to his original supposition.

He'd given up trying to figure women out.

Which was why he had no clue why she'd had a mini meltdown half an hour earlier. And why he didn't trust her complete about-face in regard to his offer.

One minute she'd been fiery and defiant, the next he'd found her in a defeated heap near the elevator.

Whoever had rung her had delivered bad news. And the thought it could've been some guy who'd devastated her rankled.

He'd assumed she was entanglement-free last night, but what if there was some guy in the picture, an ex she was hung up on? And why the hell did it matter?

Whatever had happened via that phone call, it had provided a major shake-up for her to switch from a vehement refusal to accepting his offer. It made him wonder, had it been a ruse? A plan on her part to get him to up the advance?

He didn't think so, for her devastation had been real when he'd found her crumpled beside the elevator. But his ingrained lack of trust couldn't be shaken and her vacillating behaviour piqued his curiosity meter.

Was Liza genuine or was she a damned good actress? And if so, what was her motivation?

Ultimately, it shouldn't matter. He couldn't afford to be distracted. It would take all his concentration to ensure her biography hit the shelves within a record six months. He had editors, buyers, online marketing managers and a host of other people to clue in to the urgency of this release.

Not that he'd tell them why. Having a publisher on the brink of implosion didn't exactly inspire confidence in the buyers who'd stock this book in every brick-and-mortar and digital store in the country.

He needed their backing for this book to go gangbusters following a speedy release. It would take every moment of his time making it happen.

So why the persistent niggle that having Liza stride into his office the first time, and later agree to his offer, was the best thing to happen to him on a personal level in a long time?

He'd been thinking about contacting her anyway, getting one of the company's investigative hounds onto finding her. Thankfully, that wasn't necessary. But the fact she was the WAG every publisher in town had been hounding for a tell-all? Threw him. And made him doubt his own judgement, which he hated.

Had his first impressions been correct? Was she a woman not to be trusted?

He couldn't afford to have this book deal fall through

and with Liza's abrupt about-face—shirking his offer then accepting it—what was to say it wouldn't happen again?

She'd verbally agreed to the deal but until he had her signature on a contract he wouldn't be instigating any processes.

Damn, he wished he knew her better so he could get a handle on her erratic behaviour.

She'd seemed introverted last night, reluctant to flirt, at complete odds with the image of WAGs he had.

In London, a day didn't go by without the tabloids reporting exploits of sports stars' wives and girlfriends, from what they wore to a nightclub opening to rumours of cat-fights.

The woman he'd coaxed into having a drink with him last night, the woman who'd later blown his mind with sensational sex, didn't fit his image of a WAG.

Which begged the question, what had Liza done to make her notorious?

What was her real story?

Considering he'd just emailed her a publishing contract, guess he'd soon find out.

Liza had less than twenty-four hours to come up with a plausible life story. One far removed from the truth.

She'd been in a daze on the tram ride home, stunned how quickly her life had morphed from orderly to disastrous.

Though it could've been a lot worse if she didn't have Wade's offer to agree to.

For as much as it pained her to contemplate he might have used her to get what he wanted, she'd be in real trouble if his publishing contract hadn't been on the table.

It had pinged into her inbox the moment she'd arrived home and she'd scoured the contract, expecting hidden clauses and a bunch of legalese. Surprisingly, the contract was straightforward and the sizable advance eased the constriction in her chest that had made breathing difficult since she'd taken that call from Ullric.

Once she'd forwarded it to Jimmy's manager—who also happened to be one of the best entertainment lawyers in the country—she sat down with a pen and paper, determined to have bullet points ready for her first meeting with the ghost writer tomorrow.

Wade wanted a specific kind of book: a complete tell-all highlighting the juicy, glamorous, scandalous aspects of her life as a WAG. Yet another reason why she'd have to leave Cindy out of it.

He'd also assured her the story of her life would be well written and focused on the facts, but Liza read widely and was wise enough to know ghost writers liked to embellish, taking a little fictional creativity along the way.

Let them. Considering she was doing the same thing, giving an embroidered account of her life while withholding important facts—namely Cindy's existence—she couldn't begrudge the writer that.

Why should she care? Wasn't as if the media had never invented stuff about her to sell papers or magazines.

While she'd been with Jimmy there'd been a never-ending list of supposed indiscretions. Smile at a world champion tennis pro and she was accused of having an affair. Lean too close to hear a rock star's boring diatribe at a nightclub, ditto.

She'd grown immune after a while, knowing it went with the territory. But not a day went by when she didn't feel like telling the truth and ramming her side of the story down their lying throats.

Then she'd arrive home after yet another movie premiere or restaurant opening or fashion-label launch, curl up next to Cindy on the couch, and know it was all worthwhile.

There was nothing she wouldn't do for her little sis. Including manufacture a life story to give the masses something they'd probably invent anyway, and secure Cindy's future in the process.

Liza arrived at Qu Publishing at nine on the dot the next morning, dressed to impress and armed with her extensive list.

She wanted to wow the ghost writer and to do that she'd donned her WAG persona, from sleek blow-dried hair to lashings of make-up, seamed stockings and sky-high black patent leather stilettos to a tight crimson sheath dress with long sleeves and a low neckline.

Power dressing at its best and if the reaction of the guys who passed her on Collins Street was any indication, she'd achieved her first goal: make a dazzling first impression.

She found it infinitely amusing that guys would barely give her a second glance when she did the grocery shopping with her hair snagged in a low ponytail and no make-up, wearing yoga pants and a hoodie, yet dressed in a slinky outfit with enough make-up to hide a million flaws and they drooled. Fickle fools.

As she paced the reception area she wondered if that was what had captured Wade's attention at the party. Her fake outer shell. Or was her name enough, when he'd wanted her to sign on the dotted line all along?

Then again, what he'd said had been true. *She'd* approached *him*. Engaged him in conversation. Even flirted a little, and he hadn't known her name. Not until later at The Martini Bar.

His admission had soothed her wounded ego for all of two seconds before she realised a smart guy like him would've researched her to get as much info on the WAG he wanted so badly, so would've known what she looked like from the countless pictures online.

Stupid thing was, she wanted to believe him, wanted to give him the benefit of the doubt that the way they'd hooked up at the Westin had been about a strong sexual attraction and a mutual need to escape.

But Liza had been let down by people her entire life, especially those closest to her, and had learned healthy distrust wasn't such a bad thing.

She'd idolised her dad. He'd left when he couldn't handle having a disabled daughter.

She'd idolised her mum. Yet her mother hadn't been able to handle things either. When Louisa had finally left it had almost been a relief because the tension in the house had dissipated and Liza had been more than happy to step up with Cindy.

She'd been doing it for years anyway.

While she wanted to hate Wade for using sex as a way to get her onside, part of her couldn't help but be grateful his offer had still been on the table after the way she'd stormed out of his office.

Without that contract and advance, she'd be screwed. And he'd given her a job to boot.

Not many executives would've given in to her crazy demand for a job alongside a significant contract offer, but he'd done it.

Probably out of desperation to have her agree to his proposal but, whatever his rationale, she was grateful.

He'd agreed to let her focus on marketing her biography for a start, which was a good way to ease into her new career. She might have been handed a dream job on a platter but the fact she hadn't actually worked in marketing since she gained her degree six years earlier went some way in denting her fake confidence.

If she screwed this up, not only would she have an irate publisher on her hands, she'd be fired before her job had begun.

Along with spinning a bunch of embellished half-truths for the ghost writer, she had to spend her days coming up with whiz-bang marketing plans and meeting with Wade.

She didn't know which of the three options terrified her most.

As if she'd conjured him up, Wade opened his door and strode towards her, tall and powerful and incredibly gorgeous.

She'd rubbed shoulders with some of the most handsome guys in the world, from movie stars to sporting elite, but there was something about Wade Urquart that made her hormones jump-start in a big way.

He wore his dark hair a tad long for convention and sported light stubble that accentuated his strong jaw. Throw in the deep brown eyes, the hot bod and the designer suit that highlighted his long legs and broad shoulders, and Liza wasn't surprised to find herself holding her breath.

For it wasn't the clothes that impressed her as much as the body beneath, and the fact she'd seen every inch, touched every inch, made her skin prickle with awareness the closer he got.

'Punctual. I like that.' His slow, easy grin added to her flustered state as she shook his hand and managed to look like an idiot when she snatched hers away too fast.

'I'm eager to get started.' She gestured at her bag. 'I've brought a ton of notes and pictures and stuff so we can hit the ground running.'

'That's what I like to hear.'

She fell into step beside him, having to lengthen her stride to keep up.

'I can't emphasise enough the speedy turnaround needed

on this.' He stopped outside a conference room and gestured her in. 'There's a lot riding on this book being a runaway success.'

A wave of panic threatened to swamp Liza, mixed with a healthy dose of guilt.

Inventing a bunch of lies to protect Cindy hadn't seemed so bad when she'd been jotting notes last night, but hearing the hint of desperation in Wade's voice made her wonder about the wisdom of this.

What if one of her lies unravelled? What if she was declared a fraud? Or, worst-case scenario, what if Cindy was exposed in the process?

'Something wrong?'

Everything was wrong, but Liza had to do this. It was the only way forward that enabled her to provide a safe future for Cindy while following her own dream at the same time.

She was used to depending on no one but herself and to provide Cindy with that same independence, she had to make this work.

She faked a smile that had fooled the masses before. 'Let's get started.'

With a doubtful sideways glance, he gestured her ahead of him into the room, where he introduced her to Danni, the ghost writer, a forty-something woman who reeked of efficiency.

'I'll leave you ladies to it,' he said, glancing at his watch. 'And I'll see you in my office this afternoon at one-thirty, Liza.'

'Sure,' she said, not looking forward to the marketing meeting one bit.

She might be able to fake it for Danni, but Wade had seen her naked, for goodness' sake. Not much more she could hide from him.

Over the next four hours Liza laid bare her life. The life she'd pared back, embellished and concocted, that was.

Danni taped their interview, jotted notes in a mega scrapbook already filled with scrawl and typed furiously into a laptop.

Danni asked pertinent questions, nothing too personal but insightful all the same and Liza couldn't help but be impressed.

And relieved. This biography business was going better than expected and, according to Danni, she'd have enough information by the end of the week to collate into a workable chapter book.

When they finally broke at one-fifteen, Liza had a rumbling tummy and a headache, but she couldn't afford to be late for her meeting with Wade so she grabbed a coffee from the lunch room, checked in with Shar to see how Cindy was, and made it to Wade's office with a minute to spare.

He barely acknowledged her entrance when she knocked and he waved her in, his eyes riveted to the massive monitor screen in front of him while on a speaker conference call.

Whoever was on the other end of the line was spouting a whole lot of figures that made her head spin; hundreds of thousands of dollars bandied around as if they were discussing pocket change.

She could hardly comprehend the advance Qu Publishing had offered her. It topped the other offers she'd had by two hundred grand.

Ironic, it hadn't been enough to tempt her when she'd had her investment maturing but, with her nest egg gone, beggars certainly couldn't be choosers.

'Sorry about that,' he said, clasping his hands together and resting them on the desk. 'Working on the pre-orders, which are all important.'

'How many people are interested in reading about my boring life?'

'Boring?' He spun the screen around, pointing at the spreadsheet covered in figures and highlighted colours. 'According to the orders flooding in already, you're ranking up there with Oprah and Madonna for notoriety.'

He leaned back, pinning her with a speculative stare. 'Which makes me wonder, what have you done that is so newsworthy?'

Liza shrugged, knowing he would've asked this question eventually but feeling increasingly uncomfortable having to discuss any part of her life with him.

Rehashing details for Danni was one thing; baring herself—metaphorically—to Wade another.

'Not much, really. My high-school sweetheart turned out to be a soccer superstar so we were thrust into the limelight early on.'

She smoothed a fray in her stockings, remembering how out of her depth she'd felt at the time. Photographers snapping their pic wherever they went, groupies slipping phone numbers into Jimmy's pocket constantly, autograph hunters thrusting pen and paper into his face regardless of appropriate timing.

It had been a circus but she'd quickly learned to play the game when a national magazine had offered her twenty thousand dollars for an interview.

At twenty-two and fresh out of uni it had been an exorbitant sum, and she'd grabbed it to buy a new motorised wheelchair for Cindy.

That interview had been the start. More had followed, along with interviews on talk shows, hosting charity events and appearing at openings for a fee.

Jimmy had encouraged her and with every deposit in her

investment account she'd been vindicated she was doing the right thing.

Cindy would be secure for life. Liza never wanted her sis to struggle the way she had when their parents had left them.

Being abandoned was bad enough, but left without long-term security? Liza could never forgive her folks for that.

Not that she heard from them. Her dad had vanished for good when he'd left and her mum occasionally rang on birthdays and Christmas. Liza never took her calls, letting Cindy chatter enthusiastically, while she wondered the entire time how a parent could walk out on their child. Especially a high-needs child.

'You travelled?'

She shook her head. 'No, I didn't want to become one of those women who clung to their man.'

And she couldn't leave Cindy for long stints, not that Wade needed to know that.

It was one of the things that had eventually come between her and Jimmy. He needed full-time glam eye candy on his arm wherever he went; she needed to devote time to her sister.

They'd parted on amicable terms despite what the press had said.

But her heart had been a teensy-weensy bit broken because he was the first guy she'd ever loved, the only guy she'd ever loved.

And he'd walked away, just like her folks.

Thankfully she'd developed a pragmatic outlook to life over the years and, while Jimmy continued to be plastered over the media, she was glad she'd stepped off his bandwagon.

'I thought that's what WAGs do. Pander to the whims of

their superstar partners. Hand-feed them grapes. Fan them with palm fronds.'

He was winding her up and her lips curved in an answering grin.

'You forgot being on call twenty-four-seven.'

He snapped his fingers. 'Thanks for clarifying.'

'Actually, you're not far off the mark.'

He arched a brow and she continued. 'You're on show every time you step out. Scrutinised all the time. It felt like a full-time job in the end.'

'Is that why you broke up?'

'Something like that.'

She didn't know if he was asking these questions in a professional capacity or assuaging his curiosity but for now she was happy to answer.

Sticking to the facts was easy. It was the potential landmine questions she'd need to carefully navigate.

'And then you dated a basketball star.'

She wrinkled her nose and he laughed. 'That good, huh?'

'Off the record? Henri and I had a convenient arrangement. Nothing more.'

Confusion creased his brow. 'How did that work?'

'He needed a girlfriend. I needed the lifestyle he provided.'

She threw it out there, gauging his reaction.

His eyes widened and his lips tightened, his frown deepening.

'I don't understand.'

She shrugged, as if his opinion didn't matter, when in fact it irked he thought badly of her. Not that it should surprise her. They hardly knew each other, despite one night of amazing sex. But for someone who'd spent the last umpteen years being judged by everyone, it really peed her off to add Wade to that list.

'Our arrangement was mutually beneficial. That's all anyone needs to understand.'

He recoiled as if she'd slapped him. 'I hope you'll be giving us more than that in the book.'

'My biography will be comprehensive.'

He continued to stare at her as if she'd morphed from an angel to the devil incarnate and she struggled not to squirm beneath the scrutiny.

When the silence grew painfully uncomfortable, she gestured to the stack of paperwork on his desk. 'Shall we discuss the marketing plan?'

'Yeah,' he said, his frown not waning as he spread documents across his desk and picked up his pen. 'I have a few ideas but I want to hear what you've come up with.'

As Liza ran through an impressive list of ideas, from a massive social-media blitz via popular sites to weekly bonus e-serials to Qu Publishing subscribers, Wade wondered how he could have misjudged her so badly.

Maybe he could blame it on jet lag, because he could've sworn the livewire he'd wooed into bed a couple of nights ago was far removed from the calculated, cool woman who was happy to date as part of an *arrangement*.

He'd seen a lot of interesting couples in his travels, younger women with older men in it for the money and security. Hell, he'd seen it firsthand with Babs and his dad. So why did he find the thought of Liza hooked up with some slick sports star for the sake of *lifestyle* so unpalatable?

'What do you think?'

Damn, she'd caught him out.

'Sorry, I was still pondering your Twitter tribe idea. What did you ask?'

Nice save but, by her narrowed eyes, she didn't buy it.

'With the new e-releases of any sporting personnel three months before the bio launches, why not insert a snippet from the bio into the back of those books? Build a little anticipation?'

'Sounds great.'

She'd come up with some solid ideas and he was impressed with her work ethic. Pity he couldn't say the same about the rest.

'How do you feel about the serial WAG tag?'

She stiffened in surprise. 'That's out of left field.'

He shrugged, pretending her answer wasn't important when in fact he needed to know what made her tick.

Sitting across from her, the faintest rose fragrance scenting the air and reminding him of the way it had clung to his skin after their night in his suite, he had to know who the real Liza Lithgow was.

Was she the soft, hesitant woman he'd met at the party and spent a wild, passionate night with?

Or was she a gold-digging, plastic floozy who'd do anything to further her lifestyle?

'Call it publisher curiosity,' he said, hating how her answers meant way more to him than on a publishing level.

'I've been called many things by the press over the years, serial WAG being on the tamer side.'

Her flat monotone suggested rote answers, when he wanted to know the *real* her. It annoyed the hell out of him.

'How did you put up with all that?'

'Came with the territory,' she said, darting a nervous glance at the documentation on his desk, as if she'd much rather be discussing business than her personal life.

Too bad. He wanted to know more about the investment his dad's company was riding on and right now he had the distinct feeling she was hiding something. Something that went beyond a need for some degree of privacy.

He couldn't pinpoint what it was but her general evasiveness, the look-away glances, the rote answers, seemed too trite, too polished, almost as if she'd rehearsed.

Crazy? Maybe, but he'd put his father's company and three hundred grand of his own money on the line for this book. It had to be a blockbuster and so far Liza hadn't inspired him with her careful answers and measured responses.

'You haven't told me why every publisher in Melbourne was clamouring for your exclusive story,' he said, prepared to keep interrogating her until she told him the truth.

'Don't you know?'

'Know what?'

'I slept with the entire Aussie soccer team,' she deadpanned. 'The English one too.'

He barked out a laugh. 'Don't believe you about the English. I would've read about that in London.'

'Pity my antics didn't make it all the way over there,' she said, her tone holding a hint of accusation. 'What is it you want me to say? That I danced naked at the Grand Final? That I had half the team and cheerleaders in my room one night?'

Her voice had risen and she lowered it, making him feel guilty for pushing her. 'Honestly? I have no idea why my story is so important, other than the fact I haven't given them a story before now.'

She held out her hands, as if no tricks up her sleeves. 'I've been reticent in interviews over the years. I pick and choose the ones I do and the questions I answer. Maybe that's built the mystery? Plus the fact I've dated two mega-famous Aussie sporting stars, people want to know, "Why her? What's so special about her?"'

He'd touched a nerve.

He could see it in the frantically beating pulse in her neck, in the corded muscles, in her rigid shoulders.

He could move in for the kill now he had her more animated and far removed from her trite answers, but something in her eyes stopped him.

She looked almost haunted. As if she'd seen too much, done too much, and was still reeling from it.

It made him even more curious. What or who had put that look in her expressive eyes?

'Want to take a break and meet back here at four-thirty?'

Liza nodded and stood before he'd barely finished the sentence. She was desperate to escape? Yeah, looked as if he'd definitely hit a nerve.

He watched her walk to the door, a goddess in sheer stockings, a tight red dress and heels that could give a guy serious ideas.

'Liza?'

She glanced over her shoulder and arched a brow.

'Good work on the marketing campaign.'

'Thanks.' Her smile lit her expression and made her eyes sparkle, the first genuine show of emotion all afternoon.

Interesting. Either this book or this marketing job meant more to her than she was letting on.

'See you later,' he said as she slipped out of the door with a wave, leaving him more bamboozled than ever.

Would the real Liza Lithgow please stand up?

CHAPTER SEVEN

LIZA LITHGOW'S STYLE TIPS
FOR MAXIMUM WAG WOW IMPACT

The Day Spa

For a WAG to have true wow potential at any event, a visit to a day spa beforehand is a must.

Below is a list of treatments, from the basic to the sublime.

Worth the time and money investment for body and soul.

- Waxing
- Eyelash tint
- Spray tan
- Mani and pedi (skip the basic and go deluxe)
- Footbath/reflexology
- Body scrub
- Clay body mask
- Yoghurt body cocoon
- Massage (including scalp)
- Facial

If you're too busy to attend a day spa, set aside a few hours at home and DIY.

- Cooled tea bags or cucumber slices work wonders to de-puff eyes.

- Make your own moisturising face mask: Blend yoghurt, honey, avocado and aloe vera gel, paint on face with a foundation brush, let it dry for twenty minutes and rinse. Refreshed skin!

- Condition your hair with coconut oil. You can leave it in overnight for deeper moisturizing.

- Make your own exfoliating body scrub: 1 cup raw oats, 1 cup brown sugar, 1 cup olive oil. Mix together and apply on dry skin moving your hand in slow circles. Rinse off. Smooth skin!

- Make your own hand cream: add a few drops of tea tree oil, lavender oil and olive oil to a few spoonfuls of cold cream. (For a fruity smell, add a banana.) Blend. Slather over hands, wear rubber gloves while watching TV. For better penetration, place gloved hands on a hot-water bottle.

LIZA SURREPTITIOUSLY SLID the sleeve of her dress up to check her watch.

On the plus side, Wade had stopped interrogating her during their second meeting of the day and had concentrated on marketing plans.

On the downside, it was six o'clock and she was on the verge of fainting from lack of food.

Her tummy rumbled on cue and she wrapped an arm over it. Too late. His gaze zeroed in on it. The rumbles were quickly replaced by a horde of tap-dancing butterflies as she remembered the way he'd stared at her naked body on that unforgettable night.

Damn, she'd vowed not to think about that night again, especially when working. She'd done a good job of it so far, then all it took was one casual glance from *him* and the entire evening flashed across her mind in vivid detail.

His hungry stare as he'd propped over her, their bodies joined and writhing slowly.

His sensual lips as he'd kissed and nipped her elbows, her thighs, her stomach, every zone more erogenous than the last.

His skilful hands as he'd brought her to orgasm. Repeatedly.

Great. The butterflies had stilled, only to be replaced by a fiery heat that had her gritting her teeth to stop from squirming.

'Hungry?'

'A little,' she said as her stomach gave another growl akin to a muted roar.

He laughed. 'Sorry, I'm used to working through when I'm on tight deadlines.'

His eyebrows arched when he glanced at the time on his PC screen. 'Didn't know it was so late. Want to grab a bite to eat so we can keep working?'

'Sure.'

Thank goodness she'd had the foresight to ring Shar before this meeting started. With a four-thirty start she'd had a feeling it would run late.

'Been to Chin Chin?' He shrugged into his jacket. 'I've heard it's a favourite in Melbourne.'

'Good choice,' she said, surprised they were going out for dinner. 'Food's sublime.'

When he'd suggested grabbing a bite to eat she'd expected ordered-in sandwiches while he kept her chained to the desk.

Chained... Like how he'd pinned her wrists overhead as he entered her the first time....

Uh-oh. She needed to stay work-focused. And hope to hell he didn't pick up on her sudden shift in thoughts.

'Let's go.'

He opened the door for her and as she stepped through, with him close behind, a ripple of awareness raised the hair on the back of her neck.

It disarmed her, this unexpected physical reaction when she least expected it. Several times during their meeting she'd experienced a buzz from perfectly innocuous actions like their fingers brushing when handing over documentation or a lingering glance a tad longer than necessary.

She'd been deliberately brusque, determined not to botch this opportunity, which was exactly what would happen if she acknowledged the attraction between them now he was her boss.

And not forgetting that little technicality of him potentially using her despite his protestations of innocence.

No, she'd be better off forgetting their night of scintillating sex and concentrating on getting her story straight for the book and making her marketing ideas fly.

She had enough complications in her life without adding fraternising with the boss to them.

They made small talk as they strolled down Flinders Lane and Liza tried to ignore the way people turned to stare.

Considering they were both tall and well dressed, she could attribute it to natural curiosity. Or she could acknowledge it for what it was: once a recognised WAG, always a recognised WAG.

When would people forget whom she'd dated and move

on to the next 'it' girl? Sure, she'd milked her image for all it was worth, most recently hosting a reality show that had been a ratings disaster yet was the most talked-about event on social media sites for months.

But she was done with that part of her life. Wasn't that the main reason she'd slept with Wade in the first place, celebrating putting her past behind her and moving on to a new life?

Ironic, her past had caught up with her and collided with her future.

When they arrived at the Melbourne institution, the nightly queue of eager patrons dying to try the fabulous Asian food was thankfully small but Liza knew they'd still be ushered to the bar downstairs to wait for a table to become available.

Not good. When she'd agreed to have a meal with Wade, she hadn't envisaged the two of them sitting too close in a bar.

A bar was reminiscent of their first night together and the last thing she needed right now was any reminder. Her body hummed with his proximity. Sharing a drink in a cosy setting? Not good.

Their wait for a table wouldn't be too long according to the hostess so Liza headed downstairs with Wade, trying to ignore his hand on the small of her back and the accompanying reaction that made her knees wobble a tad.

It worsened when they took a seat at the bar and their thighs brushed. Hell, what had Liza let herself in for?

'Drink?'

'Soda with a twist of lemon,' she said, desperate to reassemble her wits and not needing alcohol to add to her bedazzlement.

'Technically we're off the clock, so you can have a drink, you know.'

'Isn't this a working dinner?'

He nodded but she didn't trust the glimmer of mischief in his eyes. 'Maybe I should order you a martini again and see what happens?'

'*That* won't be happening again,' she said, squeezing her knees together for good measure.

He laughed and nudged her with his elbow, the slightest contact making her body prickle with awareness. 'Never say never, I reckon.'

'We are *so* not going there.' She glared as if she meant business.

By his answering wink, he was thinking monkey business.

'I'll let you in on a secret,' he said, leaning so close his breath fanned her ear, pebbling her skin in the process. 'It's okay to flirt outside the office. Especially after we've already—'

'No flirting,' she said, unable to suppress a smile when he blew on her ear for good measure.

'That's better.' He touched a fingertip to the corner of her mouth. 'First time I've seen you lighten up all day.'

He traced her lower lip, lingering in the middle, and she couldn't have formulated an answer if she'd tried. 'Don't get me wrong, I like how focused you are on helping us meet this all-important deadline, but today?' He pulled a funny face, complete with crossed eyes. 'You were seriously scary.'

'Was not,' she said, enjoying his antics despite her vow to keep things purely platonic from now on.

She liked the fact he could switch from mega-powerful corporate CEO to teasing. It was one of the things that had attracted her that first night, the way he lightened up when they started talking.

'Yeah, you were.' He bumped her gently with his shoulder. 'But not to worry. I've got all night to get you to loosen up.'

'All night?' She wished.

'Figure of speech.' His wicked grin said otherwise. 'Though I have to tell you, I was pretty blown away when you barged into my office yesterday. It was like all my prayers had been answered.'

Liza didn't want to go there. She should change the subject, fake an emergency trip to the loo, anything to quell the irrational surge of jubilation that he'd been happy to see her.

'We really shouldn't talk about that night. It's unprofessional—'

'Why did you bolt without leaving contact details?'

A host of callous retorts designed to maintain distance between them sprang to her lips but Liza settled for the simple truth.

'Because I didn't think you wanted more than one night.'

There. She'd put the onus back on him. No way could he admit to wanting more without appearing a little needy.

'Considering we'd only just met, I don't think either of us knew what we wanted beyond the amazing connection we shared. But later...' he shrugged and turned towards the bar, but not before she'd seen a flicker of something akin to regret darken his eyes '...let's just say I was disappointed to find you gone.'

Liza admired his honesty. He sounded so genuine she could almost believe he hadn't known her identity when they slept together.

It made her curious. What would have happened if they'd had more than one night?

'For argument's sake, let's say I left my number.'

The waiter deposited their drinks and he took a sip of whisky before turning back to face her. 'I would've called you. Asked you for a date.'

'Before or after offering me a publishing contract?'

He grimaced. 'Got to admit, that does complicate matters now I know.'

There he went again, reiterating he'd had no idea of her real identity that night at the party. Maybe she should give him the benefit of the doubt?

For when it came to liars, she had a pretty good radar. She could tell when someone was uncomfortable with Cindy from ten paces and hated when people acted as if cerebral palsy were contagious.

It had driven a wedge between her and Jimmy, between most of her friends too. Which suited her fine, because most of them had drifted away as Jimmy became more famous and their lives changed.

It had started with her school friends pulling away, girls she'd grown up with and who she'd assumed she could always count on. But the more fancy events she attended with Jimmy, the faster the snide remarks started and she found herself not invited to their parties or dinners or girls' nights out.

Being abandoned by her friends had sucked and she'd learned to cultivate light-hearted friendships with acquaintances, fellow WAGs who stuck together out of necessity. But they'd pretty much abandoned her too once she broke up with Jimmy and Henri, and she missed her old friendships more than ever.

True friends stuck around through life changes. Guess she didn't have any true friends.

'Hey, you drifted off for a second.' He touched her hand and a lick of heat travelled up her arm.

'It's more than a complication now I'm working for you and you know it,' she said, re-evaluating the wisdom of working for him when his simple touch made her skin sizzle.

'Co-workers have relationships all the time these days,'

he said, stroking the back of her hand with his thumb. 'And don't forget, the only reason you're working for me is because you blackmailed me into giving you a job.'

'Good point.' She chuckled, proud for pulling that masterstroke. 'So you're trying to get into my pants again on a technicality?'

His thumb paused and his eyes widened in surprise. 'Are you always this blunt?'

Not always. Most of her life she'd watched what she said and what she ate and what she wore, presenting a perfectly poised persona to the world, desperate no one saw behind the façade.

If she didn't let people get too close they couldn't hurt her. A motto she'd learned to live by the hard way.

So what was it about this guy that had her more relaxed than she'd ever been?

She took a sip of soda and shrugged. 'We've seen each other naked. I don't see the point in playing coy.'

He mouthed 'wow' and squeezed her hand before releasing it. 'Okay, least I can do is return the favour. I like you. You intrigue me. So while I'm in Melbourne, I'd like for us to see each other.'

Lord, Liza hadn't seen that coming. She'd thought Wade might put the hard word on her for another night in the sack. No way did she expect a quasi-relationship for the time he was in town.

She was tempted. Seriously tempted.

How long since she'd had great sex or indulged in genuine fun? Probably in the early Jimmy days, before the fame and the expectations associated with living up to the WAG label. She knew time spent with Wade would involve both sex and fun.

But what about Cindy and the lies she'd constructed to protect her?

If she started dating Wade, how long could she keep him from her place? How long before her lies unravelled and her carefully constructed story came crashing down?

She couldn't afford to have Qu Publishing renege on the contract, nor did she want to lose her first real marketing job.

Getting involved with Wade could compromise both.

'Wade, I like you—'

'I can sense a *but* coming.' He winced and pretended to clutch his heart. 'Give it to me straight. I'm a big boy, I can take it.'

She managed a wan smile. 'But I don't want to complicate our business arrangement.'

Disappointment downturned his mouth for a moment, before those lips she'd experienced over every inch of her body curved into a seductive smile.

'I understand. You don't know me that well. But the way Qu Publishing secured your book deal was by sheer persistence.'

He raised his glass in her direction. 'I don't give up easily. Challenge is my middle name.'

He clinked it to hers. 'Don't say I didn't warn you.'

Liza had been in a quandary when Wade offered to drive her home.

She'd wanted to refuse because it had been bad enough having him charm her over a delicious dinner of green Thai chicken curry and sampler plates of murtubak, slow-cooked beef and exquisite calamari.

But she'd wanted to get home fast so she could spend time with her sis before Cindy went to bed so she'd agreed.

And was now ruing the fact as he walked her to the front door.

Politeness demanded she invite him in for a coffee.

Self-preservation demanded she get rid of him ASAP.

'Thanks for dinner and driving me home,' she said, juggling her handbag from one arm to the other, hoping he'd get the hint.

'My pleasure.' He stilled her arm with a light touch on the forearm. 'Not going to invite me in?'

Damn. She admired his bluntness. But she hated being put on the spot.

'Don't think that's a good idea.'

His hand travelled up her arm in a slow caress before resting on her shoulder. 'Why? Scared I'll take advantage of you?'

'No. I just have a lot of work to do before my meeting with Danni tomorrow so—'

He kissed her, a stealth kiss that caught her completely off guard.

Her hands braced against his chest, ready to push him away as he backed her up against the front door.

But then his tongue touched her bottom lip, stroked it with exquisite precision, and she clung to him instead. Responded to his commanding mouth deepening the kiss to be sublimely erotic. Wanting more than *this*.

When his arms slid around her waist and pulled her flush against him, her body zinged with remembrance. How it felt to be pressed against his arousal, how he'd masterfully seduced her with a skill that left her breathless.

She felt weightless, floating, as he kissed like a guy who couldn't get enough. And the feeling was entirely mutual.

When Wade kissed her, when he touched her, she forgot about responsibilities. She forgot about the stress of losing her money and Cindy's security. She forgot about the long list of doctor's appointments and physiotherapy sessions and hydrotherapy at a new pool next week. She forgot about finding a replacement carer for when Shar went on holiday next.

And she existed purely in the moment, revelling in this incredibly sexy guy's desire for her.

As the blood fizzed in her veins and her muscles melted, she wanted more than this kiss.

She wanted him. Naked. Again.

The thrill of skin to skin. The excitement of exploring each other's bodies. The release that left her boneless and mindless.

Until a massive reality check in the form of her buzzing mobile switched to silent vibrated against her hip.

Shar probably wanted to head home and here Liza was, indulging in a pointless kiss that could lead nowhere.

Regret tempered her passion. She eased away. Last thing she needed was for him to think something was wrong and want to talk or demand answers she wasn't prepared to give.

'Told you I wouldn't give up,' he said, cupping her cheek in a tender moment before stepping away.

'You should,' she said, but her words fell on deaf ears as he shot her one last wicked grin before strolling down her path like a guy who had all the time in the world to woo the woman he wanted.

An hour later, Liza had bathed Cindy, assisted with her stretches and helped her painstakingly make a batch of choc-chip muffins.

Every task took double the time with Cindy's clawed elbow and hand but that never stopped her sis having a go. Liza's admiration knew no bounds and whenever she felt her patience fraying she tried to put herself in Cindy's shoes.

Being a carer over the years had been tough, but imagine being on the receiving end? Of being dependent on others for activities of daily living that everyone took for granted? Needing help with bathing and dressing, cooking and cleaning?

Not to mention the never-ending rounds of therapy and medical interventions.

Liza had it easy compared to her sis and Cindy's amazing resilience and zest for life was what drove her every day.

'Were you talking to someone outside?'

The spatula in Liza's hand froze in mid-air, dropping a big globule of muffin mix into the baking tin involuntarily.

'No one important,' she said, concentrating on filling the tin while Cindy popped choc chips into her mouth and chewed slowly.

'Sounded like a guy.' Cindy finished chewing and started making smooching noises.

Uh-oh. Shar had said they'd been busy in the kitchen when she'd arrived home but what if Cindy had seen that kiss?

'You should have a boyfriend,' Cindy said, her wobbly grin endearing. 'A proper one this time, not like those loser sports guys.'

Liza loved that about Cindy, her insightfulness. Most people saw the wheelchair and her physical disfigurement and assumed she was brain-damaged too.

While many people with cerebral palsy did suffer a degree of brain injury, Cindy had been lucky that way and she often made pronouncements that would've shocked most scholars.

'I'm too busy with my new job to date, sweetie.'

A half-truth. For the guy who wanted to date her happened to work right alongside her.

It could be convenient…if she were to lose her mind.

No, having Wade practically invite himself in sixty minutes ago reinforced she was doing the right thing in keeping things between them platonic.

She didn't want to let him into her life, into Cindy's life, when there was no future. While Cindy never talked about their folks abandoning them, it would have to hurt. The last thing she needed was Cindy bonding with Wade only to have him head back to London.

She wouldn't do that to herself—uh, to Cindy.

'I have a boyfriend.'

Liza smiled, having been alerted to Cindy's latest crush via Shar. 'You do?'

Cindy nodded. 'Liam Hemsworth. He's hot.'

'Personally, I prefer Chris.'

'No way.' Cindy popped another choc chip in her mouth. 'Though I guess that would work out well. They're brothers, we're sisters. Perfect.'

Liza laughed as she opened the oven door and popped the muffins inside. 'Tell you what. You do another ten hamstring stretches and I'll watch *The Hunger Games* with you again.'

'Deal.'

As Cindy manoeuvred her wheelchair into the next room Liza pondered her sister's observation.

You should have a boyfriend.

While she didn't need the complication, for a second she allowed herself to fantasise what it would be like having Wade fill the role.

CHAPTER EIGHT

LIZA LITHGOW'S STYLE TIPS
FOR MAXIMUM WAG WOW IMPACT

The Home

While WAGs lead a busy social life, they do occasionally entertain at home. And even if they don't, what better way to unwind after a hectic game or a rowdy after-match function than kicking back in their cosy abode?

Here are a few tips to make your home entirely livable:

- *Make your entry-way inviting.* When your guests enter your home it's the first area they see. The entry-way should make a statement, give a hint of what's to come and draw the guest into the rest of the house. Pictures on the wall are the easiest way to dress up your entry-way. Same with floor coverings. Hall tables are a nice addition as you can dress them with signature or eclectic pieces.

- *Experiment with glass.* Glass instantly adds sparkle to a room. Experimenting with shapes and heights (vases, bowls, objects) is fun, and keeping them in the same colour palette is advisable. Varying shapes in like-coloured glass can be eye-catching.

- *Mix it up.* Every object in your home doesn't have to be an heirloom. If you like quality pieces, mix them up with a little kitsch. It's okay to have your favourite collection alongside that priceless vase. The whole point of collecting is to have a passion for it, finding items you really love, so why not show them off? They're a great conversation starter too.

- *Keep window dressings simple.* Whether you go for curtains or blinds, keep them simple. Don't let them overpower your furniture. Subdued tones work best but that doesn't mean you need to skimp on quality. The simpler the curtain, the better quality the fabric should be, like linen, silk, cotton or satin. Understated elegance is the key to setting off your room.

- *Layer your bed.* Your bed is usually the focal point of your bedroom and should be treated as such. Layering different fabrics on and around the bed (from a fabric headboard to lush linens) creates an inviting room. When layering, avoid clash of texture and colour by keeping it simple. Muted tones in green, blue and white work wonders.

WADE'S WEEK HAD been progressing exceptionally well.

Danni had completed the first draft of Liza's biography, the pre-orders were phenomenal and he'd managed to sneak another dinner with Liza, albeit for business.

This time she'd driven herself so had avoided his plans

for more than a goodnight kiss on her doorstep. He didn't know whether to be peeved or glad she was so focused on her new job.

Considering he'd had his doubts about her when she'd secured this job, and her motivation behind it, he had to admit she'd impressed. Her dedication, her punctuality and her fresh ideas had given him new perspective on an industry he'd thought he knew inside out.

She was the complete professional and almost made him feel guilty for constantly picturing her naked. Almost.

They'd been too busy to catch up beyond snatched marketing meetings in the office, and for a guy who normally had his mind on the job twenty-four-seven he'd found himself being seriously distracted.

Those tight pencil skirts she wore? Disruptive, despite their sedate colours and modest below-knee length.

Those fitted jackets? The epitome of conservative fashionable chic.

Those blouses? Muted colours with barely a hint of cleavage.

But whenever she entered his office he had an immediate flashback to the night he'd seen beneath the clothes and he'd be hard in an instant.

He'd dated occasionally in London but no woman had affected his concentration like Liza. Ever.

When Danni had emailed him the first draft of her biography he'd sat up all night devouring it on his e-reader. His obsession with her should've been satisfied. Instead, the more he discovered about her, the more she piqued his curiosity.

She'd delivered exactly what he wanted in terms of a tell-all, a juicy tale highlighting behind-the-scenes gossip in the soccer and basketball worlds.

She'd changed names to protect the innocent but he knew

readers would devour the catfights and hook-ups and pick-ups, trying to figure out which real-life star and WAG inspired her stories.

This book would sell but her lack of personal details disappointed. She'd glossed over her childhood and teenage years, focusing on the glamorous drama that kicked in when her high-school boyfriend hit the big time.

He should've been glad, for she'd provided the page-turning hot gossip that sold books. But he'd be lying if he didn't admit to wanting to know more—a whole lot more—about the woman behind the fake tan and designer handbags.

If he had insight into what made her tick, he might understand her continued aloofness.

Her lack of enthusiasm at pursuing anything beyond a one-night stand surprised him. Not from ego, but for the simple fact they still shared a spark. More than a spark, if the way she'd responded to his kiss seven days ago was any indication.

So why was she holding back?

It wasn't as if he was after anything hot and heavy. He'd been upfront with her about exploring a relationship while he was in Melbourne so anything too deep and meaning-ful wouldn't scare her off.

She'd refused. But her kiss said otherwise.

She wanted this as much as he did, which begged the question, why weren't they out at a movie or dinner or at his place right now?

Instead, he had to face his worst nightmare.

With impeccable timing as always, Babs knocked on his door and he braced for the inevitable awkwardness that preceded any confrontation with his stepmum.

Ridiculous, considering she couldn't be more than ten years older than him, if that.

'Wade, darling.' She breezed into his office and made a beeline for him.

'Babs.' His terse response didn't deter her from planting an air kiss somewhere in the vicinity of his cheek.

Thank goodness. He preferred it that way. The less those Botoxed lips got near him, the better.

'Thanks for seeing me.' She took a seat without being asked. 'From what I hear we have a lot to catch up on.'

'Really?'

She hated his monosyllabic answers, which was why he did it.

'You're stalling the inevitable.' She waggled a crimson-taloned finger in his direction. 'It'd be best for all of us if Qu Publishing sold sooner rather than later.'

His fingers dug into the underside of his desk. 'I beg to differ.'

She wrinkled her nose. 'You always did.'

With a calculated pause, she leaned forward and he quickly averted his gaze from her overt cleavage spilling from an inappropriately tight satin blouse. 'It's what your father would've wanted.'

Low blow. Incredibly low. What did he expect? The woman was a gold-digging piranha and probably had already spent the money she'd anticipated from Qu's sale.

'My dad would've wanted to see his family legacy live on.' He forced a smile, knowing it would never reach his eyes. 'I'm surprised you wouldn't know that.'

The corners of her mouth pinched, radiating unattractive wrinkles towards her nose. 'We'd both be better off without a struggling business dragging us down. Digital publishing is the way of the future. Paperbacks are redundant.'

Showed how much she knew. Sure, the digital revolution was a boom for readers but, from the extensive research conducted by online companies over the last five years, there was room in the expanding market for *tree* books, as he liked to call them.

'I have figures to prove you wrong there.' He tapped a stack of documentation on his desk. 'Including record pre-orders for Liza Lithgow's biography.'

'That tart?'

Wade would never hit a woman, would never consider it, but he sure wouldn't mind clamping a hand over this vile woman's mouth and dragging her out of his office.

'Who'd want to read about her fabricated life?'

He wouldn't give her the satisfaction of asking what she meant.

'All those WAGs are the same. Fake, the lot of them. Happy to be arm candy for what they can get.'

Pot. Meet kettle.

Wade had heard enough.

'I'm not selling, Babs. The board isn't selling. They've agreed to give me three months to take this company into the black and they're men of honour.'

More than he could say for her. She wouldn't know honour if it jumped up and bit her on her nipped and tucked behind.

Her eyes narrowed, took on a feral gleam. 'You're pinning the success of this entire company on one book? Not a smart business decision. All sorts of disasters could happen before it hits the bookstores, like—'

'I really have to get back to work,' he said, standing and heading for the door, which he opened in a blatant invitation for her to get the hell out of his office.

She stood and strolled towards him, deliberately taking her time. 'I'll be at the next board meeting.'

'I'm sure you will,' he said, resisting the urge to slam the door as she stepped through it.

'What you're doing is wrong and your father would be appalled at the risk you're taking—'

This time he gave in to instinct and slammed the door.

'There's a book launch I want to suss out tonight,' Wade said, barely glancing up from his paperwork. 'We're going.'

Liza bristled. She didn't take kindly to orders, least of all from the man she could happily throttle given half a chance.

He'd been bugging her all week, using subtle charm and sexy smiles to undermine her. She'd weathered it all, had focused on work in the hope he'd forget this ridiculous challenge of trying to woo her.

He hadn't, until today. Today, he'd been brusque and abrupt to the point of rudeness and no one seemed to know why.

She should've been happy. Instead, a small part of her missed his roguish charisma.

'*We* may have other plans,' she said, in a manufactured sickly sweet voice.

He glanced up, the frown between his brows not detracting from his perfection. 'A rival company is releasing a soap-opera starlet's bio. Pays to scope out the competition, get a few ideas for what works at these shindigs and what doesn't.'

Liza hated the hint of deflation she felt that his command had been pure business and not a burning desire to spend some time in her presence outside work.

Crazy and contradictory, considering that was the last thing she wanted and she had gone to great pains to avoid any out-of-work contact since that kiss on her doorstep.

But a small part of her, the part of her that reluctantly dredged up memories of their scintillating night together, yearned for a repeat.

Needless to say that part of her didn't get a look-in these days.

'Surely you've been to heaps of book launches? What's so special about this one?'

With an exasperated sigh, he flung his pen on top of the towering stack of paperwork threatening to topple.

'I've heard they're trying an innovative giveaway. Buy the book, get a download of another free.' He pushed aside the paperwork with one hand and pinched the bridge of his nose with the other. 'I want to see how well it's received by readers who prefer to hold a tree book.'

'Tree book?'

His mouth relaxed into a semi-smile. 'Paper comes from trees. Paperbacks? Tree books.'

'Cute,' she said, a broad term that could be applied to his terminology or the man himself when he lost the 'shouldering the weight of the company on my shoulders' look.

He'd been grumpy all day but she'd weathered it, assuming he had profit margins to juggle or worry about. The fact he'd cracked a half-smile? Big improvement.

'My dad used to call them that,' he said, interlinking his fingers and stretching overhead. It did little to ease the obvious tension in his rigid shoulders.

'He built an incredible company,' she said, surprised by his rare information sharing.

While Wade seemed content to interrogate her, his personal life was definitely off-limits.

The snippets she'd learned about the enigmatic CEO had come from colleagues, co-workers who'd given her the lowdown on Qu Publishing.

A company founded sixty years ago by Wade's grandfather, a company that had produced many best-sellers under Wade's dad, but a company that had floundered when

Wade's stepmum had entered the picture and Wade had left to start his own company in London.

While no one would directly disparage Babs Urquart, Liza saw enough glowering expressions and heard enough half-finished sentences to know Babs wasn't well liked.

Apparently they blamed her for Qu's downfall. And so did their boss.

'You started out here too?'

His lips compressed, as if he didn't want to talk about it. 'Yeah. I left after a few years, started my own company in London.'

'Bet your dad was proud.'

'Yeah, though we lost touch over the last few years.' Pain flickered in his eyes and she wished she hadn't probed. 'Caught up infrequently. Snatched phone calls.'

He shook his head, the deep frown slashing his brow indicative of a deeper problem. Looked as if she wasn't the only one with parental issues. 'I resent that distance between us now. He had a heart condition. Didn't tell me 'til it was too late.'

Appalled, Liza resisted the urge to hug him. 'Why?'

Wade shrugged. It did little to alleviate the obvious tension in his rigid shoulders. 'Guess he didn't trust me to be there for him, considering I'd deliberately distanced myself from him.'

Liza didn't know what to say. She despised trite platitudes, the kind that Cindy copped from ignorant, condescending people.

And it was pretty obvious Wade had major guilt over his relationship with his dad, so nothing she could say would make it any better.

But she knew what it was like to be let down by a parent, knew the confusing jumbled feelings of pain and regret and anger.

'Kids and parents grow apart. Maybe it wasn't so much a lack of trust in you that he didn't mention his heart condition and more a case of not wanting to worry you because he cared?'

Wade's startled expression spoke volumes. He'd never considered that might have been his dad's rationale.

'So you're a glass-half-full kinda girl?'

'Actually, I'm a realist rather than an optimist.' She had to be, because it was easier to accept the reality of her life than wish for things that would never eventuate. 'And whatever or whoever caused the rift between you, it's not worth a lifetime of guilt.'

His steady gaze, filled with hope, didn't leave hers. 'I should've been there for him and I wasn't.'

A mantra taken from her mum's handbook to life.

'He loved you, right?'

Wade nodded.

'Then I think you have your answer right there.' She tapped her chest. 'If it was my heart and I had people I cared about, I'd rather make the most of whatever time we had together, even if it was only phone calls, than field a bunch of useless questions like "How are you feeling?" or "Is there anything I can do?"'

She lowered her hand and continued. 'I wouldn't care about how often I saw the person or waste time worrying over trivial stuff like the length of time since we spoke. I'd remember the good times and want to live every minute as if it were my last.'

'Dad did travel a lot the last two years...' He straightened, his frown clearing. 'Thanks.'

Uncomfortable with his praise and wishing she hadn't blabbed so much, she shrugged. 'For what? Being a philosophising pragmatist?'

'For helping me consider another point of view.' Wade

gestured at the office. 'Dad did a great job building this company and we were close. Until he got distracted.'

His frown returned momentarily and she knew it would take more than a few encouraging words from her to get him to change his mindset and let go of the guilt.

Deliberately brusque and businesslike, he shuffled papers on his desk. 'I'm here to ensure the company regains a foothold in the publishing market.'

'I thought that's why I'm here.'

She'd hoped to make him laugh. Instead, he fixed her with a speculative stare.

'How do you do it?'

'Do what?'

'Live your life under a spotlight. Fake it for all those people.'

Increasingly uncomfortable, she shrugged. 'Who said I was faking?'

He ran a hand over his face. 'Something my annoying stepmother said, about WAGs leading fabricated lives.'

A shiver of foreboding sent a chill through Liza.

What the hell was that supposed to mean? Did Babs Urquart know something? Or was she making a sweeping generalisation?

Lord, if her fabricated life ever became known they were all sunk and Wade would look at her with derision and scorn, not the continued interest that made her squirm with longing.

'Guess we all put on a front when we need to,' she said, thankful her voice didn't quiver. 'Nothing wrong with it if no one gets hurt.'

He didn't reply and his stare intensified.

'Is that what you're doing with me?' He placed his palms on the desk and leaned forward, shrinking the space between them. 'Putting on a front?'

Smart guy.

'Why would I do that?'

Yeah, as if he'd buy her feigned innocence.

'Because you're running scared. I want to date you, and I'm pretty damn sure you want to date me, but we continue to do the avoidance dance.' He beckoned her closer with a crooked finger. 'What I want to know is why.'

The longer he stared at her, his dark eyes intent and mesmerising, the harder it was to remember the question let alone formulate an articulate answer.

'Already told you. We work together. Too complicated.'

Her breath came in short, choppy punches, as if her lungs squeezed tight and wouldn't let the air out fast enough.

Her excuse for the breathlessness constricting her chest and she was sticking to it.

'Technically we don't work together. I'm here as an interim. You blackmailed me into giving you a job.' He waved a hand between them. 'You and me? We don't exactly fit the mould of corporate colleagues who shouldn't fraternise.'

He wore the smile of a smug victor. 'Got any other excuses?'

Yeah, Liza had plenty, but she'd never divulge the real reason she couldn't date Wade. Not in a million years.

'For now, don't we have a book launch to attend?' She stood, put some much-needed distance between them. 'How's that for an excuse?'

'Damn flimsy, if you ask me,' he said, his gaze sweeping over her in admiration.

'I didn't.' She swept up her portfolio and tucked it under her arm. 'Email me the book-launch details and I'll meet you there.'

His frown returned. 'It's two blocks away. Makes sense for us to go together.'

When she took too long to respond, he added, 'I'll walk

you back to your car afterwards. You know, in case you think I'll bundle you into my car and try to take advantage of you.'

She couldn't help but laugh. 'Okay.'

Wade shook his head. 'You're an exasperating woman, but if your marketing skills are half as good as your bio, Qu Publishing is going to love you.'

Her heart gave a funny little quirk at the L word tripping so easily from his lips.

As long as his publishing company was the only thing that loved her.

For as much as Liza secretly yearned for Wade, she didn't have room in her life for love.

Not now.

Not ever.

CHAPTER NINE

LIZA LITHGOW'S STYLE TIPS
FOR MAXIMUM WAG WOW IMPACT

The Hair

For the ultra-glam events like the MVP Awards (and especially if your guy is favoured to win the Most Valuable Player award) it pays to indulge in a trip to a hair salon. Even if you don't go for a fancy up-do, blow-dried sleek hair is always in vogue.

For maximum do-it-at-home WAG wow, try the loose knot. It's sophisticated and relaxed and sexy all at the same time. The perfect 'do if you're aiming for understated elegance.

Here's how you do it:

- Wash your hair.
- Add a volumising mousse to damp hair.
- Blow-dry hair from the ends to the roots to create more volume.
- Use a comb to tease the crown.
- Using fingers, gather hair in a low ponytail.
- Secure with a band.

- Fix into a loose bun with bobby pins and let strands fall.

- Finish with a light spritz of hairspray to secure.

If you're dying to try a different look but don't have the length required, hair extensions are an option.

But make sure they blend with your colour and get an expert to do them.

You don't want a clump of hair dislodging at an inopportune moment (like when the TV cameras are panning to you when your guy wins that MVP award!).

'DID YOU LEARN anything new at the book launch?'

'Yeah.' Wade screwed up his nose and rubbed his chest. 'Cab sav and spinach-feta quiche don't mix.'

Liza laughed. 'That'll teach you for scoffing an entire tray of hors d'oeuvres.'

'I didn't have dinner. I was hungry.' The corners of his mouth curved. 'Your fault.'

'How do you figure that?'

'You wouldn't have dinner with me.'

She rolled her eyes. 'That's because you said we had a book launch to attend. For *work*. Remember?'

He heaved a sigh. 'Believe me, it's all I think about.' He took her hand as they entered the underground car park. 'Next to you, that is.'

An illicit thrill shot through Liza. She shouldn't be so happy Wade ranked her next to his precious business, not when she was determined to keep him at bay, but she couldn't help it.

The guy was seriously hot and she'd bet he invaded her thoughts a heck of a lot more often than she did his.

'We're not supposed to do this, for a million reasons—'

'Can't think of one right now.'

He'd pinned her against the wall before she could blink and plastered his mouth to hers.

The feel of his commanding lips wiped all rational thought from her mind as her body responded on an innate level that scared the hell out of her.

With this one, scorching kiss she remembered in excruciatingly vivid detail how he'd kissed his way all over her body.

How he'd caressed and stroked until she'd been out of her mind.

How he'd licked and savoured every inch of her skin until she'd melted.

His hands slid over her butt and pulled her flush against him.

Damn, how could something so wrong feel so right?

Liza wriggled, needing to push him off, get in her car and head home to Cindy.

Instead, as he changed the pressure of the kiss and touched his tongue to hers, she combusted.

She arched against him, revelling in the feel of his hardness. She wound her fingers through his hair, angled his head and kissed him right back, pouring every ounce of her repressed yearning into it.

He groaned. She moaned.

His hands were everywhere. Her skin blistered with the heat generated between their bodies.

He didn't stop. She didn't care.

Until the sound of a car engine starting on the level below penetrated the erotic fog clouding her head. And she realised what the hell she was doing.

She broke the kiss and dragged in great lungfuls of air, her ragged breathing matching his.

'Don't expect me to apologise for that,' he said, resting his forehead against hers, his hands clasping her waist, leaving her no room to move.

'I would, if I hadn't enjoyed it so much.' She rested her palms on his chest, wishing she had the willpower to shove him away. 'You won't take no for an answer, will you?'

He straightened and smiled down at her. 'You're only just figuring that out?'

'Maybe I'm a slow learner.'

'Or maybe you're running from something when it'd be better to confront it and grab it with both hands?' He squeezed her waist. 'By *it* I mean you should be grabbing *me*, of course.'

Laughter bubbled up in her chest and spilled out. She loved an intelligent guy. She loved a funny guy more. Love being figurative. Totally.

'I really need to get home and work on the marketing campaign.'

He humphed. 'And I really need to get home and work on it too.'

He released her and snapped his fingers. 'Here's a thought. Why don't we head home together and do some *work*?'

She chuckled. 'Don't hold your breath expecting me to ask your place or mine.'

'Not happening, huh?'

She shook her head. 'Nope.'

He ducked his head, nuzzled her neck, and the buzz was back. 'And there's nothing I can do to change your mind?'

Her libido whimpered and rolled over.

Her mind yelled, 'Easy!'

'Uh...no,' she said, too soft, too breathy, too needy.

'Sure?'

His lips brushed the tender skin beneath her ear and trailed slowly downward where his teeth nipped her collarbone with gentle bites that made her body zing and heat pool low in her belly.

Sure? She wasn't sure of anything, least of all how she would get to her car, get in and drive home without him in the passenger seat.

'Wade, you're so—'

'Addictive?' He licked the dip between her collarbones.

'Wicked?' He deliberately brushed his stubbled jaw along the top of her breast.

'Sexy?' He edged towards her mouth, his lips teasing at the corner.

'Persistent,' she said, holding her breath as his lips brushed hers once, twice, soft, taunting.

As a car's headlights panned over them, Liza nudged him away. 'That'd be a great boost for the book's marketing. CEO AND WAG CAUGHT IN COMPROMISING POSITION UNDERGROUND.'

'All publicity's good publicity,' he said, completely unruffled while she felt dishevelled and flustered and turned on.

'Beg to differ.' She tugged down her jacket, straightened her blouse and smoothed her hair. 'Are you walking me to my car or not?'

'Lead the way.' His arm swept forward in a flourish, and as she passed him she could've sworn his hand deliberately brushed her butt.

Wade didn't play fair.

Then again, the way her skin tingled with awareness and her body seemed lit up from within, did she want him to?

Despite the urge to run from Wade as fast as her legs could carry her, Liza was glad he'd walked her to her car.

She wouldn't have made it otherwise. Her knees shook so badly after their impromptu make-out session in a dark corner of the underground car park, if it hadn't been for his steadying arm around her waist she would've definitely stumbled.

And her head was shrouded in a passionate haze, her only excuse for slipping up and not waving him away before they reached her wheels.

'You drive *this*?'

She slipped out of his grasp and fumbled for her keys. 'Yeah, why?'

'I pictured you in something swift and sporty.' Bemused, he walked around her ten-year-old people carrier. 'You could fit an entire football team in the back of this thing.'

Or a wheelchair, but that was on a strictly need-to-know basis.

'I like big cars.' She tried not to sound defensive. And failed, if his raised eyebrows were any indication.

'So it seems.'

She flicked the remote button to unlock the doors but he laid a hand on her forearm and stopped her from opening the driver's door.

'Wait.'

She couldn't. Because if she spent one more second around him in this befuddled mess she'd fall into his arms and beg for a repeat of that one memorable night they'd spent together.

'I really have to go.'

In response, he moved in closer, placing a hand on either side of her waist and pinning her between cold, hard metal behind and hot, hard body in front.

'Come home with me.'

Her heart lurched with longing but before she could protest he rushed on. 'You doubted my sincerity the first night we were together? Then let's start afresh. Make tonight our night. No work. No excuses. Just two people who are crazy about each other indulging their mutual passion.'

His heated gaze bore into her, unrelenting, demanding an honest answer. 'No complications at the office tomorrow. No second-guessing. Just you and me and an incredible night to be ourselves.'

Ah hell.

Liza was tempted. Beyond tempted.

Her body strained towards him of its own volition, miles ahead of her head in saying yes.

But what was the point? One more night would only solidify what she already knew.

She could easily fall for Wade Urquart given half a chance.

And she couldn't. Not with her responsibilities. Not with her life plan.

It wouldn't be fair to encumber a guy with Cindy's full-time care and she would never leave Cindy to fend for herself.

It was why she never considered a long-term relationship, why she would never marry.

Normally it didn't bother her. But she'd never met a guy like Wade before, the kind of guy who elicited wild fantasies, the kind that consisted of homes and picket fences and a brood of dark-haired, dark-eyed cherubs just like their dad.

'Stop thinking so hard.' He placed a hand over her heart and it bucked wildly beneath it. 'What does in here tell you?'

To run like the wind.

But she swallowed that instinctive response and reluctantly met his gaze.

She had to refuse.

But an incredible thing happened as her eyes met his.

She saw a confusing jumble of hope and vulnerability

and desire, every emotion she was feeling reflected back at her like a mirror.

No guy she'd ever been with had been so revealing and in that moment she knew she couldn't walk away from him. At least for tonight.

'Okay,' she said, mimicking his action and feeling his heart pound beneath her palm. 'But this is a one-off, okay? We don't discuss it again or bring it up at the office.'

'Okay,' he said, swooping in for a kiss that snatched her breath and quite possibly her heart.

Liza didn't remember much of the short drive to Wade's Southbank apartment. She could barely concentrate on the road with his hand on her thigh the entire time.

He didn't speak, sensing her need for silence. She couldn't speak, not without the risk of blurting how he made her feel. Uncertain and flustered and on a high.

Hell, how bad would it be come morning after another amazing night in his arms?

She shouldn't have agreed, but the part of her that had had the life she'd planned ripped away following the phone call from her financial adviser's office still craved a little indulgence.

She was doing her best: with the biography, with the marketing job, with caring for Cindy.

She deserved a little break, deserved to feel good, and Wade was guaranteed to make her feel incredible, albeit for a few hours, tonight.

His penthouse apartment was everything she'd imagined: glossy wooden floors, electrically controlled slim-line blinds, glass and chrome and leather. Minimalist chic. Reeking of money.

Not that he gave her much of a chance to study it, for the moment they stepped down into the split-level lounge room he had his arms around her and backed her against a sleek marble-topped table.

'Do you have any idea how much I want you?' he said, framing her face with his hands, staring deep into her eyes.

The depth of his need shocked her, as if he'd given her a glimpse right to his very soul.

He shouldn't want her this much. It wouldn't end well.

But she'd come too far to back out now and she couldn't even if she wanted to. For she needed him just as badly. If only for tonight.

'I have a fair idea,' she said, undulating her hips against the evidence of how badly he wanted her.

He growled. 'Tease.'

'No, a tease would do this.' Her hands splayed against his chest, caressed upwards before stroking downwards. Lower. And lower. Stopping short of his belt buckle. 'A tease would also do this.'

She slowly slid the leather belt out, toying with the buckle.

'And this.' She flicked the top button of his trousers open.

'A tease would stop here.' She inched his zipper down, the sound of grating metal teeth the only sound apart from his ragged breathing.

'But I'm no tease.' She pushed his trousers down. Slid a hand inside his black boxers. Cupped his erection.

His groan filled the air and, empowered, she went for broke.

He let her undress him until he was standing before her, gloriously naked, incredibly beautiful.

Bronze skin, rippling muscles, hard for her.

'One of us is way overdressed,' he said, taking a step towards her.

'Wait.' She braced a hand on his chest. 'I'm admiring the view.'

'Later,' he said, bundling her into his arms. 'Much later.'

CHAPTER TEN

LIZA LITHGOW'S STYLE TIPS
FOR MAXIMUM WAG WOW IMPACT

The Dream

WAGs of the New York Yankees may not harbour this same dream, but for WAGs all around the world New York City is *the* place to be.

From its iconic Manhattan skyline to its most recognised Statue of Liberty. From the Chrysler Building to the famed Empire State Building.

From its two most famous streets, Madison and Park Avenues.

There is so much to tempt a WAG.

Throw in:

The Metropolitan Museum of Art (The Met)
Central Park
The Flatiron Building
The Guggenheim
The Brooklyn Bridge
Times Square
Rockefeller Centre

Broadway
Carnegie Hall
Lincoln Centre
Madison Square Garden

And it's little wonder that most WAGs dream of being a part of New York.

So what are you waiting for? Book that airline ticket now!

LUCKY FOR WADE, he'd never had much of an ego.

For if he had it'd be smarting.

Liza had done it again. Indulged in a wild, passionate, no-holds-barred night of mind-blowing sex. And then nothing.

The next day at the office she'd reverted to the cool, dedicated woman who'd wowed him with her business ethic that first day she'd presented her marketing ideas like a veteran.

That had been four weeks ago and nothing had changed.

Admittedly, they'd been incredibly busy, with her biography having the fastest turnaround he'd ever seen in all his years in publishing.

To have a book written, copy-edited, line-edited and in ARC format within a month? Unheard of, but he'd made it happen. He owed his dad that much.

Preserving a family legacy might be the reason everyone assumed was behind his drive to save the company.

Only he knew the truth. Guilt was a pretty powerful motivator.

And despite Liza's encouraging insights that his dad had loved him and that was why Quentin hadn't shared the truth about his heart condition, Wade knew better.

His dad had known how much he despised Babs, but he'd been too much of a gentleman to bring it up or let it affect their relationship initially. But with Wade's continued withdrawal, both physically and emotionally, he'd irrevocably damaged the one relationship he'd ever relied on.

For his dad not to trust him enough to divulge the truth about his heart condition before it was too late? It hurt, deeper and harder than he'd ever imagined.

Wade regretted every moment he'd lost with his dad. Regretted all the time they could have spent together if he'd known the truth. Regretted how he'd let his superiority and judgement and distaste ruin their mateship. For that was what they'd had, a real friendship that surpassed a simple father-son bond.

Most of all, he regretted not having the opportunity to say a proper goodbye to his dad.

He'd regret his actions and the rift he'd caused until his dying day but for now he'd do everything in his power to ensure Qu thrived, as a token of respect for the man who had given him everything.

And he had the woman who'd sold her story to him to thank too.

He'd done as she said over the last few weeks. Remembered the good times with his dad.

Authors they'd signed together, books they'd published that had gone on to hit best-seller lists.

A patient Quentin teaching him golf as a teenager and the many hack games that had followed over the years.

The beers they'd share while watching the AFL Grand Final or the Grand Prix.

So many more precious memories he'd deliberately locked away because of the hurt. But Liza had been right. Holding on to guilt only made it fester and remembering the good times had gone some way to easing his pain.

She'd given him a wake-up call he'd needed and he hoped his surprise would help thank her.

He knocked on Liza's door, holding the Advanced Reading Copy behind his back. He wanted to surprise her and hoped she'd be as thrilled with how the story had turned out as he was.

He'd stayed up all night, devouring Liza's biography from cover to cover. When he'd speed read the first draft in e-format he'd done so with an editor's eye and hadn't really had time to absorb the facts beyond she'd delivered the juicy tell-all he'd demanded.

After reading the ARC last night, holding her life in *tree* format, he'd felt closer to her somehow, as if learning snippets from her childhood revealed her to him in a way she'd never do herself.

Of course, he'd hated her dating tales, insanely jealous of the soccer and basketball stars that had wooed her and whisked her to parties and elite functions, living the high life.

He had no reason to be jealous, for those guys were her past.

And what? He was her future?

Damned if he knew. It wasn't as if they were looking for anything long term. He'd spelled it out at the start and Liza did her best to maintain her distance when they weren't burning up the sheets those two times.

So why the intense disappointment she'd been willing to share part of her life with him, but only for the money?

The door opened and a forty-something woman with spiked blonde hair, no make-up and sporting a frown eyed him up and down. 'Yes?'

'Hi, Wade Urquart, here to see Liza.'

The woman's eyes widened as a sly smile lit her face. 'Nice to meet you, Wade. I'm Shar. Come on in.'

Shar ushered him through the door and it took a moment to register two things.

A pretty young woman bearing a strong resemblance to Liza was engrossed in a jigsaw puzzle alongside Liza.

The young woman was in a wheelchair.

Their heads turned as one as he stepped into the room, the young woman's lopsided welcoming smile indicative of some kind of disability, Liza's stunned expression a mix of horror and fear.

It confused the hell out of him.

Why was she horrified to see him? Was she scared he'd run a mile because she had a disabled relative, probably a sister?

The possibility that she thought so little of him irked.

He strode forward, determined to show her he was ten times the man she gave him credit for.

'Hi, I'm Wade.' He stuck out his hand, waited for the young woman to place her clawed hand in his, and shook it gently.

'Cindy,' she said, her blue eyes so like Liza's bright with curiosity and mischief. 'Are you Liza's boyfriend?'

'Yes,' he said, simultaneously with Liza's, 'No.'

Shar smothered a laugh from behind. 'Come on, Cinders, let's leave these two to sort out their confusion.'

Cindy giggled and Wade said, 'Nice meeting you both,' as they left the room.

Liza stood, her movements stiff and jerky as she rounded the table, arms folded. 'What are you doing here?'

'I came to give you this.'

He handed her the ARC, his excitement at sharing it with her evaporating in a cloud of confusion.

Why hadn't she told him about her sister Cindy? Did he mean that little to her?

They might not have a solid commitment or long-term

plans but he'd thought they'd really connected on a deeper level beyond the physical.

At the very least they were friends, and friends shared stuff like this.

As her fingers closed around the creased spine from his rapid page-turning the night before, the truth detonated.

His hand jerked back and the ARC fell to the floor with a loud thud.

'There's no mention of Cindy in your bio.'

She glared at him, defiant. "Course not. I don't want the whole world knowing about my sister—'

'What the—?' He ran a hand over his face, hoping it would erase his disgust, knowing it wouldn't. 'You're embarrassed by her.'

She stepped back as if he'd struck her, her mouth a shocked O.

Anger filled him, ugly and potent. He didn't know what made him madder: the fact she'd lied in her bio, the fact she was ashamed of her sister or the fact she hadn't trusted him enough to tell him anything.

He kicked at the ARC. 'Is any of this true?'

She flinched. 'My life is between those pages—'

'Bull.' He lowered his voice with effort. 'Leaving your sister out of your bio is a major twisting of the truth. Which makes me wonder, what else have you lied about?'

He waited for her to deny, wanted her to. But she stood there, staring at him with sorrow and regret, and he had his answer.

'I could lose everything,' he said, anger making his hands shake. His fingers curled into fists and he shoved them into his pockets. 'Your advance? Bulk of it came out of my pocket. Three hundred grand's worth.'

He should feel more panicky about the precarious position he'd placed his own company in to save his dad's—the advance was only the start, for he'd poured another half a million into the marketing budget for the bio too—but all he could think about was how Liza had lied to him. How she'd withheld the truth from him.

Just like his dad.

He'd told her about Quentin not trusting him enough, about how it affected him. Hell, she'd even given him that pep talk.

Yet she'd gone and done the same regardless.

'I earned that advance.' Her flat monotone made him want to shake her to get some kind of reaction. 'I gave you the story you wanted.'

'So what? I should be grateful?' His bitterness made her flinch. 'Should've known better than to trust someone like you.'

She paled but didn't say anything, her lack of defence riling him further.

'Guess you played me like those other poor suckers in your *biography*,' he said, not proud of the low blow but lashing out, needing to hurt her as much as she'd hurt him.

That was when the real truth detonated.

He wouldn't care this much, wouldn't be hurting this much, if he hadn't fallen for her.

A woman who didn't trust him, a woman who thought nothing of their developing relationship, a woman who'd done all of this clearly for the money only.

Reeling from the realisation, he did the only thing possible.

Turned on his heel, strode out of the door and slammed it behind him.

Liza sank onto the nearest chair and clutched her belly, willing the rolling nausea to subside.

She didn't know what was worse: feeling as if she was about to hurl or the breath-snatching ache in her chest.

This was why she never let any guy get too close.

This was why she never should've let Wade into her life.

And into her heart.

She had; despite every effort to push him away and keep their relationship strictly business, he'd bustled his way in with charm and panache and flair.

And she'd let him. She knew why too. Because for the first time in for ever she'd felt cherished. Spoiled. As if someone was looking out for her rather than the other way around.

She didn't mind being Cindy's carer but for a brief interlude in her life Wade had swept her off her feet and taught her what it felt like being on the other side.

'Double mocha or double-choc-fudge brownies?' Shar bustled into the room, pretending not to look at her while casting concerned glances out of the corner of her eye as she tidied up a stack of magazines.

'Both,' Liza said, knowing she'd be unable to stomach either but needing a few more minutes alone to reassemble her wits.

'Okay. Back in a sec.'

Breathing a sigh of relief, Liza eased the grip on her belly and stretched. Rolled out her shoulders. Tipped her neck from side to side.

Did little for the tension gripping her but at least she wouldn't get a muscle spasm on top of everything else.

Wade had ousted her lies. Worse, he thought she was ashamed of Cindy, when nothing could be further from the truth.

And the fact he hadn't let her explain, had stood there and hurled accusations at her, hurt.

Maybe she should've told him, should've trusted him

with the truth. But her motives had been pure. She'd done it all for Cindy. Would do it again if it meant protecting her sister.

Now he knew the truth, where did that leave them?

'Here you go.' Shar dumped a plate of brownies and a steaming mocha in front of her. 'Looks like you could do with a good dose of chocolate.'

'You heard?' Liza picked at the corner of a brownie, shoved a few crumbs around the plate with her fingertip.

'Enough.' Shar winced. 'Didn't sound good.'

'Is Cindy okay?'

Shar nodded. 'Yeah, she was hooked up to the computer playing a game, had her ears plugged.'

'Guess I should be grateful for small mercies,' Liza said, the severity of her confrontation with Wade hitting home at the thought of Cindy overhearing what he'd accused her of.

'You didn't tell him about Cindy.'

It was a statement, not a question, and Liza didn't know where to begin to rationalise her behaviour.

'He seems like a nice bloke.' Shar sipped at her mocha. 'Good looker too.'

'Wade's…' What? Incredibly sexy? Persistent? Thoughtful? She settled for the truth. 'Special.'

'Then why all the secrecy?'

'Because I wanted to protect Cindy.'

'From?'

'Prying. Interference.'

'Ridicule?' Shar prompted and Liza nodded, biting her bottom lip.

'You'll probably hate me for saying this, but are you sure it's Cindy you were protecting and not you?'

Liza's head snapped up; she was shocked by Shar's accusation. 'What do you mean?'

Shar screwed up her nose before continuing. 'You've

lived your life in the spotlight. TV-hosting gigs. Mingled with A-listers. Best parties. Best of everything.'

Shar paused, glanced away. 'Maybe you didn't want people knowing you had a disabled sister because you thought it would taint how you appeared to others in some way?'

'That's bull.' Liza stood so quickly her knee knocked the underside of the table and she swore.

'Then why so defensive?'

She glared at Shar. 'Because what you've just suggested is hateful and makes me look like a narcissistic bitch.'

Shar shook her head. 'No. It makes you human.'

Shar's accusation echoed through her head. Had that partially been her motivation? Was Wade right? Was she ashamed to reveal to the world she had a disabled sister?

Never in a million years would she have thought that, but if the two people in the world she was closest to—discounting Cindy—had jumped to the same conclusion, had she done it on some subconscious level?

She collapsed back onto the chair and tried to articulate her jumbled feelings. 'Because of what I've faced in the spotlight, I didn't want Cindy exposed to any of that.'

Shar pointed at the ARC lying on the floor. 'So what if you'd mentioned her in the book? Doesn't mean the media would've been beating down your door to interview her.'

'They might've.' Liza rested her feet on the chair and wrapped her arms around her shins. 'You've fielded enough calls to know how persistent they can be. It could've turned into a circus.'

'Or they could've respected your privacy and hers.'

Liza blew a raspberry. 'I hate it when you're logical.'

Shar winked. 'All part of the service.'

Now that Liza had come this far, she should tell Shar all of it.

'I did it for the money.'

'The biography?'

Liza nodded. 'That day I went to Qu Publishing's offices to tell them to stop harassing us? I had a phone call from my financial adviser's office.'

She took a deep breath, blew it out. 'My investment has gone. He scammed the lot.'

Shar blanched. 'Oh hell.'

'I said worse than that.' Liza hugged her knees tighter. 'I was still in the office. Wade found me in a crumpled heap. I had to accept his offer. The advance and royalties from the bio were the only way out.'

'Drastic times call for drastic measures.' Shar picked up the ARC off the floor and laid it on the table. 'If you didn't mention Cindy in the bio, did you stretch the truth in general?'

'A little.' She waved a hand side to side. 'Mostly stuck to the truth with the WAG side of things. Played up all that glamorous nonsense people lap up. It's what he asked for.'

'What about your folks?'

'I told the truth. Within reason.'

Even now, ten years after her mum had walked out on them, and over two decades since her dad had bolted too, Liza cushioned the hurt by justifying their appalling behaviour.

They didn't deserve it but the last thing she needed was for Cindy to realise the truth one day. That their parents had left because of her.

Cindy had been too young to know their father, had swallowed the story their mum had told: they'd grown apart and divorced. When in fact he'd been a coward, unable to cope with a disabled daughter and had taken the easy way out by abandoning them all.

As for their mum? Cindy wasn't a fool and had been stoic when she'd left. Louisa had emotionally withdrawn for years and Cindy had been philosophical, almost happy, when it had just been the two of them left.

Finding Shar at the time had been a godsend too and Liza knew she wouldn't have made it without the full-time carer and confidante.

'As long as you didn't tell blatant lies, I don't see what the problem is.' Shar picked up the ARC and flipped through it. 'What did he mean about losing everything?'

'Apparently the advance came out of his pocket.'

But from what she'd learned, Wade was loaded. Had his own publishing company in London.

Then again, she knew better than anyone that appearances could be deceptive. If his company was anything like Qu Publishing and the rest of the industry, maybe he'd taken a hit with the digital boom and was losing millions with falling print runs?

But her bio was already at the printers, ready to ship to the many bookstores that had pre-ordered by the thousands. And those pre-orders were like gold.

So what if she'd omitted Cindy? What the readers didn't know wouldn't hurt them.

He'd overreacted, probably smarting more from her omission than any real financial pressure.

Shar laid the ARC on the table and nudged it towards her. 'Maybe you should talk to him?'

'Are you kidding?' Liza shook her head. 'You didn't see how mad he was.'

'Give him time to cool off, then talk to him.' Shar took a huge bite of brownie, chewed it, before continuing. 'Besides, isn't he your boss? You'll have to talk some time.'

That was when reality hit.

She'd have to face up to work and see that devastation and disgust in Wade's eyes all over again.

The pain in her chest intensified.

Shar dusted off her hands. 'Go easy on him. I think he likes you.'

That's where the problem lay.

Liza liked him too.

Too much to be good for her.

After helping bathe and dress Cindy, Liza settled into the nightly routine of rubbing moisturiser into Cindy's dry skin.

It was their special bonding time, to relax and chat about their respective days. Liza had missed it on those evenings when she'd been on WAG duty. Guess it said a lot about her previous lifestyle that she would've rather been home with her sis than whooping it up with a bunch of fake socialites.

'That feels good.' Cindy closed her eyes and rested her head against the back of the chair as Liza spread the moisturiser evenly over her forearm with firm strokes.

'Your skin's looking great,' Liza said, always on the lookout for pressure sores or skin breakdown, common side effects with CP.

'Thanks to you.' Cindy sighed as Liza increased the pressure slightly. 'Wade seems nice.'

'Hmm.' Liza deliberately kept her strokes rhythmic, not wanting to alert Cindy to her sudden spike in blood pressure.

She didn't want to think about Wade now, didn't want to remember the disappointment and censure in his eyes as he'd stalked out two hours ago.

His accusation cut deep. To think, he'd assumed she was ashamed of Cindy…well, stuff him.

He wouldn't have a clue what it was like, trying to keep Cindy calm and avoiding stress that could potentially increase her spasticity.

Liza had seen it happen, any time Cindy was anxious, upset, agitated or excited. The medical team had advised her to avoid such situations. And that was the main reason Liza hadn't included Cindy in the book.

She couldn't run the risk of people invading Cindy's privacy, pestering for interviews and potentially increasing the likelihood of those disastrous contractures.

The changes in Cindy's soft tissues terrified Liza. The shortening of muscles, tendons and ligaments could lead to muscle stiffness, atrophy and fibrosis, where the muscles become smaller and thinner.

And if those muscles permanently shortened and pulled on the nearby bones the resultant deformities were a significant problem.

Her sis worked so hard at her exercises but Liza constantly worried about contractures, where the spasticity in Cindy's arm and leg might reach a point where the muscles required surgical release.

Cindy co-operated most days but they'd had their battles over the years, where no amount of cajoling or bribery could get Cindy to follow her exercise regimen.

Liza hated playing taskmaster but she did it. Anything to avoid seeing Cindy in more pain than she already was.

Cindy coped with the chronic pain from minor muscle contractures and abnormal postures of her joints admirably but it broke Liza's heart every time her sis winced or cried out during her routine.

Liza stayed positive and tried to encourage as much as she could, for the possibility of a hip subluxation or scoliosis from the contractures was all too real and she wanted to avoid further medical intervention for Cindy at all costs.

So including her in the biography and having Cindy agitated or overexcited, leading to contractures?

Uh-uh, Liza couldn't do it. She'd never intentionally hurt her sister or put her in harm's way and that was how she'd viewed revealing Cindy's identity to the world.

As for Shar's insinuation that maybe Liza hadn't wanted to be tainted by Cindy's disability in some way, that was off base.

Liza would've loved to raise awareness for cerebral palsy, the association and the carers, and her tell-all would've been the perfect vehicle.

But Cindy came first always and she couldn't run the risk of her spasticity worsening.

'He said he was your boyfriend.' Cindy's eyes snapped open and pinned Liza with an astute glare she had no hope of evading.

'Guys get confused sometimes.' Liza reached for Cindy's other arm and started the massage process all over again. 'Smile and they think you're crushing on them.'

Cindy giggled, a sound Liza never tired of. 'Maybe that's the problem? You've been smiling too much at Wade?'

'Could be.'

Though Liza knew smiling would be the last thing happening when they met next.

Shar was right. She had to talk to him, had to calm this volatile situation before she lost her job.

And maybe lost the guy.

CHAPTER ELEVEN

LIZA LITHGOW'S STYLE TIPS
FOR MAXIMUM WAG WOW IMPACT

The Proposal

WAGs put up with a lot to stand by their man.

So it's only fitting a WAG deserves a special proposal.

Guys, here are some of the best places in which to propose to your devoted WAG (and actually put that W—Wife—into WAG!)

- Strolling along the Seine in Paris.
- Atop the Eiffel Tower.
- Cruising the Greek Islands on a private yacht.
- Top of the London Eye.
- Sunset on Kuta Beach in Bali.
- At the ball drop in Times Square, NYC, on New Year's Eve.
- Winery dinner in the Yarra Valley, Victoria.
- Hot-air balloon, anywhere.
- Camel ride, United Arab Emirates.
- Walking the Great Wall of China.
- Outside the Taj Mahal.
- Climbing the Sydney Harbour Bridge.

- Cruising the South Pacific.
- Midnight on New Year's Eve, anywhere.
- Central Park, any time.
- Spanish Steps, Rome.
- Diamond Head, Waikiki.
- In a buré over the water, Tahiti or Maldives.
- Scuba diving in the Great Barrier Reef.

AFTER THE BLOW-UP with Liza, Wade headed for the one place he felt safe.

The office.

It had been his refuge for as long as he could remember, whether in Melbourne or London, the one place he was on top and in total control.

Family? As changeable as the wind and, as his relationship with his dad had fractured because of Babs, he'd systematically withdrawn.

Girlfriends? Chosen with deliberation, the kind of corporate women who expected nothing and were content with a brief fling.

The publishing business had been the one constant in his life, the one thing he could depend on.

And now, courtesy of Liza's lies, he could lose that too.

It had taken a full hour of checking with his legal team and exploring all possible scenarios for him to calm down.

Even if Liza's bio weren't one-hundred-per-cent accurate, according to the contract wording the readers would have no recourse if the truth of Cindy's existence came out.

He'd assumed it wouldn't be a problem but needed to know for sure. After all, how many celebrities invented backgrounds and touted it as truth?

In the heat of the moment, when he'd realised she'd kept something as important as her sister from him, he'd snapped and said he could lose everything.

He'd thrown it out there to shame her; to intimidate her into maybe telling him the truth—why she'd done it—when in fact the eight hundred grand from his own pocket wouldn't make or break him.

Now that he'd calmed down enough to rationally evaluate the situation, he might not have lost his dad's company but he had lost something equally important.

The woman he loved.

How ironic that the first time he let a woman get closer than dinner and a date, the first time he'd learned what it meant to truly desire someone beyond the physical, had turned into the last time he'd ever be so foolish again.

And a scarier thought: was he like his dad after all? Had Liza played him as Babs had played his dad?

He wouldn't have thought so, the times they'd been intimate so revealing, so soul-reaching, he could've sworn she'd been on the same wavelength.

But she'd sought him out at the very beginning. She'd blackmailed her way into a job. Had that been her end game from the start?

Was their relationship a way of keeping him onside while she milked the situation for all it was worth?

Wasn't as if she hadn't done it before. According to her bio—if any of it was true—she'd been thrust into WAG limelight by default when her high-school sweetheart became pro, but with the basketball star she'd implied they'd had an understanding based on a solid friendship and mutual regard.

Yet when he'd studied the pictures of her and Henri Jaillet her body language spoke volumes. If the cameras were trained on her Liza stood tall and smiled, while subtly leaning away from Henri's arm draped across her shoulders or waist.

In the candid shots, she stood behind Henri, arms folded, shoulders slumped, lips compressed.

By those shots, she hadn't enjoyed a moment of their relationship yet she'd done it regardless, enduring it for a year.

What had she told him at the start? *What you see isn't always what you get.*

If so, why? Had it been to support her sister? Had she deliberately thrust herself into the limelight? Had it been for the adulation or was there more behind it?

That was what killed him the most, the fact he'd felt closer to her reading the bio, as if she'd let him into her life a little, when in fact she hadn't let him in at all.

He swirled the Scotch he nursed before downing the amber spirit in two gulps. The burn in his gullet didn't ease the burn in his heart and the warmth as it hit his stomach didn't spread to the rest of him.

He'd been icy cold since he'd left Liza's, unable to equate the woman he'd fallen in love with to the woman who'd hide her disabled sister out of shame.

His door creaked open and he frowned, ready to blast anyone who dared enter. Damn publishing business, one of the few work environments where it wasn't unusual to find employees chained to their desk to meet deadlines at all hours.

'Go away,' he barked out, slamming the glass on the side table when the door swung open all the way. 'I said—'

'I heard what you said.' Liza stood in the doorway, framed by the backlight, looking like a person who'd been through the ringer. He knew the feeling. 'But I'm not going anywhere.'

He swiped a hand over his face. 'I'm not in the mood.'

She ignored his semi-growl, entered the office and closed the door.

He watched her walk across the office, soft grey yoga

pants clinging to her legs, outlining their shape, and desire mingled with his anger.

She sat next to him on the leather sofa, too close for comfort, not close enough considering he preferred her on his lap.

Her fingers plucked at the string of her red hoodie, twisting it around and around until he couldn't stand it any more. He reached out and stilled her hand, watching her eyes widen at the contact before she clasped her hands in her lap.

Great. Looked as if his touch had become as repugnant as him.

'We need to get a few things straight,' she said, shoulders squared in defiance. 'Firstly, Cindy is the most important person in my life and I'd never be ashamed of her.'

He waited and she glared at him, daring him to disagree.

'Secondly, I've spent most of my life protecting her and that's what my omission was about. Ensuring she wouldn't cop the same crap I have all these years, which may have a detrimental effect on her condition physically.'

'How?'

'Extreme emotions or mood swings can increase the spasticity in her muscles, which in turn can lead to long-term complications. Serious complications that could lead to permanent deformities.'

A tiny sliver of understanding lodged in his hardened heart, cracking it open a fraction, letting admiration creep in. And regret, that he'd unfairly accused her of something so heinous as being ashamed of her sister when in fact she was protecting her.

'And thirdly, the rest of my life laid out in the bio? True. Not fabricated. Elaborated? Yeah.' Her fingers twitched, before she unlinked her hands and waved one between them. 'But you and I? All real. Every moment, and I'd hate for you to think otherwise.'

Admiration gave way to hope and went a long way to soothing the intense hurt that had rendered him useless until she'd strutted through his door.

But he wouldn't give in that easily. It might have taken a lot of guts to confront him now, so soon after their blow-up, but he couldn't forget the fact she'd shut him out when he'd let her in.

'Prove it.'

A tiny frown crinkled her brow. 'How?'

'Let me into your life.'

The frown intensified. 'I don't know what you mean.'

'I think you do.' He shuffled closer to her on the couch, buoyed when she didn't move away. 'I want to see the real you. Not the persona you've donned for years to fool the masses. Not the woman you've pretended to be from the beginning of our relationship. The real you.'

Liza stared at Wade as if he'd proposed she scale the Eureka Tower naked.

The real her? No one saw the real her, not even Cindy, who she pretended to be upbeat for constantly. The way she saw it, her sister had a tough enough life, why make it harder by revealing when her own life wasn't a bed of roses?

Liza had always done it, assumed a happy face even if she'd felt like curling up in bed with a romance novel and a pack of Tim Tams.

So what Wade was asking? Too much.

She shook her head. 'I can't—'

'Yeah, you can.'

Before she could move he grasped her hand and placed it over his heart. 'I'm willing to take a chance on us. Without the pretence. Without the baggage of the past. Just you and me. What do you say?'

Liza wanted to run and hide, wanted to fake a smile and respond with a practised retort designed to hide her real feelings.

But looking into Wade's guileless dark eyes, feeling his

heart thump steadily, she knew she'd reached a turning point in her life.

She had two options.

Revert to type and continue living a sham.

Or take a giant leap of faith and risk her heart.

'An answer some time this century would be nice,' he said, pressing her hand harder to his heart.

'I'm taking Cindy to Luna Park tomorrow,' she blurted. 'Come with us.'

She waited, holding her breath until her chest ached.

She'd never invited anyone along to her days out with Cindy. It was their special time. To consider letting Wade accompany them, to see what the reality of being a full-time carer involved? Huge step. He'd wanted to see the real her and she'd thrown down the gauntlet.

His mouth eased into a smile and the air whooshed out of her lungs. 'Sounds good. What time?'

'Nine. We'll pick you up.'

He released her hand to rub his together. 'Great. I get to ride in the people carrier.'

'You're making jokes about my car still, even when you know it's used for a wheelchair?'

He tapped her on the nose. 'Hey, we're genuine from now on, okay? No holding back, no watching what we say. Full disclosure.'

Liza nodded slowly, wondering how he'd feel if he knew all of it.

She didn't have time to find out when he closed the distance between them and kissed her, effectively eradicating all thought and going a long way to soothing the emptiness when he'd walked out earlier.

She hated being abandoned. Dredged up too many painful memories.

She never wanted to feel that way again.

* * *

Liza didn't know what she'd expected when she'd invited Wade to accompany them to Luna Park on the spur of the moment.

She'd wanted to test him. To see how he acted around Cindy.

For when he'd walked out on her, she'd come to a few realisations. Wade was the only guy she'd ever genuinely cared about and for that reason, after seeing his disgust when she'd withheld the truth, she'd had enough of the lies and the fake life.

She wanted to be herself around him and that included Cindy. They were a package and if he couldn't handle her sister's disability Liza didn't want to get in any deeper.

Cindy was the deal-breaker.

By the way he'd teased and laughed and chatted with her sister, he'd passed with flying colours.

Liza had seen many people interact with her sister over the years. Some glanced away or pretended not to see Cindy. Some stared at her clawed elbow and wrist, at her scissored thighs, her equinovarus foot. Some patronised by speaking extra slowly or very loud. Some looked plain uncomfortable.

But from the moment they'd picked up Wade this morning he'd been at ease and, in turn, Liza had progressively relaxed as the morning wore on.

She liked not having to pretend around Wade. It was a nice change. Something she could get used to given half a chance.

While Cindy watched the roller-coaster ride with rapt attention, Wade sat next to Liza and bumped her with his shoulder.

'Having a good time?'

She smiled and nodded. 'Absolutely. I always have a ball when I'm with Cindy.'

'She's amazing,' he said, sliding his hand across her lap to grasp hers. 'And so are you.'

He waved at Cindy with his free hand as she glanced their way. 'Honestly? I don't know a lot about cerebral palsy. I'd planned on researching it last night but got caught up with conference calls.'

Liza admired his interest. Hopefully it meant his interaction with Cindy today wasn't just a token effort and he genuinely wanted to be involved in her life—which included Cindy's life too.

'It's basically a physical disability affecting movement, caused by an injury to the developing brain, usually before birth.'

The corners of his beautiful mouth curved upward. 'You sound like a medical dictionary.'

'With the hours I've spent with the medical profession over the years I reckon I could recite an entire library's worth of encyclopaedias.'

He squeezed her hand. 'What's her prognosis?'

'Normal life expectancy. The brain damage doesn't worsen as she gets older. But the physical symptoms can.'

Cindy laughed out loud as people on the roller coaster screamed when it plummeted and Liza smiled in response, never tiring of seeing her sister happy.

'Cindy's CP is pretty mild. She's diplegic, which means it only affects her arm and leg on one side. And she has spastic CP.'

Wade frowned. 'I hate that word.'

Liza shook her head. 'It's not derogatory. Spasticity means tightness or stiffness of the muscles. The muscles are stiff because the message to move is sent incorrectly to the muscles through the damaged part of the brain.'

'That makes sense.' He frowned, deep in thought. 'Can she walk?'

'A little. At home mainly, in her room, with the aid of a frame. But for Cindy, the harder she works her muscles, the greater the spasticity, so it's easier for her to get around in the wheelchair.'

Liza blew Cindy a kiss as she glanced towards them again and grinned. 'We're definitely lucky. Many CP sufferers have intellectual disabilities, speech difficulties, seizures and severe limitations with eating and drinking. Cindy's main problem is mobility.'

Wade shook his head, as if he couldn't quite believe her optimism. 'You're fantastic.' He nodded towards Cindy. 'The way you are with her? It's beautiful.'

Uncomfortable with his praise but inwardly preening, she shrugged. 'She's my sister. We've been doing stuff together for a long time.'

'What about your folks?'

She stiffened and he squeezed her hand. 'You glossed over them in your bio and you never mention them…'

Liza didn't want to talk about her flaky folks, not today, not ever. But after Wade's full-disclosure pep talk last night she'd have to give him something.

'I didn't want to make them look bad in the book. That's why I didn't say much beyond the basics.'

He frowned. 'How bad was it?'

'Dad took off when Cindy was a year old. Couldn't handle having a disabled kid. Mum progressively withdrew emotionally over the years, waited 'til I was eighteen, then she did a runner too.'

Wade swore. 'So you've been looking after Cindy ever since?'

'Uh-huh. The CP association hooked me up with Shar

shortly after Mum left and she's been a godsend. More family than carer.'

More family than her parents combined. The old saying blood was thicker than water? Give her a long, tall glass of clear aqua any day.

'Do you ever hear from them?'

She heard the disapproval in his voice and didn't want to dampen this day. 'Mum rings on birthdays and Christmas, sends money as a gift, that's about it.'

Shock widened his eyes before she saw a spark of understanding. 'That's why you took the book deal, isn't it? You support Cindy financially.'

Liza struggled not to squirm. She didn't want to discuss this with Wade, didn't want him to know her private business.

There was disclosure and there was disclosure. And for a couple that were only just embarking on a possible future, she didn't want to muddy it with her sordid past.

'We do okay,' she said, springing up from the bench and dusting off her butt. 'Come on, I think Cindy's ready for that ice cream you promised.'

Disappointment twisted his mouth before he forced a smile. 'Sure.'

But as the sun passed behind a cloud and Liza shivered in a gust off Port Phillip Bay, she wondered if her sudden chill had more to do with Wade's obvious disapproval at her reticence than the fickle spring weather.

An hour after Liza dropped him off at the office, Wade strode into the boardroom.

He couldn't get the sound of theme-park rides and Liza's laughter and Cindy's giggles out of his head, or the taste of hot dogs and mint ice cream off his tongue.

It had been an incredible morning, seeing the real Liza

for the first time, and he'd been blown away. By her dedication to her sister, by her level of caring, by her sheer joy in spending time with Cindy.

None of it was faked and it made him wonder why she'd gone to great lengths to hide Cindy's identity from him.

Sure, he bought her excuse about not wanting Cindy exposed to the kind of intrusion she'd faced with her lifestyle over the years and how emotional swings could increase the risk physically, but there had to be more to it.

He'd thought she might open up to him today of all days, for he'd seen how she'd looked at him. As if she'd really seen him for the first time.

It had made him feel ten feet tall, as if he could scale that giant mouth entrance at Luna Park and jog backwards on the roller coaster.

Then he'd made the fatal mistake of delving deeper and she'd clammed up. Shut him out, as if the last four hours had never happened.

It killed him, because he had to make some fast decisions regarding his future and he hoped to have her in it.

He knew what the board were going to say, had been sent a memo by the chairman late last night after Liza had left the office.

Everything he'd worked so hard for, everything his father had achieved, would continue.

He'd saved Qu Publishing.

Liza's biography had saved Qu Publishing.

And rather than taking her out for a night on the town to celebrate, he knew when he broke the news neither of them would feel like champagne.

It meant the end of his time in Melbourne.

The end of his relationship with Liza before it had really begun.

For now he'd seen her with Cindy he knew she'd never

leave her sister. She was too dedicated. And he wouldn't ask that of her.

What if they both came with him?

The thought exploded out of left field and he rubbed his temple, dazed and excited at the same time.

'Wade?' The chairman slapped him on the back and he dragged in a deep breath, needing to get back in the game.

His personal life could wait.

For now, he had a company to solidify.

Wade took his position at the head of the table. 'Thanks for coming, gentlemen.' He mustered a smile for his stepmother. 'Babs.'

Her lips thinned in an unimpressed line.

'As you know, thanks to the pre-orders of Liza Lithgow's biography, Qu Publishing has cleared all debts and is firmly in the black. And with projected profit margins from book sales, hardcover, trade paperback and digital, we're looking at enough capital to ensure viability for many years to come.'

He waited until the noise died down.

'So I propose a vote. All those in favour of selling Qu Publishing, raise your hands.'

There wasn't a flicker of movement at the table as a dozen pairs of eyes stared at him with admiration. All except one and he glanced at Babs, expecting to see her hand in the air.

Puzzled, he saw her hand rise above the table to hover at shoulder height before she let it fall to her lap.

'Well, looks like the vote is unanimous—'

'I want to say something.' Babs stood and Wade's heart sank. What would she come up with now to derail him?

'Quentin loved this company and I know many of you blame me for distracting him from the office these last few years.'

Gobsmacked, Wade stared at the woman who had far more insight than he'd given her credit for.

'The truth is Quentin knew he had a heart condition, one that could prove fatal at any time. He wanted to make the most of our time together and I supported that.' She paused to dab under her eyes, the first time Wade had ever seen her show genuine emotion. 'This company reminds me of what I've lost and that's why I wanted to sell. To move on with my life while holding cherished memories.'

Babs' gaze swung towards him. 'Wade, you've done a great job saving this company from the brink, but I really want out. You can buy my shares and we'll call it even.'

Wade nodded, startled into silence by this turn of events.

He hated hearing Babs articulate his biggest regret: that his dad hadn't shared the seriousness of his prognosis. If he'd known about Quentin's fatal heart condition he never would've wasted so many years staying away because of the woman now looking at him with pity.

He didn't want her pity. He wanted those wasted years back. He wanted to repair the relationship with his dad, the one he'd fractured because of his intolerance. He wanted his dad to trust him enough to tell him the truth.

But he couldn't change the past. He'd have to take control of his future instead and never repeat the same mistakes.

He didn't know if Babs genuinely loved his dad, but he could understand her need to move on with her life.

Selling her shares to him would allow them both to get what they wanted: closure for her, preserving his dad's legacy for him.

Finally finding his voice, he cleared his throat. 'Thanks, Babs, I'll have the transfer papers drawn up immediately.'

She nodded, picked up her bag and sailed out of the door, leaving the board members watching him carefully.

What did they expect? For him to cartwheel across the highly polished conference table?

He might've been tempted if not for the fact he had serious business to conduct after this meeting.

Business far more important than Qu Publishing.

Business of the heart.

CHAPTER TWELVE

LIZA LITHGOW'S STYLE TIPS
FOR MAXIMUM WAG WOW IMPACT

The Bachelorette Party

Once your sportsman has popped the question, it's time to move on to important things…like the bachelorette party!

Keep it classy.

Ditch the comedy genitalia paraphernalia.

Ditto strippers.

No club tours via bus.

Have fun with your girls without the tackiness.

- Book a swank apartment in the heart of the city, order room service, expensive champagne and watch chick flicks.
- A day spa package.
- A weekend away in a posh B&B.
- Eighties party.
- Hire out a renowned restaurant or use their private party room and indulge in fabulous food.
- River cruise.

• Cocktail party.

Recommended cocktails:

- Frozen daiquiris
- Millionaire cocktail
- Boomerang cocktail
- Bossa Nova
- Mimosa
- Pina colada
- Brown Cow
- Angel's Kiss
- Avalanche
- Chi-chi
- Romantico
- Pussy Cat
- Margarita
- Mojito
- Golden Dream
- Cosmopolitan
- Jumping Jack
- Flying Irishman

LIZA HADN'T EXPECTED Wade to show up again so soon after their morning outing.

When she'd dropped him at the office he'd been strangely withdrawn and while he'd mustered a genuine goodbye for Cindy he'd seemed almost disappointed.

She knew what the problem was. The way she hadn't been comfortable discussing her parents and supporting Cindy.

If he only knew how far she'd come in letting him get this close. She'd taken big steps forward today. Allowing him near Cindy, lowering her guard in front of him.

What did he expect? For her to blab all her deep, dark secrets at once? Not going to happen.

The fact he was waiting for her in the lounge while Shar and Cindy had a late supper on the back porch? Made her incredibly happy that he couldn't bear to be away from her for more than half a day. Or made her incredibly nervous that his impromptu visit heralded bad news.

'Drink?'

He shook his head. 'No thanks, I'd rather talk.'

'Okay.'

She perched next to him on the sofa, wondering if he noticed the threadbare patches on the shabby chintz. Seeing those patches made her angry. How hard she'd scrimped and saved, hoarding every cent away for Cindy's future, going without stuff like new furniture because she didn't deem it as important as having a failsafe should anything happen to her.

Instead, something had happened to her money and, while the advance and royalties would help, the thought of her sizable savings gone made her stomach gripe.

'Are you all right?'

'Yeah, why?' She met his gaze, knowing he was far too astute not to notice her jumpiness.

'You seem distracted.'

She tapped her temple. 'Making a to-do list for tomorrow up here. Always makes me seem scatty.'

He nodded, his grave expression saying he didn't buy her excuse for a second.

'I've got news.'

Trepidation taunted her, eliciting a hundred different scenarios, each of them worse than the last.

Pre-orders had fallen through. Bookstores had reneged. Online advertisers had pulled their backing.

'What is it?'

'With Qu Publishing in the black, I'm going back to London.'

The blood drained from her head and Liza's eyes blurred before she blinked, inhaled, steadied.

'My business is there and I've been away long enough.'

'Of course,' she said, grateful her tone remained neutral and well modulated, not shrieking and hysterical.

'I want you to come with me.' He took her hand, rubbed its iciness between his. 'You and Cindy.'

Shock tore through every preconception Liza had ever had about this guy.

He was returning to his life and he wanted her and Cindy to be a part of it?

If she didn't love him before, she sure as hell did now.

Love?

Uh-oh. Fine time to realise she loved Wade when she was on the verge of hyperventilating, collapsing or both.

What could she say? A thousand responses sprang to her lips, none of them appropriate.

She couldn't uproot Cindy. Couldn't lose Shar. Couldn't do any of this without the stability she'd worked so damn hard to maintain.

It had been her priority when her folks, particularly her mum, left. Try to maintain normality. Pretend everything was okay. That the two of them would be fine.

To tear all that away from Cindy on a whim to follow her heart?

Uh-uh, she couldn't do it.

Wade might have issued his invitation but had he really thought this through? Had he really considered what it would be like living with her and her sister? His place would need to be remodelled and that was only one of the many changes he'd have to cope with.

What if he grew tired of it? What if he couldn't handle

having Cindy full time? What if Cindy grew to love him as much as she did and then he ended it? The emotional fallout from something so major would definitely have a detrimental effect on Cindy physically.

No, one Lithgow sister having her heart broken was enough.

She'd vowed to protect Cindy and, sadly, that meant giving up her one shot at happiness.

'Your silence is scaring me,' he said, continuing to chafe her hand in his, but no amount of rubbing could stem the iciness trickling through her veins and chilling every extremity.

'I—I think you're incredible for asking us to come with you, Wade, but we can't.'

His hands stilled. 'Can't or won't?'

'Both,' she said, wondering if that was the first impulsively honest thing she'd ever told him.

She'd spent a decade carefully weighing her words, saying the right thing, doing the right thing, yet now, when it would pay to be circumspect, a plethora of words bubbled up from deep within and threatened to spill out.

'The fact you care enough to include Cindy in your offer means more to me than you'll ever know, but I can't uproot her.'

She waved to the backyard where the sound of voices and laughter drifted inside. 'She's comfortable here, safe. It's the only home she's ever known and I can't move her halfway across the world.'

He willed her to look at him, his gaze boring into her, but she determinedly stared at their joined hands.

'She'll have the best of carers. I can afford it—'

'No.' The vehement refusal sounded like a gunshot. Short. Sharp. Ominous. 'I've always taken care of her and I'll continue to do so.'

He released her hand and eased away as if she'd slapped him. 'Is it so hard to accept help? Or are you too used to playing the martyr you'd do anything to continue the role?'

His harsh accusation hung in the growing silence while a lump of hurt and anger and regret welled in her chest until she could hardly breathe.

He rubbed a hand across his face. 'Sorry, that was way out of line. But you need to realise you have a life too—'

'My life is here, right where I want to be,' she said, finally raising her eyes to meet his, seeing the precise second he registered her bleakness. 'Cindy is all I have and I'm not going to abandon her.'

'But you won't be.' He tried to reach for her and she wriggled back. 'You're not your folks, Liza, you're so much better than them. But the strain of bearing a constant load will eventually tell. It's not healthy shouldering the lot.'

He tapped his chest. 'Let me in. I'll be here for you. Always.'

That sounded awfully like for ever to Liza and it only added to her grief.

She'd be walking away from the best thing that ever happened to her.

But she didn't hesitate, not for a second. Wade was right about one thing. She wasn't her folks and there was nothing he could do or say that would make her put her needs ahead of her sister's.

She shook her head, the tears spurting from her eyes like a waterfall, spraying them. 'I can't. Sorry.'

And then she ran. Ran from the house, ran from the man she loved, ran from a bright future.

Ran until her lungs seized and her legs buckled. Even then, she kept pushing, jogging four blocks before she registered the car cruising beside her.

When she finally couldn't take another step from sheer

exhaustion, she stopped. Braced her hands on her thighs, bending over and inhaling lungfuls of air.

It didn't ease the pain.

She ignored the car idling on the kerb, ignored the electronic glide of a window sliding down.

'Get in. I'll take you home.'

Liza shook her head, willing the strength to return to her legs so she could make another dash for it.

She needed to escape Wade and his all-round goodness, not be confined in his car.

'I'm not leaving 'til you do.'

She lifted her head, mustered a glare that fell short considering sweat dripped in her eyes and her hair was plastered in lank strands across her forehead.

Then she glimpsed the devastation clouding his eyes and something inside her broke.

How could she treat this amazingly beautiful man so badly?

He didn't deserve this. He deserved a friendly parting, a thank you for giving her a job and a lifeline at a time she needed it most.

So she sucked in her bruised pride and hobbled towards the car, feeling as if a baseball bat had battered her as she sank onto the plush leather seat.

He didn't speak, intuitive to her needs until the very end, and it only served to increase her respect and love and gratitude.

When he pulled up outside her house, she mustered what was left of her minimal dignity.

'Thanks for everything.' Her breath hitched and she continued on a sob. 'I'll never forget you.'

She fumbled with the door lock, tumbled out of the car and bolted without looking back.

This time, he didn't come after her.

* * *

Wade packed on autopilot.

Suits in bags, shirts in the case, shoes stuffed in the sides, the rest flung over the top.

He liked the mindless, methodical job. Kept his hands busy. Good thing too, because otherwise he'd be likely to thump something.

Putting a hole in the wall of his penthouse wouldn't be a good idea at this point, as he didn't have time to organise plasterers to fix it.

He wanted to be out of here. ASAP. Sooner the better.

There was nothing left for him here any more. He'd done what he'd set out to do. Save Qu Publishing. Preserve his father's legacy.

Everything else that had happened? Blip on the radar. Soon forgotten when he returned to London.

Until he made the fatal mistake of glancing at the bed and it all came flooding back.

Liza on top, pinning his wrists overhead, her hair draping his chest.

Liza beneath, straining up to meet him, writhing in pleasure.

Liza snuggled in the circle of his arms, her hand over his chest, over his heart, keeping it safe.

Or so he'd thought.

With a groan he abandoned his packing and sank onto the bed, dropped his head in his hands and acknowledged the pain.

He'd deliberately closed off after he'd left her house, had driven to his penthouse in a fog of numbness. It had worked for him before, when he'd made the decision to leave the family business and strike out on his own in London.

He remembered his dad's disappointment, his surprise,

and the only way Wade had dealt with it back then was to erect emotional barriers and get on with the job.

It served him well, being able to compartmentalise his life and his emotions, forgoing one for the sake of the other.

But look how that had turned out, with his dad having a heart condition he knew nothing about and Wade distancing himself when he could've made the most of every moment.

Maybe his coping mechanism wasn't so crash hot after all?

Maybe he'd be better off confronting his demons than running from them?

Maybe he should lower the emotional barriers he'd raised to protect himself and take a chance on trusting someone again?

For that was what had hurt him the most with his dad: that their breakdown in trust had affected how he interacted with everyone, from his colleagues to his dates.

He didn't like letting anyone get close for fear of being let down, the way he'd felt when his dad had put Babs first at the expense of their relationship.

He'd never understood how Quentin could tolerate their strained relationship for that woman.

Until now.

Love did strange things to a guy and if his dad had been half as smitten with Babs as Wade had been with Liza, he could justify his behaviour.

It didn't make accepting their lost years any easier or the lack of trust he'd instilled in his dad because of his withdrawal, both physical and emotional, but it went some way to easing the guilt.

He wondered how different his life would be if he didn't run this time.

A thousand scenarios flashed through his head, the main one centred on Liza and him, together.

He'd thought he'd made her an offer too good to refuse, a magnanimous gesture including her sister. But the more he thought about it, the more he realised how selfish he'd been.

Had he really expected her to pack up, leave her support network and move halfway around the world to fit in with his life?

At no stage had he contemplated staying in Melbourne. It had been a given he'd return to London and expect her to make all the sacrifices. He should've known she'd never agree.

Maybe that was why he'd done it?

Issued an offer he knew she could never accept?

The thought rattled him.

He'd never been emotionally involved with a woman, had kept his dalliances emotion free. The way he saw it, inviting her to live with him had been a huge step forward.

But what if it wasn't forward enough?

He'd treated his dad the same way, not willing to see two sides of their story, intent on believing what he wanted to believe. It had ruined their relationship and driven an irrevocable wedge between them.

It irked, how he'd never have a second chance with his dad. But it wasn't too late to make amends with Liza....

Wade leapt from the bed and headed to the lounge room, in search of his phone.

He needed to put some feelers out, set some plans in motion, before he took the chance of his lifetime.

This time, he wouldn't stuff up.

Liza cherished movie nights with Cindy. She loved curling up on the couch, a massive bowl of popcorn and a packet of Tim Tams between them, laughing uproariously at their favourite comedies they rewatched countless times.

But tonight, not even Peter Sellers and his Birdie Num Nums in the sixties hit *The Party* could dredge up a chuckle.

Sadly, Cindy had picked up on her mood too, barely making a dent in the popcorn and chocolate biscuits when she usually devoured the lot.

'Are you sad because Wade left?'

Reluctant to discuss this with Cindy, Liza dragged her gaze from where Hrundi V. Bakshi, Sellers's character, cavorted in a pool complete with a painted elephant, and forced a smile for her sis.

'Yeah, I'll miss him.'

A tiny frown marred Cindy's brow. 'Where is he going?'

'London.'

'Wow.' Cindy's eyes widened to huge blue orbs. 'London looked amazing during the Olympics. Wish we could go.'

Cindy crammed another fistful of popcorn into her mouth, chewed, before continuing. 'Maybe we could visit Wade there?'

Stunned, Liza stared at Cindy. She'd never heard her sis articulate any great desire to travel. The furthest they'd been was Sydney when Jimmy had been up for a mega award, and Liza had spent the entire time torn between caring for Cindy and ensuring she presented the perfect WAG front when on Jimmy's arm.

It had been exhausting and she preferred to spend time with Cindy at home, while keeping her travels for WAG duties separate.

Not that they'd been able to afford it. She'd been so busy saving every cent for the future she'd never contemplated wasting money on an overseas trip.

'Wade's a good guy. He likes you.' Cindy smirked and made puckering noises. 'I think you like him too.'

Liza sighed. If only it were as simple as that.

'London's a long way away, sweetie—'

'That's what planes are for, dummy.' Cindy elbowed her. 'You should buy tickets. We should go.'

Reeling from Cindy's suggestion, Liza nudged the popcorn bowl closer and gestured at the TV, grateful when Cindy became absorbed in the movie again.

She needed to think.

Not that she'd contemplate flying to London on a holiday, not after she'd worked so hard to replace part of her nest egg for Cindy, but hearing Cindy's request opened her eyes in a way she'd never thought possible.

Had she been so focused on providing financial security she'd lost sight of the bigger picture? That in an effort to protect her sister she'd actually been stifling her?

Guilt blossomed in her chest and she absent-mindedly rubbed it, wishing it were as simple to ease the continual ache in her heart.

But since Wade had driven away last night, the pain had lingered, intensified, until she'd accepted it as a permanent fixture. Niggling, annoying, there until she got over him. Whenever that was.

Cindy laughed as Peter Sellers navigated his way around the party from hell while Liza contemplated the disservice she'd been doing her sister.

All these years she'd assumed Cindy had been content. But by her excitement about proposing a London trip, maybe Cindy was ready for adventures? Maybe she felt as if she was missing out somehow?

In building a secure life, had Liza transferred her fear of abandonment onto Cindy, ensuring her sister was cloistered rather than free to grow?

But she couldn't move to London with Wade. It just wasn't feasible or practical.

Then again, hadn't she lived a practical life the last decade? Faking smiles for the cameras, dressed in uncom-

fortable designer gear for events, pretending to like her
date when she couldn't wait to get home at the end of a
long awards night.

She'd built her entire reputation on a mirage, on a woman
who didn't exist, to the point she hardly knew the real her
anymore.

Yet Wade had taken a chance on her anyway.

He'd trusted her enough, loved her enough, to offer her
a new life and had included her sister in it.

What kind of guy did that?

An honourable, understanding, caring guy. A guy who
wasn't afraid of taking chances. Who wasn't afraid of letting people into his life.

Liza didn't like risks. Losing her folks and losing her
savings had ensured that.

And if she couldn't take risks with her life, no way would
she take risks with Cindy's.

Which brought her right back to the beginning of her
dilemma.

She loved Wade. The only guy she'd ever truly loved.

But she'd let him go because she was too scared to take
a risk, was too scared he'd eventually walk away from her.

'You're missing the best bit,' Cindy said, grabbing a Tim
Tam and offering her the last one in the pack.

'It's all yours,' Liza said, draping a hand across her sister's shoulder and squeezing tight.

Everything she did was for this incredible girl by her side
and she'd have to keep remembering that over the next few
months while her shattered heart took an eternity to mend.

She'd like nothing better than to take a chance on Wade.

But as Cindy snuggled into her side, Liza knew some
risks were too big to take.

CHAPTER THIRTEEN

LIZA LITHGOW'S STYLE TIPS
FOR MAXIMUM WAG WOW IMPACT

The Wedding

With a WAG's busy lifestyle, planning a wedding is a monumental task.

For those with mega-famous sportsmen partners, it seems the eyes of the world will be on you through-out your big day.

Here are a few tips to get you to the altar, smile intact:

- Plan well ahead. Don't leave things to the last minute. And if it's too much, hire the best wedding planner in town and delegate.

- Choose a theme for the wedding and stick to it. Makes co-ordination easier.

- If intrusive crowds on your special day are going to be a problem, consider marrying over-seas (a beach in Bali, Fiji, Tahiti).

- If paparazzi are a problem, sell exclusive rights to your wedding to one magazine and donate the proceeds to charity.

- When it comes to bridesmaids and groomsmen, less is best. Keep it simple, classy, elegant.

- Designer dress is essential.

- Trial hair and make-up months before the big day.

- Insist on tasting everything being served beforehand.

- Funky cakes may look fun on paper but stick to the classics.

- Madcap photos may appeal at the photographer's but when it's your big day captured you might not find the Groucho masks all that funny.

- Assign the rings on the day to the most responsible groomsman.

- Fresh flowers.

- Keep the guest list to close friends and relatives. Inviting the whole team may be your fiancé's priority but you don't want your wedding turning into an end-of-season trip rendition.

- Make sure your iPod is loaded with all your favourite songs and plug your ears on the way to the ceremony.

- Garter removal and bouquet throwing are yesterday.

- Prepare a classy speech. Why should your guy hog the limelight constantly?

- Most importantly, make sure you book your wedding completely out of your partner's sport

season, taking into account drawn grand finals,
replays and potential surgery due to injury.

- Look fabulous, strut down the aisle and WAG
WOW!

WADE HAD NEVER been a gambler.

He preferred to weigh the pros and cons of any decision
carefully, consider all the options, before choosing the most
logical, the most feasible.

All that sensible bull had gone out of the window when
he'd taken the biggest gamble of his life and asked Liza to
meet him here.

He didn't know if she'd show.

His message had gone through to the answering service
on her mobile and her terse 'will think about it' texted response an hour later didn't bode well.

But he'd turned up at The Martini Bar anyway, hoping
she'd take a chance.

For if there was one thing he was sure of in this godforsaken mess, it was her love.

She hadn't said it. Matter of fact, neither had he, considering she'd been too busy busting his balls and throwing
his offer back in his face.

But he'd seen it in her eyes. The adoration, the tender-
ness, the agony at the thought of never being together.

He'd been through it all, a gamut of emotions ranging
from devastation to optimism.

No more.

He might be going with his gut on this one but he'd applied logic to making it happen.

Every contingency plan had been put into place.

Now all he needed was for Liza to say yes.

He nursed his Scotch, swirled it around, instantly transported back to the night they'd met, the night they'd shared a drink here, the night that had set him down this rocky road.

For a guy who never let emotions get in the way of anything, he'd sure botched this, big time.

He took a swig of his drink and glanced at his watch. Nine p.m. on the dot. Liza was a no-show.

He'd give her ten minutes and then he was out of here.

As pain lanced his heart he thought, *Who are you trying to kid?*

He'd probably end up sitting here all night if there was the remotest possibility she'd walk in the door.

As if his wish had been granted, he saw her enter, lock eyes with him and pause.

She looked stunning, from the top of her glossy blonde hair piled in a loose up-do to her shimmery turquoise dress to her sparkly silver-sequined sandals.

Guys in the bar gawked at the doorway and he wanted to flatten them all.

He stood as she made her way towards him, torn between wanting to vault tables to get to her and sit on his hands to stop from grabbing her the moment she got within reach.

The nearer she got, the harder his gut twisted until he could barely stand.

'Hey.' She hesitated when she reached him, kissed him on the cheek before taking a seat opposite.

'Thanks for coming.' He sounded like a dufus but he sat, relieved she'd made it. 'Didn't think you'd show.'

She held her thumb and forefinger an inch apart. 'I was this close not to.'

'Why the change of heart?'

She glanced away, gnawed on her bottom lip, before reluctantly meeting his gaze. 'Because you deserved better than the way I treated you the last time we parted.'

'Fair enough.'

He liked that about her, her bluntness. She might not have been completely honest with him the last few months, but her ability to call a spade a spade when it counted meant a lot.

He hoped she'd continue in that vein for the rest of the evening; he'd settle for nothing less than the truth.

'Drink?'

'Anything but a martini,' she said, managing a wan smile.

'Sure? Because I kinda like what happens when you drink martinis.'

The sparkle in her eyes gave him hope. 'Soda and lemon for now.'

'Spoilsport,' he said, placing the order with a nearby waiter before swivelling back to face her.

'I was going to call you,' she said, her hands twisting in her lap before she slid them under her handbag. 'To apologise for the craziness after you asked me to move to London.'

'Not necessary—'

'Yeah, it is.'

The waiter deposited her soda on the table and she grabbed it, sculled half the glass before continuing. 'You caught me completely off guard. I mean, I knew you'd be heading back eventually but I didn't expect it to be so soon, and then you asked me to come along with Cindy in tow and I kinda flipped out.'

'I noticed.'

She matched his wry smile. 'I've never had anyone care about me that much to include Cindy in plans.' Her fingertips fluttered over her heart. 'It touched me right here and I didn't know how to articulate half of what I was feeling.'

That made two of them. He knew the feeling well. Bottling up true emotions, preferring not to rock the boat, seeking other outlets for his frustration rather than attacking the root of the problem.

If only he'd confronted his dad sooner, had a talk man to man, rather than skulking off to London with his bitterness. The last few years would've been completely different.

'So I want to say thanks, Wade. Your offer means more to me than you'll ever know.'

'But?'

Her gaze dropped to her fiddling hands. 'But ultimately my decision stands. I can't move to London to be with you.'

'Thought so,' he said, stifling a chuckle at her confused frown at his chipper tone. 'Which is why I'm changing the parameters of the offer.'

Her frown deepened. 'I don't understand.'

'I'm staying in Melbourne.'

Speechless, she gaped at him until he placed a fingertip beneath her chin and closed her mouth.

'I've installed my deputy as CEO in my London office. He'll run the place and answer to me.'

He sat back, rested an arm across the back of his chair, bringing his hand within tantalising touching distance of her bare shoulder. 'I'm taking over the reins of Qu Publishing. Finishing what my father started all those years ago. It's what he would've wanted.'

Another revelation he'd had while instigating steps to remain in Melbourne. It had been as if an invisible weight had lifted from his shoulders, the guilt he'd harboured in relation to the gap between him and his dad—by his doing—evaporating once he'd made the decision to run the company.

He knew it was what his dad wanted. How many times had they discussed it, before Wade had got jack of Babs and her influence over his father and had moved to London? Many times, and he'd seen his dad's shattered expression the day he'd told him of his plans to relocate and start a new business.

It had haunted him and, while they'd never broached the subject again during their brief catch-ups over the years, he'd sensed his dad's disappointment.

Yeah, the decision to stay in Melbourne was the correct one.

Now he had to convince Liza of that.

'My offer still stands. Move in with me. Give our relationship a chance.' He touched her shoulder, slid his hand along the back of her neck and rested it there. 'I love you, Liza, and from a guy who's never said those three little words before, trust me, it's a big call.'

Tears shimmered in her eyes and he scooted closer, swiping away a few that trickled down her cheeks.

'A resounding yes would be great right about now,' he said, cuddling her into his side.

Her silence unnerved him but he waited. He'd waited this long to meet the love of his life, what were a few more minutes?

She sniffled, dabbed under her eyes, before easing away to look him in the eye.

'But Cindy—'

'The parameters of my offer have changed somewhat.' He cupped her chin. 'I'm asking you to move in with me. Just you.'

Her eyes widened and she started to shake her head but his grip tightened.

'I'm blown away by your dedication to your sister, truly I am. I've never met such a self-sacrificing person. But I think you're using Cindy as a crutch. Hiding behind her. Afraid to go out into the world and take chances.' His thumb brushed her lower lip. 'Ultimately, sweetheart? That's not going to help either of you.'

Anger flashed in her eyes before she wrenched away. 'Who do you think you are, telling me what I feel and how I'm running my life?'

'I'm the guy who loves you, the guy who'll do anything to make you happy.' He laid a hand on her knee, surprised and grateful when she didn't shrug him off. 'If you'll let me.'

She glared at him a moment longer before she visibly deflated. Her shoulders sagged and her head drooped, and he moved in quickly to support her with an arm around her waist.

'Cindy wanted to go to London.'

She spoke so softly Wade had to lean closer to hear.

'It made me realise that maybe I've cosseted her too much.'

She shook her head and a few tendrils of hair tumbled around her face. 'I've spent most of my life trying to protect her but now I'm wondering...'

When she didn't speak, Wade said, 'What?'

She dragged in a breath and blew it out. 'I'm wondering if I did more harm than good, sheltering her the way I have.'

'You love her. It's natural you'd want to protect her after your folks ran out.'

'It's more than that.'

She glanced up at him, her forlorn expression slugging him in the guts. It took every ounce of his willpower not to bundle her into his arms.

'I think I used her. I liked having her dependent on me, because that way she couldn't abandon me.'

As her folks did.

Liza didn't have to say it, it was written all over her face: her fear of being alone.

'Is that why you're not doing cartwheels over my offer now? Because you think ultimately I'll abandon you too?'

She glanced away, but not before he'd seen her shock at his perceptiveness.

'I won't, you know.'

He grabbed her hand and placed it against his heart, beating madly for her, only her.

'I don't let people into my heart easily. I've never had a long-term relationship. It took me a while to trust you. I even pushed away my dad through sheer narrow-mindedness. But once I give it, it's all yours.'

He added, 'For ever.'

A tremulous smile shone through her tears. 'You're incredible, the most amazing guy I've ever met, but I've never depended on anyone before. I'd be no good at it. I'd muck up and you'd get sick of me and then—'

'Say it.'

'Then you'd leave me,' she said, so softly his heart turned over beneath her palm.

'There's no guarantees in life but how about this? I promise to love you and cherish you and look after you to the best of my ability. How's that?'

'Pretty damn wonderful.' She beamed and he could've sworn the bar lit up like a bright summer's day.

'So no more secrets, okay?'

Her face fell. 'Then in the event of full disclosure, I need to tell you what happened in your office that first day.'

He had been curious but hadn't wanted to push for answers. With a little luck he'd have plenty of time for that: the rest of their lives.

'The WAG lifestyle? Why I put up with being arm candy for Henri when we weren't in a real relationship?'

She winced. 'For the money. We had a signed agreement. I was building a sizable nest egg for Cindy's future in case anything ever happened to me.'

Yep, she was back to the abandonment issue. Considering what she'd been through with her folks he could understand that.

'That night we met? When I said I was embarking on a new life and wanted to celebrate? I was stoked to be putting my old life behind me. It had taken its toll and I was tired of faking it for everyone.'

Her fingers clenched, creasing the cotton of his shirt. 'My investment was maturing the next day and I had grand plans to tie up some of it in a guaranteed fund for Cindy in case of my death, and use the rest to modernise our place and buy her the best equipment. With that kind of monetary security, it was the beginning of a new life for me. I could finally pursue a career in marketing, my dream, and put the past behind me.'

A few pieces of the puzzle shifted and he had a fair idea what she was going to say. She would've never agreed to the publishing contract after vehemently refusing it unless she needed the money. Which meant...

'What happened to your investment?'

Her eyes darkened to indigo, filled with pain. 'My financial adviser absconded with the lot. Scammed millions in client funds.'

He swore. Several times.

'Yeah, I totally agree. The police are investigating leads but the likelihood of recovering my cash? Slim.'

'That's why you did an about-face with the publishing deal.'

She nodded. 'I needed that money as a safeguard for Cindy. It was the only way.'

He hesitated, glad they were talking things through but needing to know all of it, however unpleasant.

'I've seen how much you love Cindy, so you're not ashamed of her.' He grimaced. 'Sorry for saying that. So why did you really leave her out of your bio?'

'I always thought it was fear of her spasticity worsening and resulting in permanent deformities if her emotions careened out of control with the probable media circus.' She smoothed his shirt and let her hand fall, only to clasp his and squeeze. 'In reality? I think it's because I'm overprotective to the point of stifling. I've tried so hard to make up for our parents' shortfalls I've gone the other way and become smothering. I truly didn't want Cindy exposed to any media or ridicule, which can still happen for disabled people even in this enlightened day, so I cut her out of the story.'

'Did you ever stop to think how she'd feel if she knew that?'

Her brows arched in horror. 'I was doing it to protect her—'

'I know, sweetheart, I know.'

Maybe he needed to quit while he was ahead.

'You still haven't answered my original question.'

The corners of her mouth curved up and he had his answer before she spoke.

'I'll have to chat with Shar and see if she can become a permanent live-in carer. And I'll need a raise to cover it. Plus I still want to spend as much time as possible with Cindy.'

'Anything else?'

'Just this.'

She surged against him, grabbed his lapels, dragged him closer and kissed him.

The teasing wolf whistles of nearby patrons faded as

her lips moved on his and he wished he'd had the foresight to book a suite.

When she finally broke the kiss, he grinned. 'That's a yes, then?'

'You bet.'

She cupped his face and stared unwaveringly into his eyes. 'And I love you too. How did I get so lucky?'

'*We* got lucky.'

He kissed her again to prove it.

EPILOGUE

LIZA LITHGOW'S STYLE TIPS
FOR MAXIMUM WAG WOW IMPACT

The Indulgence

Being a WAG can be demanding.

Always looking your best to avoid incurring the wrath of ruthless paparazzi.

Constantly being scrutinised by the public.

An expectation to attend all functions with your sports-star husband/boyfriend.

An expectation to support his team.

Turning a blind eye to the women slipping their phone numbers—and worse—into your partner's pocket.

But at the end of a long day—heck, at the end of a long season—it pays to indulge in whatever makes you feel good.

- Scented candles in the bathroom—lights off—and a long hot bath.
- Glass of quality champagne.
- A raunchy romance novel designed to distract.
- A classic chick flick.

- Expensive chocolate.
- Aromatherapy oils:
  - clary sage (good for relaxing)
  - chamomile (calming)
  - grapefruit (clears the mind)
  - geranium (balancing and harmonising)
  - rosewood (uplifting)
  - neroli (calms the mind)
  - marjoram (encourages sleep)
  - vetivert (reduces tension)

Liza hopes you've enjoyed her WAG wow tips.

While she may have left her WAG days behind, she regularly indulges in the above recommendations.

Though she's rarely alone in the bath, what with Wade to keep her company...

'WOW, CHECK THIS out.'

Cindy pressed her face against the glass pod of the London Eye, where they were perched on top with an incredible view of the city spread before them.

'Amazing, huh?' Liza slung an arm around Cindy's shoulders and squeezed.

'Sure is.' Cindy tore her awestruck gaze away from the view long enough to glance up at Wade. 'Thanks for bringing me, Wade. You're the best.'

'No worries, kiddo.' He dropped a kiss on the top of Cindy's head and Liza was sure her heart flip-flopped. Could she love this guy any more?

'Hey, what about me?'

Cindy rolled her eyes. 'You already know you're the best.'

'And don't you forget it.' Liza tweaked Cindy's nose before leaving her sis alone to enjoy the view.

When Wade crooked his finger, she happily moved into his embrace.

'You're incredible, you know that?'

He smiled and nodded at Cindy. 'So I've been told.'

'Well, I'm telling you again.' Liza snuggled tighter, content in the knowledge there was no better place to be than Wade's arms. 'The way you put this trip together, checked out disabled facilities at all the hotels, did a reno on your apartment for Cindy to stay. Not to mention pulling together the digital companion novel to my bio highlighting cerebral palsy and the needs of carers to raise awareness…'

She stood on tiptoe and whispered in his ear. 'Remember how I was scared you'd leave me one day? Forget about it, babe, because I'm going to be glued to your side for life.'

He laughed and hugged her tight.

'Make that a promise and you've got yourself a deal.'

They kissed to seal it.

* * * * *

Mills & Boon® Hardback

July 2013

ROMANCE

His Most Exquisite Conquest	Emma Darcy
One Night Heir	Lucy Monroe
His Brand of Passion	Kate Hewitt
The Return of Her Past	Lindsay Armstrong
The Couple who Fooled the World	Maisey Yates
Proof of Their Sin	Dani Collins
In Petrakis's Power	Maggie Cox
A Shadow of Guilt	Abby Green
Once is Never Enough	Mira Lyn Kelly
The Unexpected Wedding Guest	Aimee Carson
A Cowboy To Come Home To	Donna Alward
How to Melt a Frozen Heart	Cara Colter
The Cattleman's Ready-Made Family	Michelle Douglas
Rancher to the Rescue	Jennifer Faye
What the Paparazzi Didn't See	Nicola Marsh
My Boyfriend and Other Enemies	Nikki Logan
The Gift of a Child	Sue MacKay
How to Resist a Heartbreaker	Louisa George

MEDICAL

Dr Dark and Far-Too Delicious	Carol Marinelli
Secrets of a Career Girl	Carol Marinelli
A Date with the Ice Princess	Kate Hardy
The Rebel Who Loved Her	Jennifer Taylor

Mills & Boon® Large Print

July 2013

ROMANCE

Playing the Dutiful Wife	Carol Marinelli
The Fallen Greek Bride	Jane Porter
A Scandal, a Secret, a Baby	Sharon Kendrick
The Notorious Gabriel Diaz	Cathy Williams
A Reputation For Revenge	Jennie Lucas
Captive in the Spotlight	Annie West
Taming the Last Acosta	Susan Stephens
Guardian to the Heiress	Margaret Way
Little Cowgirl on His Doorstep	Donna Alward
Mission: Soldier to Daddy	Soraya Lane
Winning Back His Wife	Melissa McClone

HISTORICAL

The Accidental Prince	Michelle Willingham
The Rake to Ruin Her	Julia Justiss
The Outrageous Belle Marchmain	Lucy Ashford
Taken by the Border Rebel	Blythe Gifford
Unmasking Miss Lacey	Isabelle Goddard

MEDICAL

The Surgeon's Doorstep Baby	Marion Lennox
Dare She Dream of Forever?	Lucy Clark
Craving Her Soldier's Touch	Wendy S. Marcus
Secrets of a Shy Socialite	Wendy S. Marcus
Breaking the Playboy's Rules	Emily Forbes
Hot-Shot Doc Comes to Town	Susan Carlisle

GEN STD LP

Mills & Boon® Hardback

August 2013

ROMANCE

The Billionaire's Trophy	Lynne Graham
Prince of Secrets	Lucy Monroe
A Royal Without Rules	Caitlin Crews
A Deal with Di Capua	Cathy Williams
Imprisoned by a Vow	Annie West
Duty At What Cost?	Michelle Conder
The Rings that Bind	Michelle Smart
An Inheritance of Shame	Kate Hewitt
Faking It to Making It	Ally Blake
Girl Least Likely to Marry	Amy Andrews
The Cowboy She Couldn't Forget	Patricia Thayer
A Marriage Made in Italy	Rebecca Winters
Miracle in Bellaroo Creek	Barbara Hannay
The Courage To Say Yes	Barbara Wallace
All Bets Are On	Charlotte Phillips
Last-Minute Bridesmaid	Nina Harrington
Daring to Date Dr Celebrity	Emily Forbes
Resisting the New Doc In Town	Lucy Clark

MEDICAL

Miracle on Kaimotu Island	Marion Lennox
Always the Hero	Alison Roberts
The Maverick Doctor and Miss Prim	Scarlet Wilson
About That Night...	Scarlet Wilson

Mills & Boon® Large Print

August 2013

ROMANCE

Master of her Virtue	Miranda Lee
The Cost of her Innocence	Jacqueline Baird
A Taste of the Forbidden	Carole Mortimer
Count Valieri's Prisoner	Sara Craven
The Merciless Travis Wilde	Sandra Marton
A Game with One Winner	Lynn Raye Harris
Heir to a Desert Legacy	Maisey Yates
Sparks Fly with the Billionaire	Marion Lennox
A Daddy for Her Sons	Raye Morgan
Along Came Twins...	Rebecca Winters
An Accidental Family	Ami Weaver

HISTORICAL

The Dissolute Duke	Sophia James
His Unusual Governess	Anne Herries
An Ideal Husband?	Michelle Styles
At the Highlander's Mercy	Terri Brisbin
The Rake to Redeem Her	Julia Justiss

MEDICAL

The Brooding Doc's Redemption	Kate Hardy
An Inescapable Temptation	Scarlet Wilson
Revealing The Real Dr Robinson	Dianne Drake
The Rebel and Miss Jones	Annie Claydon
The Son that Changed his Life	Jennifer Taylor
Swallowbrook's Wedding of the Year	Abigail Gordon

WALKING IN THE ISLES OF SCILLY

by
Paddy Dillon

BA DE
3/07

RA

CICERONE

2 POLICE SQUARE, MILNTHORPE, CUMBRIA LA7 7PY
www.cicerone.co.uk

© Paddy Dillon 2000, 2006
1st edition 2000
ISBN 1 85284 310 1
2nd edition 2006
ISBN-10: 1 85284 475 2
ISBN-13: 978 1 85284 475 2

A catalogue record for this book is available from the British Library.

OS Ordnance Survey® This product includes mapping data licensed from Ordnance Survey® with the permission of the Controller of Her Majesty's Stationery Office. © Crown copyright 2002. All rights reserved. Licence number PU100012932

The map on p.83 is used with permission of the Abbey Garden.

Front cover: Walkers follow a path round a heathery headland on one of the islands

CONTENTS

Isles of Scilly and Marine Park area

Marine Park area

ST. MARTIN'S

Great Ganilly

Eastern Isles

White I.

Round I.

St. Helen's

Teän

Old Grimsby

TRESCO

BRYHER

Gweal

Tresco Abbey

Norrard Rocks

Illiswilgig

Mincarlo

Samson

White I.

Porthloo

ST. MARY'S

Isles of Scilly Airport

Old Town

The Garrison

Gugh

ST. AGNES

Annet

Western Rocks

Melledgan

Crim Rocks

Bishop Rock

N

0   5 km

3 miles

INTRODUCTION

'Somewhere among the note-books of Gideon I once found a list of diseases as yet unclassified by medical science, and among these there occurred the word Islomania, which was described as a rare but by no means unknown affliction of spirit. There are people, Gideon used to say, by way of explanation, who find islands somehow irresistible. The mere knowledge that they are on an island, a little world surrounded by the sea, fills them with an indescribable intoxication.'

Lawrence Durrell, *Reflections on a Marine Venus*

Of all the British Isles, the Isles of Scilly are the most blessed. Basking in sunshine, rising green and pleasant from the blue Atlantic Ocean, fringed by rugged cliffs and sandy beaches, these self-contained little worlds are a joy to explore. They are as close to a tropical paradise as it is possible to be in the British Isles, with more sunshine hours than anyone else enjoys. There are no tall mountains, but the rocks around the coast are as dramatic as you'll find anywhere. There are no extensive moorlands, but you'll forget that as you walk round the open heathery headlands. The islands may be small in extent, but the eye is deceived and readily imagines vast panoramas and awesome seascapes. Views to the sea take in jagged rocks that have ripped many a keel and wrecked many a ship. The islands are clothed in colourful flowers, both culti-vated and wild, and attract a rich bird life, including native breeding species and seasonal migrants. And always, there is the sea.

The Isles of Scilly form the smallest of Britain's Areas of Outstanding Natural Beauty, and their historic shores have been designated as Heritage Coast. The surrounding sea is protected as a Marine Park of great biodiversity. Archaeological remains abound, not only on the islands, but also submerged beneath the sea. The Isles of Scilly are special, revealing their secrets and charms to those who walk the headlands, sail from island to island, and take the time to observe the sights, sounds and scents of the landscape. While the walks in this guidebook could be completed in as little as a week, a fortnight would allow a much more leisurely appreciation of the islands, and leave memories that will last for a lifetime.

Granite is the bedrock of the Isles of Scilly, seen at its best around Peninnis Head (Walk 3)

LOCATION

The Isles of Scilly lie 45km (28 miles) west of Land's End: a position that ensures they are omitted from most maps of Britain, or shown only as an inset. There are five inhabited islands and about fifty other areas that local people would call islands, as well as a hundred more rocks, and more again at low water. The islands are not part of Cornwall, perish the thought, but are a self-administering unit; you could think of this as the smallest county in Britain. The total landmass is a mere 16 square kilometres (6¼ square miles). The waters around the Isles of Scilly, extending as far as the 50m (165ft) submarine contour, form a Marine Park of around 125 square kilometres (50 square miles). Despite the small area of the islands, walkers can enjoy anything approaching 80km (50 miles) of truly remarkable routes around one of Britain's most charming and intensely interesting landscapes.

GEOLOGY

The geology of the Isles of Scilly can be summed up in one word – granite. The islands are the south-western extremity of a deep-seated granite mass, or batholith, that reaches the surface of the earth around Dartmoor, Bodmin Moor and Land's End. Granite is the bedrock of the Isles of Scilly, and it breaks down to form a stony, sandy or gritty soil, as well as bright white sandy beaches. In some places around the coast and occasionally inland, the

granite forms blocky cliffs and tors, rounded boulders or tilted slabs that have such a rough texture that they provide excellent grip for walkers. In other places chemical weathering of less stable minerals within the granite causes the rock to crumble, or peel away in layers. As a building material, granite has been used for centuries, but only in relatively recent times has it been possible to split the rock into squared blocks more suitable for substantial buildings.

While the Isles of Scilly escaped the Ice Age that affected much of Britain, it didn't escape the permafrost conditions that pertained south of the ice sheets, breaking up the granite tors and forming a stony, sandy soil. Nor did the islands fare too well as the ice began to melt and sea levels began to rise. It is thought that Scilly became separated from the rest of Britain around 10,000 years ago. Scilly may well have been a single landmass for a while, but a combination of rising sea levels and coastal erosion produced the current pattern of five islands and a bewildering number of rocks and reefs. Before the arrival of the first settlers, it was no doubt a wild and wooded place.

ANCIENT HISTORY

Arthurian legend points to the Isles of Scilly as the last remnants of the lost land of Lyonesse; but while a submerged landscape does exist around the islands, it was never the

The Inisidgen Upper Burial Chamber on the coast of St. Mary's is 4000 years old (Walk 3)

Lyonesse of legend. In 1752 the Cornish antiquarian William Borlase discovered and recorded submerged field systems on the tidal flats near Samson. It seems that the first settlers were Neolithic, but a more comprehensive settlement of the islands came in the Bronze Age, up to 4000 years ago. Some splendid ritual standing stones and stoutly constructed burial chambers remain from this time, and excavations have revealed skeletons, cremated remains and a host of artefacts. When the Romans began their occupation of Britain 2000 years ago, criss-crossing the land with straight roads, settlement patterns on the Isles of Scilly were in huddled formations, as witnessed today on Halangy Down and Nornour. No doubt the Romans traded with the islands, as coins have been discovered, but it seems they established no lasting presence. In later

centuries the Isles of Scilly attracted Christian hermits, leaving some of the islands blessed with the names of saints. That great seafaring race, the Vikings, also visited the islands. From time to time the Isles of Scilly have been a haven for pirates, and every now and then their retreat was smashed by the authorities of the day. In the 11th century over one hundred pirates were beheaded in a single day on Tresco!

LATER HISTORY

A Benedictine priory was founded on Tresco in the 12th century, and Henry I granted the island to Tavistock Abbey. By the 14th century the islands became part of the Duchy of Cornwall and Edward III gave them to the Black Prince, who was made the Duke of Cornwall. In the 16th century Governor

The remains of a 12th-century Benedictine priory at the Abbey Garden on Tresco (Walk 10)

Francis Godolphin was granted the lease of the islands by Elizabeth I. Godolphin built the eight-pointed Star Castle above the harbour on St. Mary's. During the Civil War, in the middle of the 17th century, Prince Charles (later King Charles II) stayed briefly at the Star Castle. Towards the end of the Civil War the islands were occupied by disgruntled Royalists who launched pirate raids on passing ships, causing the Dutch to send a fleet of ships to deal with the problem. An English fleet intercepted the Dutch, preventing wholesale destruction on the islands, and thereby gaining the final surrender of the Royalist force.

The 18th century was a time of great poverty on the islands, but despite their remoteness John Wesley visited them in the course of his preaching around the British Isles. Shipbuilding became an important occupation late in the 18th century and continued well into the 19th century. In the early 19th century the Godolphin family allowed their lease on the Isles of Scilly to lapse, so that they reverted to the Duchy of Cornwall. In 1834 Augustus Smith from Hertfordshire took over the lease of the islands as Lord Protector, and developed Tresco in particular, building the Abbey House as his residence and establishing the Abbey Garden. The successful export of flowers from the islands dates from the middle of the 19th century and has enjoyed mixed fortunes. During 1918 the Dorrien-Smith family gave up the lease on all the islands except Tresco. While fortifications on St. Mary's were strengthened in the First World War, the islands escaped lightly from the conflict. During the Second World War, however, there was a lot more activity around the islands, as submarines and warships played deadly hide and seek manoeuvres in the waters, and several warplanes were stationed on the islands.

RECENT HISTORY

In a sudden magnanimous gesture in 1949, the Duchy of Cornwall offered the sale of the freehold on most properties occupied by sitting tenants in Hugh Town. The Isles of Scilly were designated as an Area of Outstanding Natural Beauty in 1975. The Duchy leased all its uninhabited islands and unfarmed wilderness land to the Isles of Scilly Environmental Trust (now Isles of Scilly Wildlife Trust) in 1987. The Trust manages this land for conservation and recreation, safeguarding habitats for flora and fauna, while maintaining the network of footpaths over the land. The designation of a Marine Park to conserve the surrounding sea bed and marine life was another important development. The infrastructure of the islands continues to develop and tourism is an increasingly important industry, but always with due regard to the environment and the conservation of nature.

These brief notes about the history of the Isles of Scilly give only the barest

The Isles of Scilly have a most colourful
and turbulent history and heritage (Walk 10)

outline of some key events. The islands' history has been turbulent and colourful and makes an interesting and absorbing study. Be sure to visit the Isles of Scilly Museum in Hugh Town on St. Mary's for a more thorough grounding in the history of the islands, and to obtain further information.

GETTING TO THE ISLES OF SCILLY

By Road: The A30 road is the main transport artery through the south-west, pushing through Devon and Cornwall, around Dartmoor and over Bodmin Moor, to terminate abruptly at Land's End. Motorists will have to abandon their vehicles at some point as follows: at Newquay Airport; at Penzance for the ferry or helicopter flight; or at the Land's End Airport for a short flight to Scilly. Cars cannot be taken to the islands, nor are they even necessary, so enquire about secure long-term car parking, either in Penzance or at the airports. National Express buses Serve Penzance from London, Plymouth, Birmingham and Scotland. Bear in mind, if travelling on weekends, that there are no ferries or flights to or from the Isles of Scilly on Sundays.

By Rail: The rail network terminates at Penzance, which can be reached any day of the week by direct Great Western trains from London Paddington. The celebrated Cornish Scot operated by Virgin Trains, **www.virgintrains.co.uk**, offers direct daily services to and from places as far removed as Edinburgh,

Glasgow and Birmingham. Combined rail/sail deals are available through the Isles of Scilly Travel Centre. Transfers can be arranged between Penzance railway station and Land's End airport, if you chose to fly and enquire while booking your flight. A short walk around the harbour from the railway station leads to the far quay where the *Scillonian III* sails for the Isles of Scilly. Bear in mind, if travelling on weekends, that there are no ferries or flights to or from the Isles of Scilly on Sundays.

By Ship: The *Scillonian III* is a fine little ship of 1000 tonnes, sailing once each way between Penzance and St. Mary's from Monday to Saturday throughout the year. In the high season there are usually two journeys on Saturdays. Observe the regulations for carrying luggage, which should always be labelled with your destination, and clearly labelled with the name of the particular island you are visiting. Luggage can be conveyed to your accommodation in Hugh Town, but be sure to follow instructions to avail of this service. The journey usually takes 2¾ hours. It is customary for the ship's whistle to sound half an hour before each sailing to keep you on your toes! Bad weather can cause the schedule to be altered in the winter months. For details contact the Isles of Scilly Travel Centre, tel 0845-7105555; website **www.islesofscilly-travel.co.uk**

By Aeroplane: Flights to St. Mary's are operated by Skybus, using Twin Otter or Islander aircraft. Flights are available from the little airports at

14

Penzance harbour in Cornwall, from where the Scillonia III sails to the islands

Newquay and Land's End. Flights are most frequent and shortest from Land's End, operating Monday to Saturday throughout the year and taking only fifteen minutes each way. There are more flights in the high season. Flights from Newquay also operate from Monday to Saturday and take a little more than half an hour, but save a considerable amount of driving along the road. For details contact the Isles of Scilly Travel Centre, tel 0845-7105555; website **www.islesofscilly-travel.co.uk**

By Helicopter: British International offers two services from Penzance using Sikorskys. Most flights are to St. Mary's, but some operate direct to Tresco, landing at a small heliport beside the Abbey Garden. Flights operate Monday to Saturday throughout the year, with more during the high season. It is possible to enjoy some splendid aerial views of the islands using these half-hour long services. On certain winter Saturdays there may be no flights to Tresco. For details contact British International, tel 01736-363871; website **www.scilly-helicopter.co.uk**

GETTING AROUND THE ISLES OF SCILLY

Buses and Taxis: There is a bus service operating in a circuit around St. Mary's in the high season, as well as minibus and vintage bus tours around the island. There are also a handful of taxis, should you need to get to any place in a hurry. Most of the buses start from

beside a little park near the Town Hall in the middle of Hugh Town, though services can also be checked at the Tourist Information Centre. There is an airport minibus service that operates from in front of the chemist's shop a short way inland from The Quay. The off-islands are small enough to walk around on foot and walkers don't really need any other form of transport. If choosing an accommodation base on one of the off-islands, the proprietor may be able to meet you at the quay-side with a vehicle and assist with transferring luggage, but ask if this is possible when booking.

St. Mary's Boatmen's Association: Run on a co-operative basis, the Association runs several launches from Hugh Town on St. Mary's to the off-

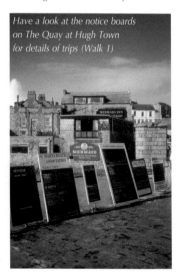

Have a look at the notice boards on The Quay at Hugh Town for details of trips (Walk 1)

islands of St. Agnes, Bryher, Tresco and St. Martin's. Launches to Bryher may also drop passengers at the uninhabited island of Samson on request. Details of services run by the Association, plus a wealth of cruises, are advertised on notice boards on The Quay at Hugh Town, as well as at the quaysides on the off-islands. Details can also be obtained from the Tourist Information Centre. The Association operates a small ticket kiosk on the Old Quay at Hugh Town. There are more ferries and cruises to more places in the high season than in the winter months. Bear in mind that the onset of stormy weather can lead to the sudden cancellation of all boat services around the islands. St. Mary's Boatmen's Association can be contacted at Karenza, Ennor Close, St. Mary's, Isles of Scilly, TR21 0NL. If specific details are needed about ferries to the off-islands, contact the following: for St. Agnes, tel 01720-422704; for Bryher and Tresco, tel 01720-422886; for St. Martin's, tel 01720-422893.

BOAT TRIPS

Quite apart from using boats as a means of access to islands and walks, why not enjoy a series of boat trips? Some trips are operated by the St. Mary's Boatmen's Association, on their large launches, while others are run using smaller boats, which usually limit their passenger numbers to twelve. Classic trips run by the St. Mary's Boatmen's Association include tours around the Western Rocks, Norrard

Rocks, St. Helen's and Teän, the Eastern Isles, and a complete circuit around St. Mary's. There are Seabird Specials for bird-watchers, historical tours, evening visits to St. Agnes for supper, and the chance to follow the popular Gig Races in the high season.

At some point during your visit to the Isles of Scilly, be sure to witness the evening Gig Races. This is the main spectator sport on the islands, when teams row furiously along a measured 2km (1¼ mile) course from Nut Rock, across the stretch of sea known as The Road, to The Quay at Hugh Town. Women's teams compete on Wednesday evenings, while men's teams compete on Friday evenings. Boats generally leave The Quay at 1930 on those evenings.

It is highly recommended that you sample some of these boat trips to broaden your experience and enjoyment of the islands, and you should make every effort to include as many of the remote islands and rock groups as possible.

TOURIST INFORMATION AND ACCOMMODATION

The Tourist Information Centre in Hugh Town on St. Mary's can provide plenty of information about accommodation, pubs, restaurants, transport and attractions throughout the Isles of Scilly. Between April and October some 75,000 people stay on the islands, and an additional 25,000 people make day trips. In August the

Accommodation around the islands ranges from luxury hotels to basic campsites

islands can run out of beds for visitors, so advance booking is always recommended. All the islands except Tresco have campsites, and these can fill too. There are abundant self-catering cottages and chalets, as well as plenty of bed and breakfast establishments and guesthouses. There are ten hotels; six of them around Hugh Town on St. Mary's and one on each of the off-islands. For full details and a full colour brochure contact the Isles of Scilly Tourist Information Centre, Hugh Town, St. Mary's, Isles of Scilly, TR21 0LL. Tel 01720-422536; email tic@scilly.gov.uk; website **www.simplyscilly.co.uk.** Another website full of information about the islands is **www.scillyonline.co.uk.**

A lot of time and effort can be spent trying to tie ferry and flight schedules into accommodation availability on the islands in the high season, and there may be a need to spend a night before or after your trip at Penzance on the mainland. Arrangements can be simplified by letting the Isles of Scilly Travel Centre handle all your booking requirements in a single package, tel 0845-7105555; website **www.islesofscilly-travel.co.uk**.

MAPS OF THE ISLES OF SCILLY

The Isles of Scilly could be explored easily enough without using maps, as the total land area is only 16 sq km (6¼ square miles), but mapless visitors would miss a great deal along the way. Detailed maps reveal alternative routes and other options to the walks in this book. Dozens of near and distant features can be identified in view, and access to all the relevant placenames is literally at your fingertips. The following maps of the islands are available in a variety of scales and styles. Ordnance Survey grid references indicate the starting point of each walk throughout this guidebook.

Ordnance Survey 1:25,000 Explorer 101 – Isles of Scilly. This map gives the most accurate depiction of the Isles of Scilly on one large sheet, including all the rocks and reefs that make up this complex group, along with a wealth of interesting and amazing placenames.

Ordnance Survey 1:50,000 Landranger 203 – Land's End, The Lizard & Isles of Scilly. This map shows the Isles of Scilly as an inset. The map offers little detail of the islands and is not particularly recommended detailed exploration, though it is a useful general map and worth having if you are also considering walking around neighbouring Land's End and The Lizard in Cornwall.

A Precious Heritage – Visitors Companion Maps to the Five Inhabited Islands, published by the Isles of Scilly Wildlife Trust. These maps show virtually all the roads, tracks and walking paths. The unfarmed wilderness land managed by the Trust is distinguished from other tenanted land. This is a most useful series of maps, but best used alongside the Ordnance Survey Explorer map.

Free leaflets containing maps of all or some of the islands can be collected from the Tourist Information Centre or picked up from other locations. Some will prove useful, others less useful, and many of them exist to highlight a variety of services and attractions around the islands. Marine navigation charts are for those who sail as well as walk, or for serious marine studies.

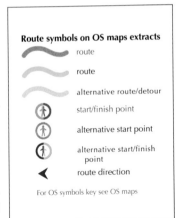

Route symbols on OS maps extracts

～～～	route
～～～	route
～～～	alternative route/detour
(walker symbol)	start/finish point
(walker symbol)	alternative start point
(walker symbol)	alternative start/finish point
◄	route direction

For OS symbols key see OS maps

The maps in this guidebook are extracted from the Ordnance Survey 1:25,000 map and an overlay shows the walking routes. A few of the maps aren't of walking routes, but show groups of small islands and rocks that can be visited on boat trips and are covered by short descriptive chapters. There are also a few small-scale plans, showing greater detail of Hugh Town, The Garrison and the amazing Tresco Abbey Garden.

THE WALKS

None of the walks on the Isles of Scilly could really be described as difficult. The only way anyone could make them difficult is by rushing through them, which surely defeats the purpose of exploring the islands when there is so much of interest to see. The walks make use of a network of paths, mostly along the coast, but sometimes inland too. They may also follow tracks and roads, but those roads are likely to be free of traffic. Sensible precautions include wearing stout shoes, possibly boots, when walking along uneven or rocky paths, and carrying a set of waterproofs in case of rain. When stormy weather whips up the waves, you can get drenched from salt spray. In any case it is always advisable to proceed with caution whenever walking close to breaking waves; there is always the chance that the next wave will break considerably higher. Unprotected cliffs also need to be approached with

caution, especially in high winds or blustery conditions. The sun can be exceptionally strong, so if you burn easily then be sure to keep your skin covered, either with light-coloured, lightweight, comfortable polycotton clothing or a high-factor sunscreen. A good sun hat is also useful, but ensure it is one that ties on so that it won't be blown away and lost at sea!

The walks included in this guidebook allow an exploration of the coastlines of the five inhabited islands, as well as some of the smaller islands. With the aid of cruises, walkers can also enjoy close-up views of the Eastern Isles, Norrard Rocks, Western Rocks and even the solitary pillar of the Bishop Rock Lighthouse. It all depends how long you stay on the islands and how much you wish to see. Walkers in a hurry could complete all these walks in a week, but two weeks would give a more leisurely chance to explore and include a number of boat trips. Better still, make two or three trips throughout the year to appreciate the changing seasons. By no means do these walks exhaust all the possibilities for exploring the islands, and there are just as many quiet and unfrequented paths left for you to discover. Apart from the walking route descriptions, there are also short descriptions of small islands that might well be visited out of interest, but where the walking potential is really quite limited.

None of the walks around the Isles of Scilly could really be described as difficult

GUIDED WALKS

Your visit to the Isles of Scilly can be enhanced by taking part in a series of guided walks that are available largely in the high season. These are walks led by knowledgeable local people, with a specific emphasis on wildlife and heritage. By joining one of these walks you have a chance to keep up to date with what is happening in the natural world. Flowers bloom and fade, birds come and go on their migrations, and a good guide will explain what is currently happening around the islands. Furthermore, there is a chance to ask specific questions on the spot. For details of guided walks, enquire at the Tourist Information Office or the Isles of Scilly Wildlife Trust Office. There are also specific wildlife cruises – some operating during the day and others departing at dusk, depending on what is likely to be sighted.

Island Wildlife Tours offers visitors the chance to discover the rich variety of wildlife around the Isles of Scilly in the company of a resident naturalist and ornithologist. Details are listed on the website **www.scillybirding.co.uk** or contact: Will Wagstaff, 42 Sallyport, St. Mary's, Isles of Scilly, TR21 0JE. Tel 01720-422212; email william.wagstaff@virgin.net

ISLAND FLOWERS

There are two broad classes of flowers on the Isles of Scilly: those grown for sale and shipment to the mainland, and those that grow in the wild. Bear in mind that wild flowers do creep into the cultivated flower fields, and some of the cultivated flowers have a habit of hopping out into the wilds! The flower industry started in 1868 when the tenant of Rocky Hill Farm on St. Mary's packed some flowers into a box and sent them to Covent Garden. Within a few years there were fields of daffodils and narcissus being grown. Visitors expecting to see fields of golden blooms will be disappointed, as the flowers are cut before they bloom. A field of wonderful blooms is technically a failed crop! To protect the tiny flower fields from wind and salt spray, tall, dense windbreak hedgerows are

Lovely to look at, but a field of flowers in full bloom is technically a failed crop!

planted. Hedging species include pittosporum, euonymus and veronica, though there are also tall shelter belts of long-established Monterey and lodgepole pines. There are flower farms on each of the inhabited islands, and some specialise in posting fresh flowers to British destinations on request. There are also bulb farms, offering a selection of hardy bulbs that are more likely to survive the journey home.

Wild flowers number around 700 species around the Isles of Scilly, making any attempt to list them here a rather pointless exercise. There are some plants that are peculiar to the islands, either growing nowhere else in Britain or being sub-species of plants that are found elsewhere in Britain. Almost 250 species are included on the Isles of Scilly Wildlife Trust Flower Checklist, which is an invaluable leaflet to carry around the islands, along with a good field guide to flowering plants. Common plants include bracken, heather and gorse on most open uncultivated areas, with bulbous cushions of thrift on many cliffs and rocky areas. Perhaps one of the most startling escapees from the flower fields are the large agapanthus blooms, which now decorate many sand dunes, growing among the marram grass. Fleshy mesembryanthemums, or Hottentot figs also creep through the dunes. The tropical Tresco Abbey Garden contains 3000 species from around the world, making that one small area alone a very special place for more careful study!

ISLAND BIRDS

The Isles of Scilly are renowned for their bird life, and while resident breeding species may be few, the islands are an important landfall for many more migrant species in the spring and autumn. Anything up to 400 species of birds have been recorded around the islands, but this includes some extremely uncommon birds that somehow find themselves well off their usual migratory routes. Almost 150 species are included on the Isles of Scilly Wildlife Trust Bird Checklist, which is an invaluable leaflet to carry around the islands, along with a good field guide to birds.

Seabirds are, of course, plentiful. Herring gulls, greater and lesser black-backed gulls and kittiwakes are fairly common. Four species of terns are present, including Arctic terns on their amazing round-the-world migrations. Cormorants and shags frequent isolated rocks and cliff ledges, easily spotted because of their habit of holding their wings outstretched for long periods. By taking a wildlife cruise you can see great 'rafts' of shags far out to sea, and maybe also smaller 'rafts' of Manx shearwaters.

Auks include guillemots and razorbills, sleeker and more slender than the comical puffins that are eagerly awaited each spring by bird-watchers. During the breeding season male puffins have rainbow-hued bills, used for courtship display, aggression against other males, and for digging burrows. Like the Manx shearwater,

Gulls are everywhere around the islands, but there are plenty of rare birds to see

puffins nesting on dry land live in mortal fear of gulls. Storm petrels and fulmar petrels nest in isolated places, out on remote rocky ledges or on the island sanctuary of Annet. With their amazing flying dives, gannets provide the most startling feeding display of any of the seabirds. While most people imagine them spearing fish with their bills, they actually seem to catch fish while swimming back to the surface. The inter-tidal flats, especially around the shallow lagoon in the middle of the Isles of Scilly, attract a host of waders. Piping oystercatchers probe the sands, while turnstones, naturally, prefer to look beneath stones in search of food. Sanderlings, sand pipers, whimbrel and ringed plovers may also be seen on the sands, with rock pipits preferring the higher, drier regions of the beaches. 'Seabird 2000' was a comprehensive count of all seabird species around Britain that took place during the years 1999–2001. Counting the birds around the Isles of Scilly involved volunteers visiting most of the exposed rocks around the islands.

While there are no great freshwater lakes on the Isles of Scilly, there are several small pools and ponds. Many of these attract waterfowl and some have been equipped with bird hides to aid observation. A few uncommon species of herons have been spotted around the islands. Snipe, redshanks and green-shanks are attracted to water, along with moorhens, ducks, geese and swans. Water rails are commonly spotted, and it is worth looking out for little egrets in the autumn. Reeds and willows surround many of the pools, so a variety of warblers, wagtails and flycatchers find them a favourable habitat. Kingfishers, though extremely uncommon, often startle birdwatchers with a sudden flash of iridescent blue.

There are plenty of birds to be spotted around the fields and hedgerows. Wrens, though tiny, are really quite numerous. Blackbirds and thrushes, swallows and martins, finches and tits all favour these habitats, while more open spaces may feature redwing and fieldfare. Stonechats prefer spiky gorse bushes. Cuckoos are often heard earlier in the Isles of Scilly than main-land Britain, and the poor rock pipits often find themselves raising cuckoo chicks. Birds of prey include kestrels, merlins, peregrines and hobbies. Birds that you shouldn't expect to see include owls, magpies and wood-peckers, but occasionally a true rarity blows in from distant climes. For up-to-date details of birds around the islands, check the website **www.scillybirding.co.uk**

ISLAND ANIMALS

Apart from domestic farm stock and pets, very few animals are seen around the Isles of Scilly. A few rabbits maybe, but little else, unless a few bats are spotted as they hunt for insects at dusk. One peculiar little creature is the Scilly shrew, which is a distinct variation from its mainland cousins. Animals that have been introduced to the islands include hedgehogs, which are present only on St. Mary's, and slow worms, present only on Bryher.

MARINE PARK WILDLIFE

Although the waters around the Isles of Scilly are protected as a Marine Park, few visitors are aware of the importance of this habitat. Four special areas within the Marine Park have been identified. The Western Rocks are described as super-exposed and can support only the hardiest communities of plants and animals. St. Agnes and Annet have pebbly seabeds around them, supporting a range of rare seaweeds.

Seals can sometimes be approached quite closely on boat trips around the rocks

The east coast of St. Mary's has sheltered bedrock providing a habitat for solitary corals, branched sponges, delicate sea fans and other similar species. Despite their 'roots' and plant-like appearance, these species are actually animals. The flats around Samson, Tresco and St. Martin's are the shallowest waters around the Isles of Scilly, with rich communities of seaweeds and animals. An abundance of hard-shelled molluscs include scallops, limpets, razor shells, cowries and periwinkles. Sea urchins are numerous, but live in deep water and only occasionally are their shells cast ashore. Crabs and lobsters are common.

There are a surprising number of large mammals in the sea around the islands. Grey seals can be observed resting on remote shores and tidal ledges. Dolphins and porpoises are occasionally spotted around the islands, but more often favour the open ocean, as do more rarely spotted pilot and killer whales. The chances of seeing marine species are of course increased by taking one of the wildlife cruises advertised around the islands.

FISHING

Fishing is now a minor occupation around the Isles of Scilly, but it is interesting to see what species are caught. Dogfish and rays are present, and their egg cases can be found on the shores. Plaice, sole, skate, mackerel, cod, monkfish, pollock, turbot, mullet and hake are all caught. There are conger eels and squid, and every so often peculiar species such as marlin and sea horses make their way into these waters. Commercial shrimping and prawning is restricted to three months in the summer. Very occasionally huge basking sharks are seen, their enormous mouths filtering the water for the tiniest marine organisms. These sharks used to be hunted for the oil in their livers, and became something of a rarity, though they seem to be on the increase again. Most of the fish caught commercially are packed away to the mainland, but local fishermen do supply some of the hotels, guesthouses and restaurants with fresh catches. Crabs and lobsters are lifted in traditional pots.

ISLES OF SCILLY WILDLIFE TRUST

The Isles of Scilly Environment Trust was formed in 1985, and by 1987 had secured a 99-year lease on all the un-farmed wilderness land owned by the Duchy of Cornwall. This includes substantial areas of St. Mary's, St. Agnes and Gugh, Bryher and St. Martin's, as well as all the uninhabited islands and rocks. Tresco, which is leased to Robert Dorrien-Smith, is not managed by the Trust. The organisation became the Isles of Scilly Wildlife Trust in 2001.

The remit of the Trust is wideranging, but basically encompasses maintaining a balance between wildlife conservation and recreation. Staff maintain the footpath network on the islands, and have an ongoing programme to control bracken and gorse and to replenish the native tree cover. Visitors can help by contributing to a tree-planting scheme. Ancient monuments need to be cleared of scrub and protected from damage, important nesting sites for birds need to be kept free from interference, and constant monitoring of the environment is necessary. It all takes time and it costs money. Visitors to the Isles of Scilly are invited to become Friends of Scilly. It is also worth visiting the Trust office in Hugh Town, where a wealth of interesting publications can be purchased. Staff also occasionally lead walks and wildlife trips. Information can be obtained on The Quay in Hugh Town, or contact the Isles of Scilly Wildlife Trust, Carn Thomas, Hugh Town, St. Mary's, Isles of Scilly, TR21 0PT. Telephone 01720-422153; website **www.ios-wildlifetrust.org.uk**

THE DUCHY OF CORNWALL

Many visitors to the Isles of Scilly wonder about the role of the Duchy of Cornwall, since mention is made of this body virtually everywhere. The Duchy is a series of estates, by no means all in Cornwall, but throughout Britain, which exist to provide an income to the heir to the throne. Established in the 14th century, the extent of land controlled by the Duchy has varied through the centuries, but has always included the Isles of Scilly. As the islands' landlord, the Duchy has always raised its revenue through the sale of leases and collection of rents on the land. Some of the earliest rents were paid in the form of salted puffins! It is probably through the influence of Prince Charles that the Duchy has an increased awareness of the environmental and aesthetic value of the land in its control. Information boards can be studied in the harbour waiting room at Hugh Town, outlining the role of the Duchy in the life of the islands. The Duchy office is at Hugh House on the Garrison above Hugh Town on St. Mary's. Members of the Royal Family have occasionally used a secretive little bungalow nearby for informal holidays. Its location used to be jealously guarded by islanders, but now they gleefully point it out to visitors!

PLAN OF THIS GUIDE

The plan of this guidebook is simple. The first few walks are on St. Mary's, taking in a town trail around Hugh Town, a stroll around The Garrison, then more extended walks around the coast and along the nature trails of St. Mary's. The rest of the islands are visited in a roughly clockwise direction, with Gugh and St. Agnes being explored in turn. Short chapters describe some of the smaller islands and groups of islets and rocks; and as visits must be on boat trips, no walking routes are offered. Thus, the guidebook works its way around Annet and the Western Rocks, Samson, Bryher and

the Norrard Rocks. Tresco and the little islands of St. Helen's and Teän give way to St. Martin's and the Eastern Isles, bringing this delightful tour around the Isles of Scilly full circle. Although of limited extent, it takes a lot of time to explore.

SAFETY MATTERS

It is highly unlikely that anyone could get lost in the Isles of Scilly, although it might be possible to get on the wrong ferry and land on the wrong island, or become marooned on an uninhabited island! Apart from that, while walkers may occasionally be unsure exactly which headland or bay they have reached, they cannot be much more than an hour's walk from wherever they started. Apart from minor cuts and grazes, accidents are unlikely, though care needs to be taken around cliff coasts, and special care needs to be taken in any case while walking beside the sea. If tempted to walk along beaches, or visit rocks and islets at low tide, always ensure that there is an easy escape route before the tide flows again. In the event of accident, the police, fire service, ambulance or coastguard can be summoned by dialling 999 (the European 112 works also). Be sure to give a full account of the nature of the accident, as well as your own contact details so that the emergency services can stay in touch with you. A little forethought will ensure an accident-free trip.

WALK 1
Hugh Town Trail

___

Distance   2.5km (1½ miles)
Start   Harbourside Hotel on The Quay – 902109

The main settlement on St. Mary's used to be Old Town, but during the construction of the defences around the Garrison, people drifted onto the narrow neck of land between the harbour and Porth Cressa, and Hugh Town grew throughout the 17th century. Hugh Town is by far the largest settlement on the Isles of Scilly. In a sense it is the islands' capital, even though it only has the appearance of a small town or large village.

A stroll around Hugh Town is something you should complete at the start of any exploration of the Isles of Scilly, so that you become aware of the islands' greatest range of services, and know where to find things and how the place operates. Hugh Town, for all its small size, is packed with history and heritage and all kinds of interesting corners. Most buildings are built of granite, the bedrock of the islands, and they stand cheek by jowl on a narrow neck of land between the Garrison and the larger part of St. Mary's. Take special note of all the slide shows that are offered in the evenings in the high season. Knowledgeable local people present these talks; people with a passion for the history, heritage, flowers and wildlife of the islands.

The Quay is an obvious place to start this walk. Those who reach the Isles of Scilly using the *Scillonian III* place their feet on this stout granite quay before walking anywhere else in the islands. The Quay connects Rat Island to Hugh Town, with the oldest parts closest to town, dating from 1603, but don't rush straight into town. The Harbourside Hotel sits on **Rat Island,** offering food and drink here at the start. The ferry waiting room beside the hotel is full of informative panels about the history and natural history of the islands, and these are well

29

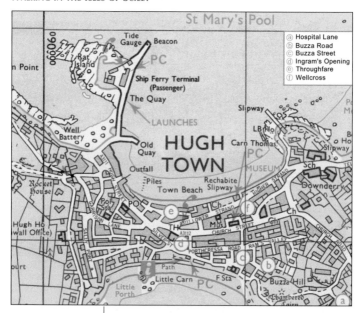

worth a few minutes of study. Some panels also offer information about the Isles of Scilly Wildlife Trust and Duchy of Cornwall.

While following The Quay towards town, take note of all the notice boards advertising ferries to the off-islands, wildlife cruises, evening cruises and all the rest. There is a small stone kiosk on the **Old Quay** where tickets can be obtained for the off-islands launches and cruises run by St. Mary's Boatmen's Association. For most other cruises and trips, either book in advance or pay on board. Ten o'clock in the morning is the busiest time in high season, when everyone flocks down to the quays for their tickets and the launches take their first eager passengers to each of the off-islands.

Turn left at the **Mermaid Inn** and walk along **Hugh Street.** The Pilot's Gig Restaurant if off to the right, but continue straight onwards, passing the Atlantic Hotel, which is on the left. Hugh Street is like a canyon of granite and it is fortunate that space is limited, so few vehicles use it. The **Post Office** stands beside a rugged granite arch and bears a stone marked 'VR 1897'. A fine granite terrace of houses continues on that side of the street, while the Isles of Scilly Steamship Company office is on the left. A group of gift shops are clustered around a road junction. The Bishop & Wolf is a bar and restaurant to the right, but keep left to reach a more open square. The **Town Hall** stands to the right, carrying a date-stone of 1897, and the small green space in the middle of Hugh Town serves as the town park. Taxis, small tour buses and splendid vintage buses may be parked here, should anyone fancy a quick spin around St. Mary's along its rather limited road network.

Keep left of the little park, following **Lower Strand Street,** passing Armorel Cottage and its huge aloe plant. The **Custom House** is to the left, and the Star of the Sea Catholic Church is to the right. A toilet block stands beside a short promenade path, where there are fine views across the harbour, while inland, shops give way to a terrace of houses. The **Lifeboat Station** is tucked under a granite tor and is served by a short path. If you follow it, then you have to return afterwards. The latest lifeboat is called *The Whiteheads* and is usually moored out on the harbour.

The road called **Higher Strand** climbs uphill, but turn sharply right at the top to discover the Isles of Scilly Wildlife Trust office. When this is open, a wealth of literature about the flora and fauna of the islands is available. The staff are very helpful if you have any particular questions or interests. They may have a series of wildlife walks or cruises planned, so ask for details. Just around the corner is the **Parish Church** of St. Mary the Virgin, dating from 1835, and a cylindrical granite tower, which was once a windmill, can be seen on Buzza Hill. Walk straight down into town along Church Street. The Hotel Godolphin is on the right, as well as the **Methodist Church.** There may be a notice posted at the church detailing evening slide shows. The Bell Rock Hotel is on the left.

The **Isles of Scilly Museum** stands on the right, in a rather faceless modern building. Don't be put off by the façade, as the interior is absolutely packed with interest. There are plenty of items relating to the history and heritage of the islands, as well as exhibits detailing the flora and fauna. Usually, some of the flowers and shrubs that grow around the Isles of Scilly are arranged in jars or pots, changed every few days, so that you can be absolutely sure about identifying the wealth of species that can be spotted outdoors. Leaving the museum, the Church Hall is on the right, and again there may be a notice detailing evening slide shows. A terrace of granite guesthouses leads back to the little park and the **Town Hall.**

Turn left and climb up a few steps on an embankment to see **Porth Cressa Beach.** There is a toilet block to the left and the Porthcressa Inn is to the right. Walk back down the steps and turn left along **Silver Street,** behind the Town Hall, and head back into the middle of Hugh Town. Turn left at Mumford's, where books, maps, postcards and the like can be bought. To the right is the **Tourist Information Centre.** Obtain all the information you need about accommodation options, ferries, buses, taxis, pubs and restaurants, as well as checking the opening times and prices of attractions around the islands.

Follow **Garrison Lane** uphill. The police station is on the right, but turn left along **Sallyport.** Look for a sign above a passageway marked 'Garrison Through Archway' to be led through a terrace of houses and under the Garrison Walls by way of the low-roofed Sallyport. Emerge onto a narrow road near **Hugh House,** which is the Duchy of Cornwall office. Turn left to reach the **Garden Battery** and enjoy a view over the rooftops of Hugh Town, appreciating just how compact the little town really is. Follow the road past the **Higher Battery** and turn left uphill. Visit the Powder Magazine Exhibition and learn about the fortifications of the Garrison, or continue up to the **Star Castle Hotel.** While walking back downhill afterwards, pass through an old archway dated 1742 at **Gatehouse Cottage.** Walk downhill past

St. Mary the Virgin Parish Church is one of three churches in Hugh Town

Tregarthen's Hotel, which was founded by Captain Tregarthen. He used to bring passengers to the Isles of Scilly 150 years ago, whenever he brought supplies from the mainland. There was a catch; his guests couldn't leave the islands until he went back to the mainland for more supplies! Turn left below the hotel to return to the harbour where the town trail started.

Facilities in Hugh Town

Most services and facilities on the Isles of Scilly are concentrated around Hugh Town. If you can't find what you need here, then you probably won't find it anywhere on the islands. Anything else must be brought from the mainland!

- There are six **hotels** around Hugh Town, as well as the largest concentration of **guest houses**, **bed and breakfast** establishments and **self-catering** lodgings in the islands.
- The only two **banks** available in the Isles of Scilly are Barclays and Lloyds (the latter with an ATM) and both are in Hugh Town. The **Co-op** offers a cashback service.
- There is a **post office**, **chemist** and **newsagent**, as well as a number of **shops** selling provisions, crafts and souvenirs.
- Although several **pubs**, **restaurants** and **cafés** are available, in the high season it is wise to book in advance for meals.
- There is an interesting **museum** in town.
- The **police station**, **hospital** and all administrative services for the Isles of Scilly are located around Hugh Town.
- **Churches** include St. Mary the Virgin (Church of England), Our Lady Star of the Sea Catholic Church and the Methodist Church.
- **Toilets** are located on The Quay, on The Strand and at Porth Cressa.
- **Tour buses** that make circuits around St. Mary's, as well as taxis, run from clearly marked stands in the centre of Hugh Town, near the Town Hall. **Ferries** to the off-islands all depart from The Quay, along with specific boat trips.

WALK 2

The Garrison Wall

___

Distance 2.5km (1½ miles)

Start Garrison Gate in Hugh Town – 901106

The promontory to the west of Hugh Town is almost completely encircled by a stout, granite defensive wall bristling with batteries. The Garrison was developed in stages over three centuries, but the most significant starting date is 1593, when Governor Francis Godolphin built the eight-pointed Star Castle. Additional walls and batteries were built around the promontory, with more appearing during the Civil War. The Garrison held out as a Royalist stronghold until 1651. Other islands holding out to the bitter end included Jersey, in the Channel Islands, and Inishbofin, off the west coast of Ireland. The Garrison came to resemble its present form during restructuring associated with the Wars of the Spanish Succession and the Napoleonic Wars. During the two world wars, there were few alterations, except for the positioning of pillboxes into some of the batteries. Even while it was manned by soldiers, the Garrison Wall provided a leisurely walk for 18th- and 19th-century visitors, and it still does so admirably today. English Heritage produces an excellent leaflet map and guide to the Garrison, and a visit to the Powder Magazine Exhibition is highly recommended.

Accommodation is available within the Garrison Wall at two remarkably different locations. The Star Castle Hotel is one of the more exclusive hotels in the Isles of Scilly, offering some rooms with four-poster beds in keeping with the history of the place. The hotel also has a Dungeon Bar! Standing high on the headland is the Garrison Farm campsite, the only campsite on St. Mary's, and one of only four campsites available around the Isles of Scilly.

A steep, stone-paved road runs up from **Hugh Town** to the **Garrison Gate.** Look for the date 1742 carved in stone above the moulded archway, below a little bellcote. The

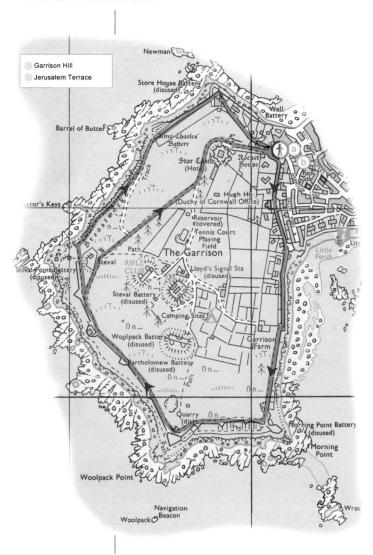

ⓐ Garrison Hill
ⓑ Jerusalem Terrace

Newman

Store House Battery
(disused)

Well
Battery

Barrel of Butter

King Charles'
Battery

Rocket
House

Star Castle
(Hotel)

ctor's Keys

Hugh Ho
(Duchy of Cornwall Office)

Reservoir
(covered)

Track

Breakw

Tennis Court
Playing
Field

Path

The Garrison

Steval

RIFLE
CLUB

Lloyd's Signal Sta
(disused)

St val Point Battery
(disused)

Steval Battery
(disused)

Camping Sites

Little
Porth

Woolpack Battery
(disused)

Garrison
Farm

Bartholomew Battery
(disused)

Garrison
Path

Quarry
(dis)

Morning Point Battery
(disused)

Morning
Point

Woolpack Point

Navigation
Beacon

Woolpack

Wras

Guardhouse and **Gatehouse Cottage** stand just inside the archway. Visit the Powder Magazine Exhibition straight ahead, if an in-depth study of the fortifications is desired, otherwise turn left to start walking clockwise around the walls. A narrow road rises to the **Higher Battery,** where there is a view over the rooftops of Hugh Town. Walk to the **Garden Battery,** which is in front of **Hugh House,** the Duchy of Cornwall office. A little further along, the road passes over a **Sallyport:** a narrow, low-roofed passageway beneath the wall. It is worth taking a peek under the wall at this point, but beware of the low headroom if you are tall. The next battery is the **Upper Benham Battery,** which overlooks Porth Cressa Beach.

Continue along a stony track parallel to the Garrison Wall, passing the **Upper Broome Platform.** Trees flank the track as it passes the **Lower Broome Platform.** At this point the wall takes a slight step back from the cliffs, and the line of an older breastwork can be distinguished along the cliff-top. The **Morning Point Battery** occupies a rocky promontory with sweeping views; its cannons had clear lines of fire to the north, east, south and west. While walking around the southern portion of the Garrison Wall, the wall is again a step back from the cliff and the line of another older breastwork can be seen.

Mounted cannons aim across St. Mary's Sound from the Woolpack Battery

A granite archway gives access to the Woolpack Battery on the Garrison Wall

The **Woolpack Battery** stands on another rocky promontory offering a good range for cannon fire. Two big cannons here were salvaged from a wreck. Views across St. Mary's Sound take in Gugh, St. Agnes, Annet and the distant Bishop Rock Lighthouse. Walk to **Bartholomew Battery** and up past **Colonel George Boscawen's Battery.** Look out for a peculiar structure partly buried underground; this was an engine room that generated power for a series of range-finding searchlights in the early 20th century.

Further along the track there is a fork, and walkers can go either way. Following the track uphill to the right leads quickly and easily past some wind-blasted pines to reach the **Star Castle.** Following the line of the Garrison Wall, however, it ends quite suddenly below the **Steval Point Battery.** Bear right and continue along the cliffs, looking at the breastwork and batteries that preceeded the Garrison Wall, dating from the Civil War period. The course of the wall resumes at the **King Charles' Battery,** and can be followed to the Store House Battery in front of **Newman House.**

Although the Garrison Wall continues along the cliffs from Newman House to Hugh Town, walkers have to leave it and head uphill to return to the **Garrison Gate.** To visit the eight-pointed **Star Castle,** turn sharply right just before reaching the Garrison Gate and follow the road uphill. The castle has been a hotel since the 1930s and is one of the most unusual places you could choose as an accommodation base in the Isles of Scilly. There are further wanderings that can be made on the high ground within the Garrison. There is a campsite and access to an early 20th-century hilltop battery. When explorations are complete, simply walk back through the **Garrison Gate** to return to **Hugh Town.**

Facilities in the Garrison

The Garrison lies immediately west of **Hugh Town**, so all the facilities of the town are readily available as detailed in the Hugh Town Trail. However, contained within the Garrison Wall are the **Star Castle Hotel**, the Garrison Farm **campsite**, Powder Magazine Exhibition and a pottery studio.

WALK 3

St. Mary's Coast

Distance   16km (10 miles)
Start   Town Hall in Hugh Town, 903105

The longest coastal walk available in the Isles of Scilly is around St. Mary's. It takes most of the day to complete, and while not particularly difficult, there are a lot of ups and downs, and ins and outs along the way. There are also plenty of interesting things to see: notably old fortifications, a host of ancient burial cairns and a well-preserved ancient village site. Anyone running out of time, could detour inland onto a road and hope to intercept the bus service, but carry the current bus timetable if you plan to do this.

The scenery around the coast varies tremendously, taking in cosy little coves, awesome granite headlands, areas of woodland and open heath, and always, always the surging sea. With a favourable tide a short detour onto Toll's Island, connected to St. Mary's by a sandy bar, is possible. While Salakee Down and Tolman Point can be explored, there is no access to the coast near the airport. Once Old Town is reached, the walk could be cut short and the road can be followed quickly back to Hugh Town, on foot or by bus, saving the rugged Peninnis Head for another day.

Walkers who feel fit and still have energy to spare on returning to Hugh Town, can of course extend the walk and complete a lap around the Garrison Wall, as outlined in Walk 2. The addition of the Garrison Wall walk ensures that walkers really do cover the entire coastal circuit of St. Mary's.

For anyone based in Hugh Town, the **Town Hall** makes a good reference point for the start of this walk, but by all means start from wherever you are staying, or from The Quay if arriving by ferry. Face the little park and keep to the left of it, following **Lower Strand Street** and passing

Armorel Cottage with its huge aloe plant. There is a short promenade path beside the road, with fine views over the harbour. The **Lifeboat Station** is tucked under a granite tor and is served by a short path. If you follow it, then return afterwards and walk up the road called **Higher Strand,** passing the secondary school and continuing downhill. Turn left as signposted for **Harry's Walls,** maybe following other signs to make a short detour uphill to see the remains of this unfinished 16th-century fort. The track along the shore passes **craft studios** and joins a road. Turn left to follow the road uphill, over-looking Newford Island and enjoying widening views across the harbour.

Turn left along a path to pass Juliet's Garden Restaurant above **Porthloo,** with its delightfully flowery terrace. Three gates lead through fields to reach an open slope above the sea. Bracken and brambles flank the path as it approaches **Carn Morval Point,** then the path cuts across a heathery slope. There are views of Annet, Samson, Bryher, Tresco, St. Helen's, Round Island, Teän and St. Martin's. Also notice that there is a nine-hole golf course a short way uphill. Follow the path down through bracken, until diverted inland and uphill on **Halangy Down.** Here you can inspect the remains of an ancient

Walkers brave the storm as they walk around Carn Morval Point on St. Mary's

41

Bear in mind that you could continue inland by road to the Telegraph Tower to catch a bus back to Hugh Town.

village site, admiring inter-linked round houses and little paths between them. The site is around 2000 years old. On the brow of Halangy Down is **Bant's Carn** burial chamber; a much older structure dating back some 4000 years.

Head for some tall masts on the brow of Halangy Down and go through a gate. Turn right to walk uphill. ◀

Watch for a sign on the left pointing along a track to show the way to the Innisidgen burial chambers. Follow this track along, then left and downhill. When it reaches the shore, continue along a path through marram grass and bracken. The **Innisidgen Lower Chamber** is perched on a grassy bank to the right, then you follow a path up a slope of bracken to reach the **Innisidgen Upper Chamber.** This is a more impressive structure, with views out to St. Martin's and the Eastern Isles, and tall, dark Monterey pines on the slope above.

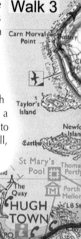

Follow the path further around the coast, across another slope of bracken, to reach **Block House Point.** There are the scanty remains of an old block house and breastwork defences on the slope. The path moves inland around a little valley above **Watermill Cove.** Stay high on another series of paths through more bracken then descend to a sandy beach overlooking **Toll's Island.** A sand bar links the little island to St. Mary's at low tide, so it might be possible to include it in the circuit. A path leads to **Pelistry Bay** and turns around a couple more rugged headlands, where intriguing rocky tors are passed on the way to **Porth Wreck.** It is worth climbing straight uphill from this rugged little cove to see a burial chamber on top of **Porth Hellick Down.** This is the largest of eight burial cairns; the other seven being difficult to locate on the ground sloping towards Porth Hellick. Curiously, views from the mound extend across most of St. Mary's, but none of the other islands are in view. There are some huge boulders of granite on the heathery down, as well as rocky points extending into the sea, and towering tors around **Porth Hellick.** One of the most prominent tors is known as the Loaded Camel.

While walking round the shingly embankment at the head of Porth Hellick, pass a memorial stone to Sir Cloudesley Shovell, a Rear-Admiral in the Navy until his death nearby in 1707. A fleet of twenty-one ships was sailing to Portsmouth on 22nd October 1707 and would have made it safely past the Isles of Scilly if Shovell hadn't ordered the fleet to heave-to and take soundings. Four ships, including the Shovell's flagship *Association*, were wrecked on the Western Rocks. Shovell escaped in a barge, along with his greyhound and a large treasure chest, but suffered another wrecking while making for St. Mary's. His body was brought ashore and buried at Porth Hellick, then later removed to Westminster Abbey for reburial. Some 1670 sailors were drowned that night, and the incident remains one of the worst of almost a thousand wreckings around the islands. The exact site where the *Association* sank was not discovered until 1967.

Walkers follow the coast of St. Mary's from Pelistry Bay round to Porth Wreck

Pulpit Rock is one of a series of bizarre granite formations on Peninnis Head

There is access to the Higher Moors nature trail from Porth Hellick; refer to Walk 4 for more details. Watch for a path climbing uphill from **Porth Hellick**, flanked by bracken, and passing through a gate. The path is flanked by hedgerows as it climbs to the buildings at **Salakee**. Turn right and walk down the access road to reach a junction with another road. Turn left to follow this road, passing the **airport access road**. The road leads past the Old Town Inn on its way into **Old Town**. A break could be taken at the Old Town Café at a road junction.

Old Town used to be the main settlement on St. Mary's, with Castle Ennor as its main defence. The castle site is now lacking any stonework and Old Town is a mere village, since most inhabitants drifted to Hugh Town in the 17th century. Walkers who have had enough for one day can save the walk around Peninnis Head for another day, and either walk back along the road to Hugh Town or catch a bus if one is due.

To continue with the walk, turn left along the road at the head of **Old Town Bay,** then left again to pass the **Old Church.** Labour Party members may wish to pay their respects to a past Prime Minister, Harold Wilson, who is buried in the churchyard and who had a great affection for the Isles of Scilly. Follow the path flanked by tall hedges as it passes a couple of fields, then it passes the spiky tor of **Carn Leh.** Continue along the path, staying just above the rocky coast rather than climbing higher on **Peninnis Head.** There are huge blocky outcrops, towering tors, precariously perched boulders, great flat slabs and areas of strangely fluted water-worn granite. Pulpit Rock and the Outer Head are places of bizarre rock-forms well worth a few moments of careful study. This is one of the most amazing landscapes on St. Mary's.

Pass below the little **Peninnis Lighthouse** and take in a view of Gugh, St. Agnes and Annet across St. Mary's Sound. Walk further round the headland to see the Garrison Wall and Bryher in the distance. The path leads around the coast, diverting uphill and inland to avoid an eroded stretch of coast, then it runs down to the beach at

Porth Cressa. Call a halt to the walk here, as the **Town Hall** is just a step inland. There are abundant offers of food and drink at various pubs and restaurants, the nearest being the Porthcressa Inn. Walkers who feel able to continue can complete the walk around the **Garrison Wall** too, referring to the route description in Walk 2 to complete the circuit all the way around St. Mary's.

Facilities around St. Mary's Coast

Facilities around the coastline of St. Mary's are sparsely scattered once Hugh Town is left behind, but the following places could be of interest.

- There are craft studios a short way out of Hugh Town, as well as **Juliet's Garden Restaurant** above Porthloo. The only other places offering food and drink are near the end of the walk, at the **Old Town Café** and **Old Town Inn**.
- **Accommodation** is sparse around the coast, being limited to a couple of guesthouses, self-catering cottages and chalets a short distance inland.
- **A bus service** makes a circuit around the island's roads and could be used to split the route at easily accessible points such as Telegraph or Old Town.

WALK 4

St. Mary's Nature Trails

Distance	8km (5 miles)
Start	Old Town Café, 914102
Map	See walk 3

This walk challenges the view that all the walks around the Isles of Scilly must be within sight of the sea. There are two nature trails on St. Mary's: the Higher Moors and the Lower Moors. These trails are for the most part enclosed by patchy woodlands, hedgerows or reed beds. Views from them tend to be of nearby farmland, and only at a couple of corners do they run close enough to the sea for walkers to be able to see it.

Starting from the little village of Old Town, only a short walk from Hugh Town, walkers can enjoy the Lower Moors nature trail first. Farm tracks and quiet roads can be used to reach the Telegraph Tower, which is the highest point on the Isles of Scilly, then link with the Higher Moors nature trail. This leads almost to the sea at Porth Hellick, but leafy paths and tracks link with roads that lead back to Old Town to complete a circuit where there are only a few glimpses of the sea and attention is focussed on the inland parts of the island.

The Old Town Café stands at a crossroads in the little village of **Old Town.** Walk inland along a quiet little road with a rough surface. After passing only a few houses, a gate allows access to the **Lower Moors** nature trail. Follow a path between bushes and reed beds, and look out for two **bird hides** off to the left overlooking a small reedy pool. There is also a **wooden boardwalk** through the reeds, which makes a loop and rejoins the main path further on.

Using the bird hides there is the best chance of observing the waterfowl on the pool. Mallard and moorhen are common, with heron, redshank and water

Telegraph Tower stands on the highest
point in the Isles of Scilly at 51m (166ft)

rail seen on occasion. The reeds also attract a variety of warblers, and flycatchers are often present in numbers. Thrushes and blackbirds favour the more willowy areas. The wetlands are covered in reeds, rushes and sedges, with interesting orchids, irises and other species that prefer wet ground.

A gate at the end of the path leads onto a road. Cross over the road and go through another gate to continue. A short stretch of the nature trail weaves through a flowery field to pass through a gate onto another road. Turn right along a dirt road, flanked by trees as it rises. Reach a junction with another road. Turn left to follow this road gently uphill, keeping an eye peeled for kestrels searching for small prey in the surrounding fields. Avoid other roads heading left and right, and aim for the cylindrical granite building called the **Telegraph Tower.** This stands on the highest point in the Isles of Scilly, amid houses and an array of communication masts, at a mere 51m (166ft). There are bus services in this area.

Backtrack along the road a short way and turn left. The tarmac quickly gives way to a stony track, then turn right to pass a farm at **Content.** Walk straight along the track to reach the next road, then turn left to pass the **Sage House** nursing and residential home. When a triangular road junction is reached at **Maypole,** keep right, then turn right down a narrower road. This leads into **Holy Vale,** where tradition asserts that there was once a convent or monk's cell. There are a few houses in the vale, surrounded by gardens of exotic vegetation worth a moment of study.

There is a detour that could be made at this point to include a visit to the Longstone Heritage Centre in the middle of St. Mary's. A couple of little notices giving route directions from Holy Vale will be spotted, but basically just turn right at the bottom of the road, then left to pass houses and follow a narrow path along the edge of a woodland. When a broader track is reached, simply turn right and walk up to the **Longstone Heritage Centre.** There are plenty of old photographs and displays relating to the history and heritage of the Isles of Scilly, as well as

a café, souvenir shop and putting green. After making a visit, retrace your steps into **Holy Vale** and continue the walk.

The road in Holy Vale gives way to a narrow path that runs through the **Holy Vale Nature Reserve.** Trees stand very close together on either side of the narrow path, and the roots can be slippery underfoot. The path is on an earthen embankment above a marsh, and the place seems like a jungle. It is one of the few places around the Isles of Scilly where you can walk among tall, densely planted trees. Emerging from the trees, cross a road and go through a gate to continue along the **Higher**

Moors nature trail. The path is gritty underfoot as it passes through reedy and bushy areas then there is a boardwalk section and two **bird hides** off to the left, overlooking a reedy pool. Again, it's worth taking a break to study the waterfowl, though noisy black-headed gulls sometimes invade the pool. While going through a gate at the end of the path you are within a few paces of the shore at **Porth Hellick,** not far from a monument to Sir Cloudesley Shovell.

Swing round to the right after passing through the gate, following a path through bracken away from the shore. The path goes through another gate and is flanked by hedgerows. Walk uphill to the buildings at **Salakee** and turn right to walk down the access road to reach a junction with another road. Turn left to follow this road, passing the **airport access road.** The road leads past the Old Town Inn on its way back to **Old Town.**

Facilities on the Nature Trails

Facilities in the heart of St. Mary's, along the Lower Moors and Higher Moors nature trails, are quite limited. A short bus journey or a brisk walk leads quickly back to Hugh Town where the fullest range of services is available.

- **Old Town** offers food and drink at the **Old Town Café** and **Old Town Inn**. There are also crafts and galleries around Old Town. The **Longstone Heritage Centre** has a restaurant a little off-route above Holy Vale.
- **Blue Carn Cottage** provides bed and breakfast accommodation at Old Town, while **Atlantic View** and **Shamrock** offer bed and breakfast near Telegraph.
- The **airport minibus** runs between Hugh Town, Old Town and the airport. The airport has a café.

WALK 5

The Gugh

Distance   (4km) 2½ miles
Start   The Quay on St. Agnes, 884086

Sometimes you can walk over to The Gugh, more often simply referred to as Gugh, and sometimes you can't. It all depends on the state of the tides. A high tide covers a sand and shingle bar that links Gugh with St. Agnes, and the water in Porth Conger and The Cove merges to become a single channel. Although The Bar is out of water for more time than it spends underwater, that is no consolation if you arrive just as it sinks beneath the waves. Tide tables are available from the Tourist Information Centre in Hugh Town. Gugh is the smallest of the inhabited Isles of Scilly, having only two households. It is a rugged little island, with so few people walking its paths that they are quite narrow in places. A circuit around the island takes only an hour or so, and if The Bar is clear then it is easy to combine a quick spin around Gugh with a walk around the entire coastline of St. Agnes.

There are no direct ferry services to The Gugh, so this walk has to start at The Quay on **St. Agnes.** Follow the concrete road inland past a toilet block, then pass the **Turk's Head** pub. Watch for a track leading downhill on the left, leading onto the shingle of **The Bar** and across to **Gugh,** but also watch the tide and be very wary if it is advancing while you are on the island. The two houses on the island are seen very clearly as they both face The Bar. Note the curious shape of their roofs, which are intended to shed powerful gales in such an exposed location.

When setting foot on **Gugh,** turn left to walk clockwise around the island, taking in the northern end first. Either scramble on the rocks at the end of the point, or

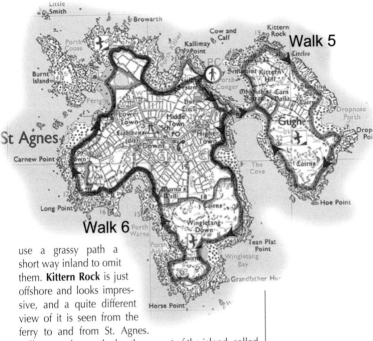

use a grassy path a short way inland to omit them. **Kittern Rock** is just offshore and looks impressive, and a quite different view of it is seen from the ferry to and from St. Agnes.

Follow a path over the heathery crest of the island, called **Kittern Hill,** where the most extensive views are available from the island. Descend gently to a prominent standing stone known as the **Old Man of Gugh.** This is a Bronze Age ritual monument with a distinct lean to one side. Away to the west is a burial chamber known as **Obadiah's Barrow,** whose excavation yielded a crouching skeleton and a dozen cremation urns.

On reaching the rugged **Dropnose Porth** there are two options. One is to cut inland across the island and return directly to **The Bar.** The other is to continue around the coast and pass **Dropnose Point.** Once past Dropnose Point, follow a path across a grassy, bouldery slope to pass **Hoe Point.** After turning the point, walk alongside **The Cove,** with a view back to St. Agnes.

55

A launch service passes between the island of Gugh and a rock called The Cow

Reach **The Bar** and cross over, then either turn right to return to the **Turk's Head** and The Quay, or turn left to explore other parts of **St. Agnes.** To continue walking all the way round the coastline of St. Agnes, refer to Walk 6.

Facilities on Gugh

There are no facilities. No ferry, no toilets, no accommodation, and no shops, food or drink. Bear this in mind if in danger of being stranded by a rising tide!

WALK 6

St. Agnes

Distance	6.5km (4 miles)
Start	The Quay on St. Agnes, 884086
Map	see Walk 5

St. Agnes looks deceptively small on the map but its coastline is heavily indented and the whole island seems to be surrounded by rugged tors of granite. The beaches are often rough and cobbly, but there are a couple of small sandy coves. With a favourable tide, walkers could combine a walk around St. Agnes with a shorter walk around the neighbouring island of The Gugh, as described in Walk 5. The two islands are connected by The Bar; a ridge of sand and shingle that spends more time out of the water than in it.

There are some curious features around St. Agnes, such as the natural granite sculpture called the Nag's Head, the cobbly spiral of the Troy Town Maze, and a very prominent disused lighthouse dominating the island from a central position. Views on the western side of St. Agnes take in the little island bird sanctuary of Annet and the awesome jagged Western Rocks that have wrecked many a ship. Further explorations in that direction are best accomplished on the occasional trips run by knowledgeable local boatmen. The tiny Burnt Island, however, can be visited when the receding tide exposes a rough and cobbly bar on the north-western side of St. Agnes.

Leave **The Quay** and follow the concrete road inland past a toilet block, passing the **Turk's Head** pub. Watch for a track running downhill on the left, leading onto the shingle of **The Bar** that connects St. Agnes to Gugh. ▶ Turn right at **The Bar,** and follow a path through some trees above the shore. Drop down onto a sandy beach at **Cove Vean,** then continue along a path through

If the tides are favourable, walkers can cross over to Gugh and walk round the island, but refer to Walk 5 for a detailed route description.

The Nag's Head is a natural sculpture that happens to look like a horse's head

bracken and over rock outcrops to reach heathery, bouldery slopes around **Wingletang Down.** The cove of Wingletang Bay is more often referred to as the **Beady Pool**, earning its name from the little beads that can still be found on the beach from a 17th-century wreck. The southernmost point of St. Agnes is turned at **Horse Point.**

Walk around the rough and bouldery coast, then wander round the little cove of **Porth Askin.** After passing a big granite tor, follow a well-trodden path around **Porth Warna,** crossing a few stiles. The cove is named after St. Warna, who arrived in a coracle from Ireland and is regarded as the patron saint of shipwrecks. After passing **St. Warna's Well** and turning round the head of the cove, keep an eye peeled to the right, and you can detour inland a short way to see the **Nag's Head.** This is a natural pillar of granite that just happens to have a strange protuberance shaped like a horse's head.

Continue along a rugged path around rocky headlands at **Long Point.** Tors of granite have long ridges extending into the sea. Views take in the Western Rocks, the Bishop Rock Lighthouse and Annet. The Western Rocks seem to fill the sea with jagged teeth ready to rip the keel from any vessel that dares approach them. Annet is a long, low, uninhabited island, protected as a nature reserve for important colonies of sea birds. Note the **Troy Town Maze,** which is made of cobbles pressed into the short grass in the shape of a spiral. It dates from 1729 and was made by a local lighthouse keeper, apparently based on an earlier design.

After walking round **Carnew Point** the tors are smaller and a cobbly path above the beach leads past the **Troy Town Farm** campsite to St. Agnes' Church. Note the long slipways here, which were formerly used for launching lifeboats. The infamous Western Rocks have wrecked hundreds of vessels, and for many years volunteers from St. Agnes were the only people capable of reaching survivors in time. Most people are content to follow a dirt road onwards and return to **The Quay,** but keen walkers can explore another rugged stretch of low coastline.

Continue along the coast and a cobbly tidal bar can be used, at low tide, to reach **Burnt Island.** An extensive pebbly seabed at **Smith Sound** is colonised by rare species of seaweed and supports rich communities of marine animals, even if some of them look like plants! Walk further around the northernmost point of St. Agnes, passing a pool where a variety of birds can be spotted, then the cobbly paths give way to more even walking surfaces. Reach a track and turn left to follow it back to the **Turk's Head** and **The Quay.**

Walkers who have the time and inclination to explore further can follow a concrete road up to **Higher Town,** through the centre of the island. There are interesting places offering food and drink, such as Covean Cottage with its delightful restaurant. There is also the Post Office & General Store at the top of the road in **Middle Town.** The stout, white, disused lighthouse can be approached on the highest part of the island. A blazing beacon was maintained from 1680, continually improved through the centuries with the use of oil and electricity, until a revolving light shone out to sea. This was extinguished in 1911 in favour of the little Peninnis Lighthouse over on St. Mary's.

Facilities on St. Agnes

- The Turk's Head serves **food and drink** near The Quay and provides the nearest thing to **hotel accommodation** on St. Agnes. Covean Cottage provides **bed and breakfast** accommodation and operates a **restaurant** at Higher Town. The Parsonage offers **bed and breakfast** accommodation at Middle Town, where there is also the Post Office & General Store, as well as the Bulb Shop, which sells bulbs, flowers, arts and crafts. Troy Town Farm **campsite** is at Lower Town, close to St. Agnes (Church of England). There are **self-catering** cottages and chalets on the island, while **toilets** are located beside The Quay.
- Apart from St. Mary's Boatmen's Association, **ferries** to and from St. Agnes are operated by *St. Agnes Boating,* tel 01720-422704. Evening Supper Cruises are operated from St. Mary's to the Turk's Head on St. Agnes.

Boat Trip – Annet and the Western Rocks

Annet is uninhabited and access is restricted. Landings are not allowed from 15th March to 20th August, but there are occasional boat trips and Seabird Specials that take visitors close to the island. There are some rugged cliffs along the eastern side of Annet that are populated by shags and cormorants, but the most interesting features are largely unseen. The island is covered with cushioned clumps of thrift and beneath it are hundreds of burrows that have been excavated by shearwaters and puffins.

Local boatmen only take visitors to the Western Rocks on days of flat calm

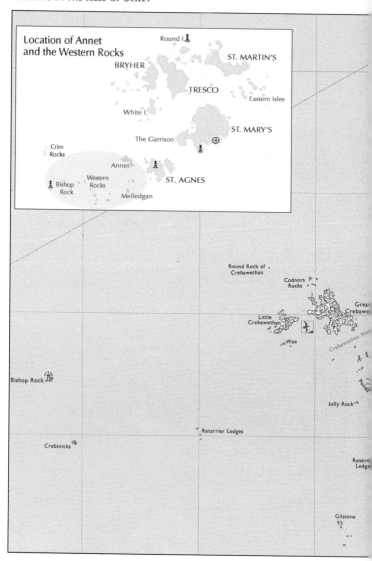

Location of Annet
and the Western Rocks

Round I.

BRYHER

ST. MARTIN'S

TRESCO

Eastern Isles

White I.

ST. MARY'S

The Garrison

Crim
Rocks

Annet

Bishop
Rock

Western
Rocks

ST. AGNES

Melledgan

Round Rock of
Crebawethan

Codnors
Rocks

Great
Crebawe

Little
Crebawethan

Wee

Crebawethan Nea

Bishop Rock

Jolly Rock

Crebinicks

Retarrier Ledges

Roseve
Ledge

Gilstone

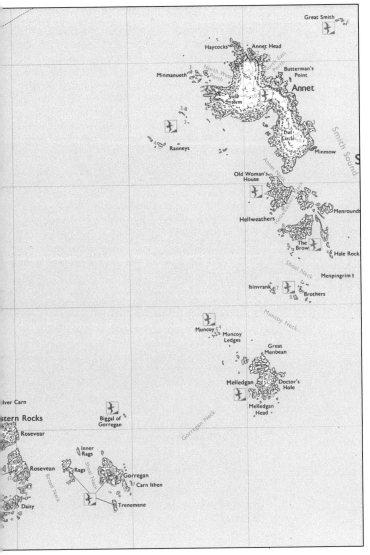

Great Smith

Haycocks • Annet Head

Minmanueth
North West Porth
North East Porth

Butterman's
Point

Annet

Field
System

Ranneys

Hut
Circle

Minmow

Smith Sound

S

Old Woman's
House

Hellweathers

Menrounds

The
Brow

Hale Rock

Shoal Neck

Menpingrim

Isinvrank

Brothers

Muncoy Neck

Muncoy
Muncoy
Ledges

Great
Menbean

Melledgan

Doctor's
Hole

Melledgan
Head

Iver Carn

stern Rocks

Biggal of
Gorregan

Gorregan Neck

Rosevear

Inner
Rags

Rosevean

Rags

Shoal Neck

Gorregan

Broad Neck

Carn Ithen

Daisy

Trenemene

Puffins will only come ashore during the breeding season, spending the rest of the year far out to sea, where they are seldom spotted by people. Shearwaters also spend the entire day far out at sea, coming ashore to their burrows only at nightfall, for fear of attack by gulls during daylight hours. Naturally, following each breeding season, Annet is covered with the rotting remains of chicks as well as any adult birds that fall victim to the gulls. Anyone landing on Annet, early or late in the year, is asked to tread carefully for two reasons: first, so that you don't turn an ankle, and secondly, so that you don't destroy one of the precious nesting burrows.

Annet and neighbouring St. Agnes are as close as visitors usually get to the vicious-looking fangs of the Western Rocks, unless they take a boat trip out to them. Some of the names of the rocks sound quite innocuous, such as Rosevear, Rosevean and Daisy, while others sound very threatening, such as the Hellweathers. The most distant groups include the Crim Rocks, Crebinicks and, of course, the Bishop Rock with its slender granite pillar lighthouse.

The first attempt to build a lighthouse on the Bishop Rock, using cast iron, was unsuccessful, and the structure was torn from the rock during a gale in 1850. The granite pillar dates from 1858, but needed extra height and girth adding in 1887. The lighthouse builders lived in small huts, now in ruins, on Rosevear, sailing to work whenever the weather would allow. Lighthouse keepers tended an oil lamp until the switch was made to electricity in 1973. The light has been automatic since 1992 and it is no longer serviced by boat, but by helicopters, which land on the precarious helipad on top of the lantern.

Visitors to the Isles of Scilly soon discover that boatmen only take tours to the Western Rocks and Bishop Rock Lighthouse on rare days of flat calm, pointing out shipwreck sites, grey seals and birds along the way.

WALK 7

Samson

Distance 2.5km (1½ miles)
Start Bar Point on Samson, 879133

Samson is uninhabited and has no landing pier, but it is also quite a popular destination and can sometimes be quite busy with explorers. There are only a few trodden paths, and anyone trying to make a complete coastal circuit will find that some parts are overgrown with bracken and laced with brambles! However, there are enough paths to allow a decent exploration of the northern half of the island, as well as both the North Hill and South Hill. When arriving on one of the launches, be sure to listen very carefully when the departure time is announced. Landing is usually achieved by running the launch slightly aground on the sandy Bar Point, then passengers have to walk the plank pirate-style down onto the beach!

The Isles of Scilly Wildlife Trust manages Samson as a nature reserve and is keen to preserve its flora, fauna and archaeological remains. Neolithic pottery has been found. Bronze Age burial chambers and alignments of cairns date back as far as 4500 years. At low tide on the sandy Samson Flats you can distinguish ancient field systems – testimony to rising sea levels over the millennia. An early Christian chapel and burial site lies on the beach at East Porth. South Hill is divided into small fields by drystone walls, and a number of ruined farmsteads can be seen. In the 18th century the population was almost fifty, but around 1855, Augustus Smith of Tresco evacuated the last elederly inhabitants and the island has been uninhabited ever since. Smith tried to create a deer-park on Samson, but it wasn't a success.

Invasive bracken covers former fields, but provides cover for wood-sage and bluebells. Cushions of thrift grow on rocky parts of the island, and spiky marram grass covers the dunes. Heather covers most of North Hill. Colonies of lesser black-backed and herring gulls populate the slopes of South Hill. Oystercatchers, dunlin, redshank and whimbrel can be spotted on the tidal flats. Ringed plover and grey plover are often present, along with curlew, turnstone and sanderling. Wrens can be spotted among the drystone walls, while rock pipits, stonechats, dunnocks, kittiwakes and terns can be seen from time to time. Kestrels will overfly Samson in search of prey, sometimes joined by the occasional merlin or peregrine.

When stepping ashore on **Bar Point,** walk up the sandy beach and drift to the left, then either walk along the beach for a while or come ashore to pick up a narrow coastal path. The path runs along the foot of North Hill to a grassy, sandy depression in the middle of the island, known as **The Neck,** between East Porth and West Porth. Anyone wanting to continue around the southern coast of Samson should bear in mind that there is no real trodden path through the bracken and brambles, and the beaches are uncomfortably cobbly underfoot. Oddly enough, it was the southern half of the island that was formerly divided into small fields and intensively cultivated in the 19th century.

From **The Neck** in the middle of Samson, a path can be followed up a slope of bracken onto the crest of South Hill. This path passes a couple of **ruined houses,** whose empty doorways and windows can be used to frame interesting views of Tresco and Bryher. Look carefully at the ground to distinguish the shapes of ancient hut circles and burial chambers, while a rugged little scramble over blocks of granite leads to the top of **South Hill,** where the whole of the island can be viewed in one sweeping glance.

Follow the path back down through the bracken to **The Neck** then drift to the left to pick up another coastal path beside West Porth, leading to **Bollard Point.** Swing to the right

and climb uphill to reach the heathery top of **North Hill.** Take the time to inspect a number of small burial chambers around the summit, then walk down to **Bar Point** when you see the launch approaching to collect passengers. Be warned that when the tide is ebbing, the boatmen want everyone on board quickly to avoid being beached between tides.

The ruined interior of one of the last inhabited cottages on Samson's South Hill

Facilities on Samson

- There are no facilities on Samson: no toilets, no accommodation, no shops, food or drink.
- **Ferries** are provided on an occasional basis, so check before planning this walk. Take note of the departure time to avoid being stranded!

WALK 8

Bryher

Distance 9km (5½ miles)
Start   Church Quay on Bryher, 882149

The launches serving Bryher sometimes complete a circuit, dropping passengers at Samson and Tresco too, allowing walkers to enjoy a spot of island-hopping. Bryher looks small on the map but its heavily indented coastline offers a good day's walk. There are some amazingly rocky points, as well as fine views of the spiky Norrard Rocks off the western coast. Heavy seas occasionally pound Hell Bay when westerly gales are blowing. Initially, it looks as though it is possible to walk from Hell Bay to Shipman Head, but the sea has cut a deep and narrow channel through the headland, effectively making Shipman Head into an island; thus denying access to walkers. Although the population of Bryher is quite small, the island offers a good range of services including accommodation, food and drink.

A walk around the south-west of Bryher leads walkers as close as they can normally get to the Norrard Rocks, unless one of the occasional boat trips is taken out there, as described in the next chapter. The rocks have the appearance of a sunken mountain range with only the peaks showing. The largest rocks are Mincarlo, Maiden Bower, Illiswilgig, Castle Bryher and Scilly Rock. Access to the Norrard Rocks is prohibited from 15th March to 20th August, to protect breeding seabirds. Gweal is a small island separated from Bryher by the narrow channel of Gweal Neck, with access available any time visitors care to reach it by boat.

The route around Bryher is described from Church Quay, but depending on the state of the tides, your launch may well drop passengers at Anne Quay. Even if starting at Church Quay, listen to any announcement the boatman makes, as you may need to be collected from Anne Quay later in the day.

Church Quay is sometimes left high and dry above the water by the ebbing tide. **Anne Quay** was constructed with the help of Anneka Rice on the popular *Challenge Anneka* series on BBC television. As anyone would expect, Church Quay was constructed close to a church, so take a peek inside **All Saints Church** while following a narrow dirt road inland and uphill. Climb up to a cross-roads and turn left over a rise. Walk downhill and turn left down a track, then turn left again along a concrete road to pass **Veronica Farm.**

A coastal track is lined with agapan-thus blooms in summer, while fleshy-leaved mesembryan-themum swathes the ground around **Green Bay.** A coastal path passes banks of bracken and brambles around **Samson Hill.** Turn around **Works Point** on the southern end of Bryher, and enjoy views of Tresco, St. Mary's, Gugh, Samson, the Bishop Rock and Norrard Rocks. Continue walking around **Stony Porth** and enjoy the exceptionally rocky scenery around **Droppy Nose Point.** The sea beyond is filled with the spiky shapes of the **Norrard Rocks.**

Leaving **Droppy Nose Point,** follow a path over the crest of **Heathy Hill** and walk around the lovely curve of **Great Porth,** passing a rocky tor along the way. The Golden Eagle Gallery is passed, and there are houses and headlands nearby, as well as the **Hell Bay Hotel.** A large pool also catches the eye, and a path leads between the pool and **Stinking Porth** in the direction of Gweal Hill. Either follow a rugged coastal path looking across a narrow channel to the little island of Gweal, or climb to the top of **Gweal Hill** to enjoy more wide-ranging views. The panorama takes in the northern end of Bryher, parts of Tresco, and the Day Mark on St. Martin's, followed by St. Mary's and the Garrison Wall, Samson and St. Agnes, Annet, the Bishop Rock Lighthouse and Norrard Rocks.

Follow a path away from **Gweal Hill,** through marram grass and bracken, around the cove of **Popplestone Neck,** to rise over the heathery slopes above the rocky coast of **Hell Bay.** The sea is often uneasy around Hell Bay, and the shape of the bay seems to make

Great Porth and Gweal Hill seen near the Hell Bay Hotel on the west of Bryher

View of Tresco from cliffs that flank Shipman Head Down on the north of Bryher

the waves pile up, so that they crash into the rocks and send spray spouting skywards. There are attractively rocky headlands ahead that may also be battered by heavy seas. Follow the path onwards, as if aiming for the most northerly point on the island at **Shipman Head.** However, a rocky point is reached where a deep and rocky channel can be seen to separate Shipman Head from the rest of Bryher. The sheer-walled rocky chasm, known as **The Gulf,** has a boulder jammed in its throat and cannot be crossed safely by walkers.

Retrace steps then follow paths that drift to the left, continuing over **Shipman Head Down.** There are lovely views over the channel separating Bryher from Tresco, taking in Cromwell's Castle above the Tresco shore and King Charles' Castle on the heathery slopes above. Both these fortifications can be visited by following Walk 9. It is also possible to see the lighthouse on Round Island peeping over Castle Down on Tresco from time to time. Stay high on the heather moorland until overlooking some houses. Descend and keep to the right of the houses to pass through a field on a trodden path. There may be tents pitched, as the field is used as the island **camp site.**

A walker stands proud on a granite outcrop on Shipman Head Down on Bryher

When a track is reached, most walkers will turn left to reach the Fraggle Rock Café and Bar. However, it is worth turning right up the track, then turning left along narrow paths to reach the top of **Watch Hill.** The ruins of an old watch-house remain on the hill, alongside a more modern water tank. A splendid panorama from the hill overlooks northern Bryher, northern Tresco, Round Island, St. Helen's and St. Martin's. The Great Pool can be seen in the middle of Tresco. St. Mary's and the Garrison Wall are in view, followed by Gugh, St. Agnes, Samson, southern Bryher, Annet, the Bishop Rock Lighthouse and Norrard Rocks. Retrace steps down the hill and follow the track down to the **Fraggle Rock Café & Bar.**

Continue walking along the dirt road away from the café and bar, noting the left turn for the **Bryher Stores & Post Office** if any provisions are needed. The dirt road gives way to a concrete road in places. If your launch is collecting passengers from **Anne Quay,** then turn off to the left to wait for it, but to return to **Church Quay,** follow the road uphill past a telephone box and the **Vine Café.** Walk down to a crossroad and turn left to walk back down past the church to reach Church Quay.

Facilities on Bryher

Facilities on Bryher are concentrated in a band across the middle of the island, rather than on the southern or northern parts of the island. They include the following.

- **Toilets** are located beside Church Quay. **All Saints** (Church of England) is above Church Quay. The **Vine Café** stands inland between Church Quay and Anne Quay. **Soleil d'Or** provides bed and breakfast accommodation near Anne Quay, and there are a few **self-catering** cottages and chalets around the island. **Bryher Stores & Post Office**, as well as the **Fraggle Rock Café & Bar** and the island **campsite**, are all found at the end of the road above Anne Quay.

- **Bank House** offers bed and breakfast accommodation on the western side of Bryher, and the nearby **Hell Bay Hotel** offers accommodation, food and drink. The Golden Eagle Gallery is also located on the western side of the island.

- Apart from St. Mary's Boatmen's Association, **ferries** to and from Bryher are operated by Bryher Boat Services, tel 01720-422886.

Boat Trip – The Norrard Rocks

The Norrard, Northern or Northward Rocks, lie scattered throughout the sea to the west of Bryher and Samson. They can be viewed easily enough from Gweal Hill on Bryher, where the little island of Gweal is also prominently in view. Landings on Gweal are possible any time of the year, but none of the launches usually land there, so it might require the special hire of a boat. The Norrard Rocks are remarkably spiky in certain profiles and have the appearance of a sunken mountain range, with only the topmost peaks showing.

The little island of Gweal with some of the jagged Norrard Rocks also in view

The Norrard Rocks are closed to visitors during the breeding season, from 15th March to 20th August, but in any case landings aren't normally made on any of them.

The rocks include Mincarlo, Castle Bryher, Illiswilgig, Seal Rock, Maiden Bower, Black Rocks and Scilly Rock. Seals are often seen around the rocks, resting on low ledges, and puffins can be spotted in the early summer well away from disturbance. The occasional tours around the Norrard Rocks include unusual views of Samson and Bryher, and will often include a landing on Bryher or Tresco as a bonus.

Westward Ledge

Sharp Rock

Little

North Cuckoo

Eastward Ledge

South Cuckoo

Murr Rock

The Flat

Scilly Rock

Horse Rock

Gweal

Gweal Ledges

Westward Ledge

Stippit

Maiden Bower

Black Rocks

12

Round Rock

Murr Rock

Garden of Maiden Bower

Seal Rock

Gerwick

Jacky's Rock

Seal Rock Neck

Outer Neck of Gerwick

26

Castle Bryher Neck

Castle Bryher

Buzza Rock

Picket Rock

Illiswilgig

Rocks of Illiswilgig

Middle Ledge

Northern (Norrard) Rocks

Mincarlo

Biggal

WALK 9

Tresco

Distance	10km (6 miles)
Start	Carn Near Quay on Tresco, 893134

'Tropical Tresco' is a term often heard around the Isles of Scilly. It refers to the fact that all manner of tropical plants grow lush and healthy at the Abbey Garden, on a south-facing slope sheltered by windbreak trees and bushes. The name of Augustus Smith is forever associated with Tresco. He took over the lease of the island in 1834, and as Lord Protector of the islands he was responsible for great improvements, though not always with the full support of the islanders. He introduced compulsory schooling, the first in Britain, and there were fines for non-attendance. A monument to Augustus Smith can be visited on a hilltop near the Abbey Garden.

Tresco is a fertile island, with regimented lines of tall, dark Monterey pines providing the tiny flower fields with shelter from the winds. There are sweeping sandy beaches around the southern coast, and surprisingly extensive moorlands in the north. Fortifications abound around the coast, with reminders of the 17th-century Civil War in the shape of King Charles' Castle and Cromwell's Castle. The Abbey House is one of the most substantial buildings in the Isles of Scilly, but it is not open to the public.

It takes all day to walk around Tresco properly, and maybe even a whole weekend if anyone wants to make really detailed explorations of the coastline and still be able to have a good look round the Abbey Garden. The ruin of a 12th-century Benedictine priory lies at the heart of the garden, but see the separate description of the Abbey Garden for details. Tresco can be reached directly by helicopter from Penzance on the mainland; cutting out the need to use St. Mary's as an intermediate stepping-stone.

Launches to Tresco usually berth at the Carn Near Quay on the extreme southern point of the island. However, note that the launches sometimes berth at New Grimsby,

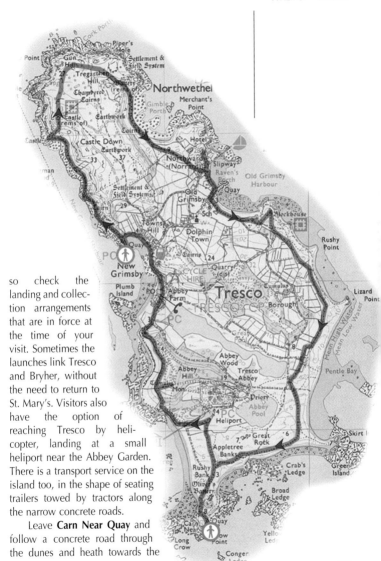

so check the landing and collection arrangements that are in force at the time of your visit. Sometimes the launches link Tresco and Bryher, without the need to return to St. Mary's. Visitors also have the option of reaching Tresco by helicopter, landing at a small heliport near the Abbey Garden. There is a transport service on the island too, in the shape of seating trailers towed by tractors along the narrow concrete roads.

Leave **Carn Near Quay** and follow a concrete road through the dunes and heath towards the

Abbey Garden. A little hill on the right bears the remains of **Oliver's Battery** – one of a handful of reminders of the Civil War.

Warning The road passes a little heliport, where warning signs, lights and barriers alert you to incoming flights. Do not enter this area when a helicopter is operating, and do not wave to, or otherwise distract the pilot. Ensure that you keep hold of any items that might blow away or become entangled in the helicopter rotors.

Once past the heliport, the **Abbey Garden** is to the right, but this walk makes a circuit of the island by turning left. Follow the concrete road, taking a right fork to avoid a stretch of road that has fallen into the sea. There are echiums and agapanthus growing in the sandy soil, as well as fleshy-leaved mats of mesembryanthemum creeping along the ground. Slopes of bracken and brambles give way to higher stands of pines. A short diversion to the right, along a path flanked by rhododendrons on **Abbey Hill,** allows walkers access to the Smith Monument, a slender pillar of granite boulders raised in memory of Augustus Smith. If no diversion is made, then keep following the concrete road onwards and enjoy the views across the channel to Bryher.

The road runs gently downhill and there is a glimpse to the right of the **Great Pool** in the middle of Tresco. Keep left at a junction beside the Estate Office and Post Office. On the approach to **New Grimsby,** a right turn inland leads to the New Inn, and could also be used to short-cut across the island; otherwise keep straight on to reach the **Quay Shop,** café and toilets. There are occasional launches between the quay at New Grimsby and the neighbouring island of Bryher: easily the shortest ferry journey anywhere in the Isles of Scilly.

To the right of the quay follow a signpost for King Charles' and Cromwell's Castles. A narrow path runs through bracken and heather above a bouldery shore. It leads to **Cromwell's Castle** first, which is a cylindrical stone tower on a low rocky point. Steps allow access to the roof, and cannons aim across the channel. A rugged path climbs up the heathery slope a short way inland to reach the ruins of **King Charles' Castle.** This hilltop fort was constructed in the middle of the 16th century to defend the narrow New Grimsby Channel between Tresco and Bryher. During the Civil War, a century later, it was captured by the Parliamentary army and partially demolished. Stones from the building were used to build Cromwell's Castle at the foot of the hill, in a much better position to defend the channel.

Cromwell's Castle on Tresco, built towards the end of the 17th-century Civil War

79

There are fine views around the northern end of Tresco from King Charles' Castle, taking in rocky Men-a-vaur, Round Island and its lighthouse, St. Helen's and maybe a distant glimpse of Land's End. St. Martin's leads the eye to the Eastern Isles, then the southern end of Tresco gives way to St. Mary's. Gugh and St. Agnes are followed by Samson and Bryher, with the distant Bishop Rock Lighthouse also in view.

Follow the heathery path northwards to **Gun Hill,** enjoying superb views back along the channel to St. Mary's, as well as across the channel to Shipman Head at the northern end of Bryher. Turn right and walk across the short heather using any narrow paths you can find. Disturbed ground along the way marks old, small-scale excavations for tin ore. Pass a couple of granite tors and rocky points as height is gradually lost. A coastal path leads through bracken around **Gimble Porth,** then a sandy path leads inland between fields. Turn left down a concrete road to pass some holiday chalets. Another left turn leads to the **Island Hotel,** if anyone fancies taking a break for food and drink in style. There is exotic vegetation around the hotel and lovely views from the outside terraces. If a break at the hotel isn't required, then turn right along the coastal road to reach the quay at **Old Grimsby.**

Turn right alongside some houses at Old Grimsby. Go inland as far as St. Nicholas' Church if you want to visit it, otherwise turn left beforehand along another concrete road. A sign on the left points along a track for the **Old Block House,** which sits on a rocky outcrop on top of a low hill. A Royalist force was ousted from this little fortification during the Civil War – the Parliamentary force arriving via the little island of Teän. The structure overlooks the Island Hotel and the little islands of Northwethel, Men-a-vaur, St. Helen's and Teän. St. Martin's fills much of the view, leading the eye round to the Eastern Isles and across to part of St. Mary's.

Follow grassy paths away from the **Old Block House,** through the bracken and roughly parallel to the coast. Walkers could drop down onto the sandy beaches either side of **Lizard Point** and continue to the promontory of **Skirt Island.** Note the tall, dark Monterey pines inland, and the tiny flower fields beyond them. Bracken gives way to marram grass and there may be agapanthus blooms in the dunes. While following the path parallel to the coast, there are views of the **Abbey House** away to the right. When the concrete road is reached at the southern end of the island, a left turn leads quickly to the **Carn Near Quay.** If there is still plenty of time to spare, then you could turn right and follow the road back across the **heliport** and explore the **Abbey Garden,** but it really needs at least a couple of hours to do justice to the place. Birdwatchers who find they have time to spare could check around the **Abbey Pool,** which attracts a ducks, geese, swans and other waterfowl.

Facilities on Tresco

- Most of Tresco's facilities are concentrated in a band through the middle of the island, between New Grimsby and Old Grimsby, and they include the following. The **Quay Shop** and café, selling provisions and souvenirs at New Grimsby, with toilets alongside. The **Gallery Tresco** is nearby, along with the **Post Office** and **Estate Office**. The **New Inn** offers food, drink and accommodation a short distance inland. **St. Nicholas'** (Church of England) stands amid fields in the middle of Tresco. The **Island Hotel**, near Old Grimsby, offers accommodation, food and drink. There are a couple of **self-catering** lodgings and time-shares on Tresco, but no guesthouses, bed and breakfast establishments or campsite. The Abbey Garden is on the southern half of Tresco and incorporates the **Garden Café**. There are **toilets** alongside.
- Direct **helicopter** flights are available to Tresco from Penzance, operated by British International, tel 01736-363871. Apart from St. Mary's Boatmen's Association, ferries to and from Tresco are operated by Bryher Boat Services, tel 01720-422886.

WALK 10

Tresco Abbey Garden

This isn't exactly a walking route, but the Abbey Garden is quite extensive and visitors have to walk around it to appreciate it to the full. It is probably rather ambitious to try and combine a thorough exploration of the Abbey Garden with a complete coastal walk around Tresco, but anyone staying on the island for a couple of days will doubtless find time to do both with ease. There is an abbey, or more correctly a priory, in the middle of the garden, but little remains apart from a couple of archways and low walls. This 12th-century structure was founded by Benedictine monks and was quickly brought under the control of Tavistock Abbey. Its ruinous state may have little to do with the 16th-century Dissolution of the Monasteries, as the site may have been abandoned long before that time. The people of Tresco used the priory site as a burial ground in the 17th century, until they acquired a cemetery alongside the new church of St. Nicholas.

Augustus Smith was responsible for planting the Abbey Garden from 1834. He not only collected plants himself, but also obtained specimens from Kew Garden and encouraged seafarers to bring back flowers and shrubs from exotic climes. There are well-established trees from Australia, New Zealand, South America, South Africa and the Mediterranean. Arid areas have been created for cacti, while nearby terraces overflow with cascades of colourful flowers. Look out for ericas, proteas, lampranthus, cistus and many more. Most plants are labelled, if you find yourself puzzled by the bewildering number of species. The following route outline is only a suggestion, but it makes use of most of the paths and takes in all the varied areas of the garden. There are around 3000 species of plants in the Abbey Garden, and over 20,000 individual plants on the 7 hectare (17 acre) site, which is a bewildering number even for a dedicated botanist!

On entering the Abbey Garden there is a shop and ticket counter, toilets and the Garden Café. The old priory ruins lie well to the right, in the oldest part of the garden, but most visitors find themselves drawn first towards the Valhalla Museum. This is an interesting corner, where

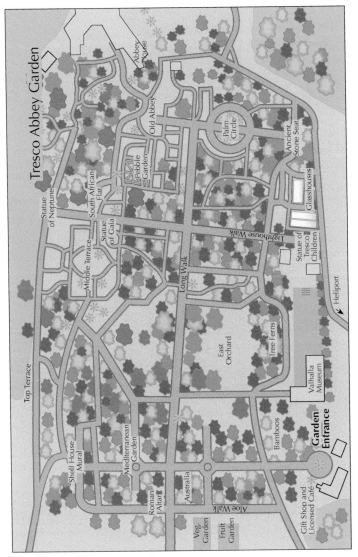

Tresco Abbey Garden

Abbey House

Old Abbey

Palm Circle

Ancient Stone Seat

Statue of Neptune

South African Flat

Pebble Garden

Middle Terrace

Statue of Gaia

Glasshouses

Lighthouse Walk

Statue of Tresco Children

Long Walk

Top Terrace

Heliport

East Orchard

Tree Ferns

Shell House Mural

Mediterranean Garden

Roman Altar

Australia

Aloe Walk

Valhalla Museum

Bamboos

Garden Entrance

Veg. Garden

Fruit Garden

Gift Shop and Licensed Café

*The exotic Tresco
Abbey Garden was
planted by Augustus
Smith from 1834*

figureheads from shipwrecks have been restored and
mounted around a courtyard. Other items of archaeological or antiquarian interest lie scattered around, including
cannons and signal guns. This is very much a hands-on
type of museum, where visitors can touch and feel many
of the exhibits.

Walk beyond the museum, passing tree ferns, and
intersect with the Lighthouse Walk. This could be
followed straight uphill, ending with flights of steps, to
reach a statue of Father Neptune on the Top Terrace.
Tall, dark Monterey pines provide a windbreak along the

top edge of the garden. Turn left along the Top Terrace, then left again, to descend to the Middle Terrace. Here there are two options and of course, both are recommended. Explore the terraces of the Mediterranean garden and continue down to the Long Walk, then turn left and left again to reach a statue of Gaia. There is an exit back onto the Lighthouse Walk, which can be followed back up towards the steps.

Turning right away from the steps leads to a couple of arid areas such as the Pebble Garden and the West Rockery. Narrow paths lead either down to the priory ruins or through the Pump Garden to reach the Long Walk again. Crossing the Long Walk, another path can be followed to the Palm Circle, or you can retire to the Garden Café for something to eat or drink.

As there are literally dozens of species arranged in compact formations throughout the garden, any attempt to list the species here is pointless. In broad terms, expect to see palms of all types, acacias, eucalyptus, bananas, mimosa, aloes, yucca, ice plants, cacti, honeysuckle, cinnamon, and flowers of every colour and scent. Exactly what can be see depends on the season and on how much time is spent looking, as some species are shy and retiring, occupying little niches in the rockeries. Colours change throughout the year as different species come into bloom, maybe none more startlingly than the New Zealand flame trees. On hot summer days there are exhilarating fragrant scents carried on the breeze from a range of aromatic plants.

Facilities at the Abbey Garden

Facilities at the Abbey Garden includes the **Valhalla Museum**, the **Garden Café** (with toilets) and a well-stocked **shop** selling souvenirs and books aimed at gardeners and those with an interest in flowers. The **heliport** alongside, said to be the only 'garden heliport' in the world, offers direct flights between Tresco and Penzance, operated by British International, tel 01736-363871.

Boat Trip – St. Helen's and Teän

It is believed that the little islands of St. Helen's and Teän were once joined to St. Martin's, maybe even as late as the 11th century. The water between the islands is quite shallow at low tide, but that is not to say that anyone should chance wading across. St. Mary's Boatmen's Association offers occasional tours around the small

islands of St. Helen's and Teän, and landings are some-times possible. The tours include Round Island, but without landing. Trips around the islands usually include a landing at Tresco or St. Martin's.

St. Helen's is a small and rugged hump between the northern ends of St. Martin's and Tresco. Its most notable feature is the remains of an early Christian church site, hermitage and burial place. The church, or oratory, dates from the 10th century, but there are earlier hut sites and cairns around the island. A ruined brick structure known as the Pest House was built in the 18th century. Seafarers suffering from illness or fever were likely to be put ashore there, where they would be unable to infect the rest of the ship's crew or the local island population. There is an interesting annual pilgrimage to St. Helen's on the Sunday closest to St. Ellid's Day, 8th August. Ellid lived on St. Helen's, and it was on this island that the Viking Olaf Trygvasson was converted to Christianity. He origi-nally came to plunder the south-west of England and exacted a hefty tribute from the English King Aethelred the Unready. Olaf later became the King of Norway, and is remembered as one of three missionary kings along with Håkon the Good and Olaf the Stout. No doubt his conversion on St. Helen's dictated the manner of his rule.

While landing on Teän is generally unrestricted, local boatmen have been observing a voluntary restric-tion between 15th March and 20th August. The beaches above the high water mark are used as nesting sites by ringed plover and terns, whose eggs are often indistin-guishable from pebbles. There is a ruined early Christian chapel on the island. In 1684 a Falmouth family settled on Teän and the succeeding generations continued its occupation, along with occasional settlers from St. Martin's, but today the island is uninhabited.

WALK 11

St. Martin's

Distance 10km (6 miles), or including White Island 12km (7¼ miles)
Start Higher Town Quay on St. Martin's, 931152

St. Martin's has a dense arrangement of tiny flower fields on its southern slopes, and rather wild and uncultivated northern slopes. The two main settlements are Higher Town and Lower Town, and launches could use one or both quays when landing and collecting passengers. The walk around the island allows visitors to see, at relatively close quarters, how intensively cultivated the flower fields can be. There is a choice of paths on the northern side of the island, where walkers can either follow a narrow coastal path or switch to a broad, grassy path that slices through the bracken covering the higher parts of the island. The red and white Day Mark on St. Martin's Head is about as close as anyone can normally get to Land's End and mainland Britain while exploring the Isles of Scilly.

With favourable tides, explorations of St. Martin's could also include White Island (pronounced 'wit'). This rugged little island is just north of St. Martin's and at low water a crossing can be made over the cobbly White Island Bar. The island has some impressive rocky headlands, and some parts are covered in deep, spongy cushions of thrift. There are also ancient field systems and cairns to inspect, as well as old kelp pits where seaweed was burnt to produce potash and other minerals. A thorough exploration of White Island would add another 1¼ miles (2km) to the walk around St. Martin's.

Although this walk starts at the Higher Town Quay, be sure to listen for any announcement the boatman makes: visitors might be collected from the Lower Town Quay later in the day, or vice-versa, in which case restructure the walk.

Walk uphill from **Higher Town Quay** on a winding concrete road, enjoying views down to the beach before turning left at a junction in **Higher Town.** Pass the Polreath café and the Post Office & General Stores. The road bends right to pass **St. Martin's Church,** but walk straight onwards beforehand, down a grassy, hedged track. When a point is reached where tracks cross, turn right to pass the white **school** building and rise gently to rejoin the road. Turn left then left again down another grassy, sandy track. At the bottom, either stay on dunes covered in marram grass, or walk along the beach. Either way, just beyond a granite tor is the **Lower Town Quay.** In the event of alighting from the ferry at this point, read the route description from here.

St. Martin's on the Isle Hotel at the Lower Town Quay incorporates the Round Island Bar and Teän Restaurant, named after the two little islands visible offshore. Teän is closest, while Round Island is easily identified because of its prominent lighthouse. The island tucked away behind Teän is St. Helen's. Either walk along a narrow path in front of the hotel, or use a broader track behind, to continue around the coast to **Tinkler's Point.** While walking round the bouldery **Porth Seal,** pass a water trough and a gate, then continue along a broad, grassy track with a view out to White Island. Note the spiral designs and other shapes that have been made by pressing beach cobbles and old ropes into the grass near the **White Island Bar.**

If the tide is out, walkers can cross the cobbly tidal bar and explore **White Island,** adding an extra 2km (1¼ miles) to the walk around St. Martin's. There are only vague paths around **Porth Morran,** passing old kelp pits and leading to an ancient cairn on the highest part of the island. On the return, it is worth seeing some of the rocky little headlands on the eastern side of the island. There is also an ancient field system on the narrowest and lowest part of the island. Climb over the rugged little hill at the southern end of the island before walking back across the cobbly **White Island Bar** to return to St. Martin's.

A coastal path leads around the broad, sandy beaches of **Little Bay** and **Great Bay.** The path is narrow and runs through bracken or heather, laced with honey-

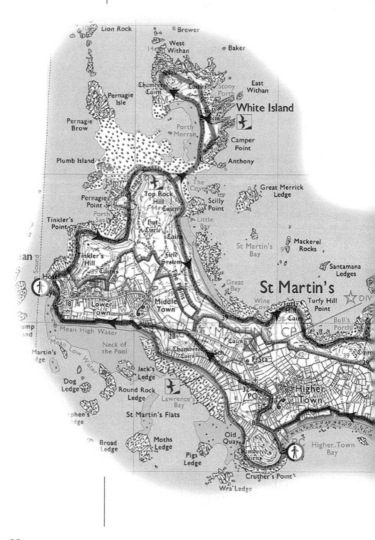

suckle and other plants. If the path prooves too narrow, then use other paths to move inland and follow a broad, grassy track along the crest of the higher downs. The lower coastal path runs above a rocky shore and turns around **Turfy Hill Point.** Climb to the rocky little top of **Burnt Hill** beyond Bull's Porth or simply continue along the narrow path. There is a short, steep, rugged climb onto the heathery, rocky point of **St. Martin's Head.** The headland is crowned with a prominent red and white **Day Mark** and a ruined building. Although the Day Mark bears a date of 1637, it was actually constructed in 1683.

Views from the Day Mark stretch far across the sea to Land's End, with the Eastern Isles arranged in an attractive cluster closer to hand. Beyond St. Mary's is a distant view of the Bishop Rock Lighthouse. Samson and Tresco can be seen, along with Round Island and White Island. Follow a well-trodden path away from the **Day Mark.** Look away to the left across **Chapel Down** to can spot what appears to be a standing stone on the heathery slopes. Approach it and try to distinguish the shape of a carved face. The stone is thought to be an ancient statue-menhir, maybe 3000 years old, but it was only discovered and re-erected on this spot in 1989.

Follow the well-trodden path from the Day Mark to a triangular junction of tracks, then turn left and walk downhill. The track becomes sandy and is flanked by tall hedges as it runs back to the Higher Town Quay. Along the way, pass signs announcing the Little Arthur Farm Trail, Little Arthur Café

St. Martin's Church is located at Higher Town on the island of St. Martin's

and St. Martin's Vineyard. These places are all open to
the public if you follow the directions on the signs. **Little
Arthur Farm** is run according to green principles and
offers a café on site, while the vineyard is the only one
to be established in the Isles of Scilly and is a developing
concern. There are toilets and a sports pitch just before
the **Higher Town Quay** is reached.

If it is necessary to return to the Lower Town Quay
for the return ferry, then either retrace steps along the
route that was followed earlier in the day or follow the
concrete road between **Higher Town, Middle Town** and
Lower Town. This road passes most of the facilities on St.
Martin's, except for those located at the eastern end of
the island.

Facilities on St. Martin's

There are three settlements on St. Martin's: Higher Town, Middle Town and
Lower Town. Most of the island's facilities are at Higher Town, though there
are important facilities at Middle Town and Lower Town as follows.

- **Higher Town** has the **Polreath Guest House** and café, the Post Office
  & General Stores, St. Martin's (Church of England) and Methodist
  Church. The Glenmore Gift Shop and North Farm Gallery deal in arts
  and crafts. **Toilets** are down beside the quay. **St. Martin's Vineyard** and
  the **Little Arthur Café** are a little further outside the village. The island's
  campsite is located at Middle Town, in former flower fields.
- **Lower Town** features **St. Martin's on the Isle Hotel**, offering accommodation and incorporating the Round Island Bar and Teän Restaurant.
  Ashvale House also offers bed and breakfast accommodation nearby,
  and has a gallery. The **Seven Stones Inn** is a little further inland. Self-
  catering lodgings and chalets are also available.
- In addition to St. Mary's Boatmen's Association, **ferries** to and from St.
  Martin's are operated by St. Martin's Boat Services, tel 01720-422814.

Boat Trip – The Eastern Isles

Boat trips often sail around the Eastern Isles, allowing close-up views of shags and cormorants on rocky ledges or feeding out at sea. The lower rocks and ledges are often used by seals, many of them reluctant to move until the rising tide gently lifts them from their resting places. The isolated rocky islet of Hanjague stands as a lonely Scilly sentinel, with the next landfall to the east being Land's End on the mainland. Many of the boat trips that explore the Eastern Isles also include a landing on St. Martin's.

The little island of Nornour was a largely unregarded island until a storm in 1962 suddenly unearthed a well-preserved ancient settlement site. Dating from the 1st century, the site yielded Roman coins and pottery, and the beach was strengthened against further erosion to preserve the inter-linked stone dwellings. Interesting door-jambs and hearth-stones are easily identified. The water between Nornour and Great Ganilly completely recedes at low tide, and when the ancient village was inhabited the landmass may have been much larger. Occasional boat trips land on Nornour, while visitors with their own boats often choose to land on the larger islands of Great Ganilly, Great Arthur and Little Arthur. Legend says that King Arthur was buried here after his final battle, again pointing to the existence of the lost land of Lyonesse. You don't have to believe in Lyonesse, but while enjoying the peace and tranquillity of the Eastern Isles there is no harm dreaming about the place!

Little Gan

Great
Ganinick

Littl
Ganin

The rocky islet of Hanjague is a solitary Scilly sentinel in the Eastern Isles

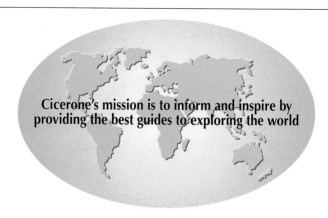

Cicerone's mission is to inform and inspire by providing the best guides to exploring the world

Since its foundation over 30 years ago, Cicerone has specialised in publishing guidebooks and has built a reputation for quality and reliability. It now publishes nearly 300 guides to the major destinations for outdoor enthusiasts, including Europe, UK and the rest of the world.

Written by leading and committed specialists, Cicerone guides are recognised as the most authoritative. They are full of information, maps and illustrations so that the user can plan and complete a successful and safe trip or expedition – be it a long face climb, a walk over Lakeland fells, an alpine traverse, a Himalayan trek or a ramble in the countryside.

With a thorough introduction to assist planning, clear diagrams, maps and colour photographs to illustrate the terrain and route, and accurate and detailed text, Cicerone guides are designed for ease of use and access to the information.

If the facts on the ground change, or there is any aspect of a guide that you think we can improve, we are always delighted to hear from you.

Cicerone Press
2 Police Square Milnthorpe Cumbria LA7 7PY
Tel:01539 562 069   Fax:01539 563 417
e-mail:info@cicerone.co.uk   web:www.cicerone.co.uk